THE DREAD PIRATE FLEUR & the Ruby Heart

www.**kidsatrandomhouse**.co.uk

THE DREAD PIRATE FLEUR & the Ruby Heart

SARA STARBUCK

Illustrated by Adam Relf

RED FOX

THE DREAD PIRATE FLEUR AND THE RUBY HEART
A RED FOX BOOK 978 1 862 30702 5

First published in Great Britain by Red Fox,
an imprint of Random House Children's Books
A Random House Group Company

This edition published 2009

1 3 5 7 9 10 8 6 4 2

The Random House Group Limited supports the Forest Stewardship Council
(FSC), the leading international forest certification organization. All our titles that are
printed on Greenpeace-approved FSC-certified paper carry the FSC logo. Our paper
procurement policy can be found at www.rbooks.co.uk/environment.

Set in Bembo

Red Fox Books are published by Random House Children's Books,
61–63 Uxbridge Road, London W5 5SA

www.**kids**at**randomhouse**.co.uk
www.**rbooks**.co.uk

Addresses for companies within The Random House Group Limited can be found at:
www.randomhouse.co.uk/offices.htm

THE RANDOM HOUSE GROUP Limited Reg. No. 954009

A CIP catalogue record for this book is available from the British Library.

Printed in the UK by CPI Bookmarque, Croydon, CR0 4TD.

To Tom, with love
I wish you fair winds
and following seas,
ever and always

CHAPTER 1

The Pandora Inn, Truro, Cornwall, 1692

'Wake up, girl. Wake up *now*. There's no time left.'

Fleur opened her eyes to see her father staring down at her. Even in the shadowy gloom of the starless night she could see fear blazing in his eyes like fire.

'Father?' she mumbled groggily. 'What's wrong?'

At that moment someone thundered on the door downstairs. The boom roared and echoed relentlessly around the silent bowels of the old inn and Fleur shivered; it was as if the devil himself wanted to get in. She sat up in bed and watched her father stride over to the window and peer down through a gap in the curtains.

'Father, what's happening?'

The hammering downstairs grew even louder and the solid oak front door cracked as it buckled under the pressure. Her father stared down at the rabid gaggle standing outside and sighed as if exhausted. Fleur noticed then that he had thrown on a pair of breeches under his nightshirt and a huge cutlass hung from his belt; the blade glinted menacingly. He turned to face his daughter and began to speak.

'Child, I hoped that this day was never to be. But here we are.' His voice was rough with sorrow and anger. 'I've been lying to you.'

Fleur opened her mouth to speak, but at that moment a heavy cloud scudded away from the moon and its light poured in through the flimsy curtains. Her father stood in the pooling moonbeam, like a terrible dark thing trapped in a silver cobweb. His face was drained of all warmth and joy, his entire being racked and crippled with emotion. She shivered again and curled into herself. Who *was* this person? This wasn't her beloved father, a kind and gentle man. Fear fluttered in her belly, for he was all she had left.

'I'm sorry, Fleur, but I lied because I had to and that's

all there is to it.' He came towards her and sat on the edge of the bed, then reached out and touched his fingertips to hers. There, for a moment, was a glimpse of her beloved daddy.

'I don't understand. What have you lied about?' she said.

He shook his head and almost smiled. 'Almost everything. I'm not who you think I am.'

'Yes you are,' she replied defiantly. 'You're my father, the landlord of the Pandora Inn.'

He nodded. 'Aye, girl, I am that. But I am also so much more and it's almost time for me to own the truth.'

They heard the inn's door begin to crack; the crowd below started shouting.

'Give yourself up, you land-loving turncoat. We know you're in there.'

A pistol was fired into the night.

'We've come from hell and we'll carry you back there with us. Henry the Heartless, come and meet your maker!'

'But, Father, listen, it's all right,' Fleur said with relief. 'They ain't looking for you. They're calling for Henry the Heartless, not John Morgan. Shouldn't we just let 'em in?'

She started to get up but her father pushed her back onto the bed. Their eyes met and a chill seeped into her heart, for she knew in an instant that John Morgan had never really existed at all.

'I'm sorry, daughter,' he said quietly, 'but there's no time left. My real name is Henry Hart, although some will know me as Henry the Heartless.' His voice faltered with emotion. 'We have but moments together. Child, do you trust me?' He gripped her arms tightly, bruising them.

'Aye, Father,' she said firmly. 'More than anything.'

He nodded and released his grip. 'I cannot stop what is about to happen but I have made provision for you.'

Terror squeezed at Fleur's heart so tightly that she could barely breathe. 'What do you mean? What's going to happen?'

He stared into her eyes with such intensity that she fell silent.

'You'll have to be patient for a while, but someone *will* be coming for you.'

'Who?' she asked.

A smile brushed his lips as he looked down at his daughter with love and pride. She belonged to him, that much was evident, with the same tumble of thick black curls as his own, the pale, delicate face, and a wildness about her that could never be tamed. But those huge, brilliant green eyes were all her mother's.

'There's too much to explain. But I have asked him to tell you everything. It will be all right, I promise you.'

Fleur nodded and tried to speak but her bottom lip trembled as she tried not to cry. None of this made any sense. Her father stared down at her and suddenly his steely expression crumbled and softened. He swept her into his arms and she buried her face in his chest. He smelled as he always did, of pipe smoke and the Cornish sea. She felt his ragged breath; his heartbeat thundered like the hooves of a runaway horse, and she knew then that he was scared too. She had to let him know that she would be brave; she couldn't let him down.

'Daddy,' she whispered. 'Oh, Daddy, I don't understand any of this but I promise to do as you ask and have patience. I know that you will always look after me.'

A mighty sob roared through his body and he was almost overwhelmed, but he took a deep breath and steadied himself. 'I know you will, my brave girl. You're my daughter, never forget that. You will hear all sorts of things said about me, but you are the only person who knows me for who I am. Your mother believed in me.' His voice cracked as he remembered his beloved Rose, lost to them both years ago. 'And I hope you can do the same. I *was* the man they will say I am . . . once; but that was long ago and much has changed. I put all the darkness behind me and hunted out the light. I chose to be a good man.'

He reached for the gold locket around Fleur's neck and flipped it open. Inside was a tiny sketch of Rose. He stroked the beautiful face staring back at him with a fingertip and closed his eyes. It was enough to give him the strength he needed. Suddenly the door downstairs exploded and the raggle-taggle group stormed into the inn: there were huge crashes as they started smashing everything up. Fleur and her father sprang apart.

'Remember, you can choose who you want to be too,' he said. 'My blood runs through you like salt in the ocean.' He smiled to himself, a small, sad smile. 'I have oft wondered whether I have caged you, stripped you of your fins. I see you stare into the sea as if you belong among the waves. And you do, my fearless mermaid. And yet I wanted you to have a better life, a safer life. But I always feared they would find me and so I have taught you much of what I am and what you could be without you ever fully realizing it. All those skills will be of use shortly. I just hope that I've taught you enough. I have always loved you, my beautiful Fleur.'

Bottles were thrown at the wall and doors kicked down as the cries for Henry the Heartless grew louder. The storm was almost upon them. Something wild flitted through her father's eyes and his body tensed. He was almost lost to her.

'Daughter, you have to hide.'

'No!' Fleur exclaimed. 'I can't leave you.'

'You have to.'

Fury surged through her suddenly and she stamped her foot with frustration. 'No, Father, let me fight next to you,' she begged. 'You know I am capable and fast – and stronger than any girl has any right to be. I can help you.'

He squeezed her shoulders tightly and smiled sadly. 'No, my little rebel. There are too many of them and you are no match for animals like these. They're ruthless to the core and will show you no mercy.'

'But why teach me all those fighting skills if I can't use them at the right time?' demanded Fleur.

'This ain't the right time,' he replied firmly. 'But remember what I taught you well because you'll be needing everything I armed you with soon enough.'

Fleur clung to him as the tears finally poured freely down her face. 'But I—'

'You have to live, Fleur. Don't you see? I have to know that you will survive or this will have all been for nothing.' He stared down at her in anguish. 'I would have my soul boil in hell for you.'

Footsteps thundered up the stairs.

'There's nowhere to hide.' Fleur looked around in panic.

Her father walked over to a small cupboard and flung it open. She peered into a tiny space cluttered with clothing and frowned.

'But it's too small.'

Her father bent over, swept the clothes aside and gently pushed the back of the cupboard to reveal a compartment big enough to hide someone.

'What's this?' she exclaimed.

'It was built just in case,' he replied gravely.

Feet stormed across the landing.

'I love you, Fleur,' her father whispered hoarsely. 'Remember, I promise by all that is great and good that he *will* be coming for you – you're not alone.'

They embraced once again quickly, and then she crawled into the space. Her father closed both doors firmly but Fleur pushed the secret panel open slightly so that she could see through the cracks in the cupboard door.

'Henry the Heartless,' a voice roared, 'has all the fight gone out of you now ye be a lubber?'

Fleur heard the sound of a sword being drawn and someone else began to speak. It was a few moments before she realized that it was her father. His voice was harsh with fury.

'Oh, I have all the fight I need,' he said. 'I've been waiting for you to come, you ratty sea dog. What's been keeping you?'

As footsteps entered the room, the space thickened with tension.

'Aye, you say that, but you ignored the message we left for you.'

'You thought I'd come because you summoned me? Hah! You're more stupid than I remember then. I'd rather dangle from the yardarm than answer to anyone.'

Through the crack Fleur watched her father toss back his unruly mane of black hair and laugh. It was so strange hearing him being called Henry. The men inched towards him like shadows following the dying sun. They were a strange, battle-scarred assortment, wearing a mixed bag of colourful, ill-fitting clothing. Nasty weapons hung from them like leaves on trees.

'Where is he, Henry?' someone asked evenly. 'Tell us or we'll give you a bellyful of pickling brine.'

Fleur shuffled forward slightly to see who was speaking. He was huge and brutish, with a straggly mess of dirty red hair and a broad beaked nose. He was a striking man, handsome almost, but there was a cruel arrogance about him. He wore an eye-patch and two of the fingers on his left hand were missing.

'Where is who?' Fleur's father replied bluntly. It was almost as if he was enjoying it.

'You know who we mean,' someone spat at him.

Fleur's father laughed dangerously and she stared at him in amazement. He was changing before her eyes. He'd always been a strong, proud man, but now, silhouetted against the moon, he looked even taller. Pride and fear ran through her as goose pimples erupted over her body.

'Say his name. If you dare . . .' her father replied quietly.

The men laughed nervously.

'You'll be thinkin' we believe in the legend, won't you?' Someone sneered. 'That if we say his name out loud, he'll come and have our hearts' blood.'

'Say his name then, if you think it nonsense,' Henry retorted.

Swords were drawn. The flame-haired man walked over to him and stood so close that he recoiled from the reek of his enemy's foul breath. The man leaned in and spoke in a venomous tone. 'William Hart − or should I say, William the Heartless?' He looked about the room theatrically. 'See, it wasn't that hard − and hell's bells, what a surprise, he hasn't turned up.'

'He'll wait until you're sleeping,' snarled Henry. 'But don't worry, he'll wake you before he kills you. It'd be no sport for him otherwise.'

'But that's not always been the case, has it?' The man replied.

With one hand Henry raised his cutlass like a wand; with the other he held a huge staff aloft. Fleur tried not to gasp out loud as she watched him spin the stick in his hand as if it were as light as air. She had never seen it before, even when her father had taught her stick-fighting in the woods nearby. The staff was a strange thing indeed: it was almost as long as Fleur herself and appeared to be forged from a wealth of curiosities. The bottom half was made from different types of wood, with ancient-looking sharks' teeth embedded at its base. At the centre of the staff was a wide ring of gold set with a huge ruby. The top half seemed to be made from a huge snaking tusk that spiralled into a sharp point. Fleur couldn't take her eyes off the blazing ruby. It blinked in the shadows like the bloodied eye of something ancient and timeless; she could feel it seek her out in her hiding place. Her father stood between her and the motley crew like a giant rock. His hands didn't shake and she could feel the energy surrounding him like a magnetic field. He was a warrior.

There was a pause, like the lull before a storm, and then all hell broke loose. Swords swished and glinted as they were drawn, and then everyone was upon Henry at once. She watched as he fought them off, one by one, and couldn't believe what she saw. She had often witnessed him take on drunks at the inn; she had observed his discipline and strength when he taught her how to protect herself. But this was like nothing she had ever seen before. It was as if he was possessed; a whir of lightning dancing in chaos. His sword blazed and clinked as if it had a life of its own and the staff twirled about in a lethal dance. He was untouchable. Men lay dead at his feet.

But then a pistol was fired – two shots – and he cried out with pain. His knees buckled beneath him and he sank to the floor. Fleur tried not to scream and leaned forward to see who had shot him. A wiry man wearing a blue bandana was carrying the smoking pistol. He spat out a stream of vile oaths before shuffling backwards to join the other men. He had his back to Fleur, so she couldn't see his face, but through the rents in his filthy shirt she could see tattoos of hangman's nooses and skulls inked onto his back. She wiped away her tears and narrowed her eyes to stare at the crude black images: she would never forget those tattoos – she owed as much to her father.

The red-haired man stood over Henry and laughed. 'Did you think we'd forgotten about your fighting skills, Hart? I was prepared to lose a few men finding out if you were still as talented after all these years, but I'm not stupid. I can see time hasn't stolen anything from you.'

'It's stolen everything,' Henry replied mournfully, struggling to sit up and spitting out a mouthful of blood.

The man kicked him down again and held a long thin rapier to his neck. 'Tell us where he is,' he demanded.

'I don't know,' Henry replied.

'Tell us or we'll kill you.'

Henry laughed. 'I'm already dead.'

The red-haired man pushed the sword in a little deeper and a couple of beads of blood glistened at Henry's throat.

'Some folk say you had a child. What if we found the brat and fed him piece by piece to the sharks?'

The laughter stopped abruptly. 'I don't have no children,' Henry hissed through gritted teeth. 'Why would I want to bring life into this godforsaken world? You can choke me and let me rot, but you won't find no family of mine. All you have is me.'

'I'll grind your mealy-mouthed jib into the dirt until you're barely breathing and then we'll rip this inn apart. The last sound you'll hear will be your own cries for mercy.'

Fleur tried to swallow away the fear that choked her.

'Be damned.' Henry groaned, spat out more blood and laughed with everything he could muster. 'You'll never catch William. And I will never turn on him. Now finish me, before I find the strength to kill you all.'

They were the last words that Henry spoke. With a bloodcurdling cry the one-eyed man plunged his blade into Henry's throat and the other men soon joined in. Fleur turned away and bit her hand until she tasted blood – it was all she could do to stop herself from shouting out. But she was done with crying; fury burned within her, and instead she wanted revenge on every man left standing in that room. As she cowered in the secret cupboard, listening to them rip her home apart, a name echoed around her head like a whisper: *William Hart, William Hart, William Hart . . .*

She wasn't alone. Someone was coming for her.

CHAPTER 2

Henry's funeral was a small affair, and to everyone but Fleur he was still known as John Morgan. A fistful of regulars at the inn turned up to pay their respects, but the Morgans had no family or close friends. They'd always kept themselves to themselves and now Fleur knew why. She stared blindly down at the wooden coffin that was about to be lowered into the earth. She hated to think of her father being nibbled on by rats, even though he was dead.

The memory of that horrible night haunted her, chasing behind like a stalking wolf. After the men killed her father, they had stolen the strange staff and set about destroying the only home she had ever known. It was only when she'd heard the flames crackling and licking the ageing timbers of the inn that Fleur had finally left. She had walked through the burning building carrying nothing but her father's beloved bow and a leather quiver of arrows slung across her back – as though the flames couldn't touch her; as though she was already a ghost.

Despite the warmth of the spring morning, Fleur was frozen. The Puritan preacher was rambling on about fire and brimstone, but she heard none of it. She didn't know what was to happen to her now: she was only eleven and had nowhere to go. A week had passed since her father's death and she was beginning to wonder just when this mysterious man who shared her father's real name was going to come for her. Maybe he too had been killed?

Sadness pinned her down, dragging her to the depths of despair. She could barely remember her mother, Rose, who had died when Fleur was three. She only had fragments of her, like the shards of a broken mirror – too few to see the image. Instead she remembered her smile. Its warmth never seemed to fade. Since Rose's death it had been just the two of them: John Morgan and his daughter, whose name was the only delicate thing about her.

Fleur had always hated being treated like a girl and much preferred the rough and tumble of boys' sports. Her father had indulged her, imparting the same skills he would have to a son, and she had loved it. He had taught her about weapons: she could assemble and fire a pistol and use a sword. She could fire arrows, fight with a staff and defend herself against attack, using skills Henry had told her he had picked up on his travels, before she was born. He had taken her out in his tiny sailing boat and insisted that she became a capable sailor. Fleur had learned how to tie every knot there was and to plot a course by using navigational charts or by staring up at the moon and the stars. She knew how to turn an hourglass to find out the time, how to judge the speed of a ship by casting astern a knotted rope fastened to a plank and counting the knots. She could measure the depth of the sea, steer a ship, mend and manage the sails to catch the wind. She could also dress wounds, cook, climb and swim.

Of course, fellow villagers had gossiped that John Morgan needed a wife to curb his daughter's wild ways. And there had been plenty of women who were more than willing to marry the handsome loner. But there was no replacement for Rose. And there was no hope of Fleur ever acting like a girl.

Hot tears stung her eyes and she lowered her head to hide them. She wore her mother's locket around her neck and her father's hunting bow across her shoulders. They were the only keepsakes she had to remember them by. She had her memories, but she knew that they would dim over time, and the solidity of these precious objects helped her feel that her parents were still around somehow. She shifted the weight of the bow across her back and let herself remember happier days spent firing arrows with the deadly accuracy of a seasoned predator. They'd had a rabbit for their pot most nights thanks to her hunting skills.

The preacher had been droning on but Fleur suddenly became aware of a sudden hush; a ripple of feverish whispers swept through the small group. Even the preacher eventually stopped talking – a rare thing, for he loved the sound of his own voice. Fleur opened her eyes and saw him staring into the distance with a look of pure terror. She turned to follow his gaze and a chill ran through her.

A man strode towards her with the force of a tidal wave. The world seemed to shrink and shift aside for him, such was his presence. In his slipstream walked a boy who looked a couple of years older than Fleur, and four swarthy-looking men wearing ill-fitting sailor slops, worn buckled shoes and sea coats. But she barely glanced at the others: she couldn't take her eyes off their leader. Each step he took seemed to suck the life from everything around him. He was a black hole, an explosion of energy drawing everything into him. As he drew nearer, Fleur's heart began to race and her chest constricted. It couldn't be . . . Surely not . . . No one would play such a cruel trick. She was thinking the same thought as everyone standing in silent shock around her: it was as if her father had risen from the grave he had yet to be buried in. And by the look of things he'd been to hell and back.

Fleur gasped out loud and her legs felt weak. She forced herself to stare at the face she never thought to see again. The man was identical to her father, except for the raven hair that fell down his back in knotty tangles, the ragged scar etched into his left cheek and the black eyes that were as icy and barren as the underworld he had crawled from. He wore a riotous crimson *justaucorps* coat and a violet sash. Such bold colours had been banned under the Sumptuary Law and no one but the upper classes was allowed to wear them. The law had been passed to prevent commoners imitating the appearance of aristocrats. But this well-dressed man was clearly a classless savage. A notched and blood-besmirched cutlass swung dangerously under his skirt, his buckled shoes shone from polish and he wore stockings, breeches and a tricorn hat bearing a bright red feather. Thick gold earrings dangled from both ears and his fingers were heavy with bejewelled rings.

He came to a halt and scanned the group. As he did so, the preacher mouthed the word 'devil' and held up his Bible.

The man roared with laughter. 'You think that little book will save you?'

The preacher remained silent and still, but a tremble betrayed him. The man stared at him until he closed his eyes, then snatched the leather-bound Bible away and threw it into the empty grave.

'If there be a God, he can collect that himself.' He scanned the group and narrowed his eyes when he saw Fleur. 'Are you Fleur? Speak quickly, lassie. I might look like your father but I haven't his patience.'

Fleur stood firm and met his gaze. It was like being hurled into the stars. 'I am she.'

He squinted and walked towards her. 'Aye, I can see that now I've clapped eyes on thee.' He pointed at the bow at her back. 'Is that Henry's?'

She nodded. 'Who are you?' she asked.

A smile played on his lips. 'You dare ask me that, child?'

She nodded. 'I first took you for a ghost.'

He studied her again. 'I am a whisper on the wind. That's all you need to know for now. But I am also a man of my word and I made an oath to your father that I intend to keep. Do you have the stomach for a journey, girl?'

Fleur looked around the group of people she barely knew and realized then that this was what her father had told her would happen. *He* had come to get her. This was William Hart. Her mind was bubbling over. The resemblance between her father and this man was too great for them to be anything but brothers. And they shared the same name. This man was her uncle; he was all she had; he was her family. But why hadn't she heard about him before? All she knew for certain was that she had to trust her father. He would never let anything bad happen to her; even death couldn't stop that.

'Well, have you had your tongue pruned?' William snarled.

She ignored the gentle hands pulling her away from him and stepped forward. She raised her chin and met his steely gaze. 'I was wondering when you were going to show up.'

This time there was definitely a flicker of life in those dead shark eyes. 'Well, you be coming with us then,' he said firmly.

With that he threw a fistful of coins onto the ground beside the preacher's feet. They lay there guiltily, the assorted plunder of fortune surely gathered from every country in the world: pieces of eight, castellanos and doubloons from Spain, ducats from Sicily, pagodas from India, moidores from Portugal, and the more familiar shillings, sovereigns, guineas and pounds from England.

William nodded at the holy man. 'I presume this will buy his body and your silence?'

The preacher's eyes widened hungrily when he saw the amount of money lying next to him, and he nodded. No one dared say anything. The four men standing behind William walked over to the coffin and started to pick it up. The boy scowled at Fleur, then turned to help the men balance the coffin solidly on their wide shoulders. Mary, the woman who had tried to hold Fleur back, could stand it no longer. She had always been kind to Fleur and her father, and had agreed to let the girl stay in her tiny house until after the funeral.

'But where are you taking Fleur?' she asked William

Hart. 'And what are you going to do with John's body?'

'John?' he questioned, and then a look of realization passed over his face. 'Oh, you mean Henry.'

Mary looked confused. 'Henry?'

Her husband pulled her back gently but William looked at her curiously. 'If you must know, woman – and I am telling you because you clearly knew my brother – I am taking him to be buried where he belongs. John was never his real name, y'see. His name was Henry Hart.'

This time a gasp rippled around the group and Fleur kept hearing the same word muttered in fearful awe: *pirates*. Mary paled and choked on her words and this time let her husband pull her away.

'Mary, what's wrong?' Fleur's face was full of concern and confusion.

'Get away from me, child,' Mary said, pushing the girl away. 'I let you into my home. Don't you understand the risk I was taking?'

'What do you mean?' Fleur asked.

'You're a Hart!' Mary said through gritted teeth. 'Pirate blood! You're bad stock, girl. You'll never be nothing but trouble.'

Fleur turned to face her uncle. 'I don't understand.'

He simply grinned infuriatingly, motioned for his men to follow him with the coffin and then strode off. He called out to her over his shoulder: 'You will, girl. That you will.'

'But my father was an innkeeper!' she shouted after him, stamping her foot hard.

William stopped in his tracks and whipped round to face her. 'No, he wasn't.'

Fleur bit her lip and asked the question she already knew the answer to: 'Were you both pirates?'

William threw back his head and roared with laughter; his men joined in. '*Were?*' he said. 'Were and am, girl. Pirate captains at that.'

It hit her like a thunderbolt. No wonder the villagers had been struck with terror. She'd heard their whispers over the years, the stories of murderous mutiny and foul robberies on the high seas. Pirates were ruthless, feared more than any sea monster. They would sell their souls for a chest full of treasure. And her father had been one once. No wonder Mary had told her she was bad stock. Fleur turned to the group of Cornish villagers in shock, but no one would meet her eye. She wasn't welcome, that was clear. And yet to follow this stranger, whose very name seemed to cause fear in those around her . . . ? But she had no choice. It was her father's plan for her. And she clung to that thought as she began to walk away.

Fleur looked back one last time at the sleepy Cornish village where she had lived for her entire life, and without another word left behind everything she had ever known.

CHAPTER 3

Despite the weight of the coffin, William's men followed him effortlessly as he set off at a brisk march in the direction of the sea. Fleur chased after them, gathering up her skirts so that she could match their pace – this was evidently a man who didn't like to be kept waiting. She tried to catch up with the boy, but he ignored her completely. Instead she watched him striding ahead, his mop of blond hair shining gold in the sunlight, his dirty bare feet scrambling along the shingly path as if he felt no pain. The group made a strange procession, weaving along the scrubby headlands like a colourful ribbon fluttering in the breeze.

Finally William stopped on some rocks near a small cove and turned to face them. 'Fleur, come here,' he barked.

She picked her way over to him. 'Yes?'

He indicated that his men should stop for a while. 'Drink your grog, men, and rest. You too, Tom. You'll be needing your energy soon enough.'

The men lowered the coffin to the ground and began passing round a bottle of rum mixed with water. The boy, Tom, sat down nearby.

William peered down at Fleur. 'You're definitely a Hart, but I see your mother in you too, girl. You've got her emerald cat-eyes.'

'Did you know my mother?' she asked hopefully.

Her uncle abruptly shook his head. 'No, I didn't know her at all.'

Fleur's smile faded a little and she wondered whether he was lying. 'And what about you?' she pressed on, interested to know if she had any other kin. 'Were *you* ever married? Do I have any cousins?'

William's face darkened. 'My brother and I parted ways a long time ago.' He eyed her with contempt, any previous warmth gone completely. 'He chose a different life to me and it would have been dangerous for him to know my whereabouts. Death would have met him sooner.'

Fleur suddenly remembered what the men had said to Henry on the night of his murder. 'That's what they said, the men who killed my father. They kept asking him where you were.' Her voice faltered and she swallowed. 'But he wouldn't tell them, and so they . . . they . . .'

'Killed him,' William finished abruptly. He pulled a small brass telescope from a pocket and stared out to sea. 'Now then, can you remember anything of those men?'

Fleur thought back to the dreadful night. 'They were dressed like your men,' she said. 'And they were covered with tattoos and talked like sailors. And' – Fleur swallowed hard as she remembered – 'they were ruthless. Especially their leader. He was an animal. And he stole this strange staff my father was using.'

Her uncle spun round to face her and spoke through gritted teeth; Fleur noticed that his men were staring at her too, listening intently.

'What staff?' he growled, then turned to address the others. 'Drink your grog, men, and close your ears.'

'I don't know,' said Fleur. 'It was an incredible thing and Father was fighting with it. I hadn't seen it before. I thought maybe he'd taken it from one of the men who attacked him.'

'That staff belongs to my family,' spat William.

Fleur couldn't suppress a small shiver of delight. Family meant *her* now, even if that wasn't what her uncle had been thinking. 'Please, sir,' she began nervously – he was clearly fuming – 'why did my father have the staff? If it's some sort of family heirloom thing, how come he never even showed it to me?'

William glared at her. She got the distinct impression that he was trying to decide whether or not to tell her.

'In truth, I didn't know he had the damned thing,' he admitted finally.

'But why?' Fleur asked.

He spat on the floor. 'Oh, I'm sure he thought he had good reason,' he muttered. 'The staff is very special, girl, if the carrier is worthy. It was carved by Jacob Hart, the first ever pirate. Your great–great–great–great . . . awell, anyway, you're related. Old Jacob saw more of the world than any man before or since, and his weapon was made from the spoils of his travels. Treasures from the four corners of the earth. 'Tis rumoured to be fused together from the wood of three sacred trees. The Tree of Creevna, whose limbs are a charm against drowning. The Djambu Baros, a tree that reaches up as high as heaven. And the tree of Yama' – William's face was suddenly stern – 'the Tree of Death that grows in hell.'

Fleur frowned, trying to make sense of this fantastic

story. 'It had something at the top. A sort of spear,' she remembered. 'What's that?'

'A narwhal horn,' said her uncle, nodding gravely. 'From a "corpse whale", as the men call 'em, 'cause they have the colour of drowned sailors. And that spiral tusk you saw is hard and sharp enough to make a few corpses of its own. It'll punch a hole in pack ice, or the belly of a ship. A handy tool for an enterprising sea captain.'

'And what about the gold?' Fleur asked. 'There was gold too.'

William's eyes flashed with passion as he warmed to his subject. 'That's Inca gold. Sir Francis Drake . . .'

Fleur shrugged.

'A family friend,' he went on. 'He captured a Spanish galleon filled with gold. Only it went down, gold and all, after an earthquake sent a great wave to turn the ship over. All of it except for one little bit, that is' – his eyes sparkled greedily – 'a little bit of gold from the coffers of the last Inca king.'

Fleur thought back to the magnificent gemstone that had called out to her in the shadows. 'And a stone set in it . . . a red one. A ruby, I think. And there was something strange about it. I could feel it in my bones, sir.'

William looked at her strangely. 'What do you mean?'

She shrugged. 'I'm not sure really – it just felt like it was alive or something.'

He peered down at her even more intently. 'The ruby is the stone of nobility and nothing but a measure of the family's standing. Tell me,' he said, quickly changing the subject, 'the man that ordered Henry's death – was his hair red? And was he missing a few fingers on one of his hands and maybe an eye an' all?'

'Yes,' said Fleur, shutting her eyes tight against the memory.

A storm cloud of rage passed over her uncle's face. Fleur could almost see the anger rising from him like steam. Then he stared vacantly out to sea again. She could sense him longing to be out on the water, free of the land that tied him down.

'Alexander Blood,' he muttered. 'Damn him to the depths. That mutinous rogue has always been a plague to me and mine. Our argument goes back generations. I swear that revenge will be mine and death and damnation will be his. The Hart staff will be returned to us – after I've run it through his heart, that is.'

Fleur opened her mouth to ask more questions but William silenced her.

'Did Henry ever speak of his past or his family?' he asked.

She shook her head. 'I didn't even know you existed.' She looked up at the familiar face and sadness flooded her. 'Were you twins?'

'Aye.' William nodded. 'Born within moments of each other.' He stared into the distance, lost in the past. 'We were the dread pirates of all the oceans for a time,' he said. 'We had the fastest galleon and a crew of hungry sea dogs: we could take whatever we wanted.' He took a pipe from his pocket and started loading it up with tobacco. 'Henry was better than I. He could navigate our ship through seas so violent that no one but demons should have survived. He fought with as much honour as violence and he was a great leader of men.' William studied Fleur's face, trying to recapture his brother there. 'He was more of a gentleman pirate, your father – although, let's be honest, a pirate is a pirate and there's none of us that are that virtuous.'

Fleur felt sad for her father. She remembered their last night together, when she had seen his true self. She had witnessed the transformation, the spark that had reignited something primal and powerful within him. Had he really been happy as John Morgan? It sounded as if he had once been a very different man, riding the waves and taming the swirling depths. 'So what happened?' she asked quietly.

William's face hardened and his eyes grew black and cold again. 'There are some things best left for history to nibble on, child. He made his choice and time ran away with it. But know this' – he peered at her with such intensity that she began to tremble – 'the father you knew isn't who he really was. Henry will always belong to the ocean; he will always be a pirate captain. I'll be taking his body to be buried where he belongs.'

He stood up and started to walk away but Fleur followed him.

'And where's that then?' she asked.

William motioned for Tom to join them. The boy picked up a leather bag and obediently made his way over.

'To the island of Ile aux Forbans in the heart of the Indian Ocean, where there be a resting place for pirates and the like. I'll be dropping you off before I bury my brother.'

Fleur watched Tom pull some dirty clothes from the bag, followed by a sharp knife. She felt cold as he held the blade up to the light to catch a sunbeam, but raised her chin defiantly. 'I want to see him buried. After all, he was my father as well as your brother.'

William shook his head adamantly and took a deep lungful of pipe smoke. 'No.'

'*No?*' exclaimed Fleur. 'Why not?'

He shrugged and sent a mouthful of smoke spiralling up into the air. 'My promise was to make sure you got to a safe place and that's all there is to it. D'ye understand?'

Anger raged inside Fleur. She put her hands on her hips and faced him. 'Where are you taking me?' she demanded.

William stared at her for a long time while Tom fidgeted nervously. Finally he spoke.

'Henry made arrangements for you years ago. Just after you were born he gave a treasure chest full of gold to a distant cousin of ours. She was married to a lubber with a failing sugar plantation in St Kitts in the Caribbean. He asked that in repayment she must take you in as her own if 'twas ever necessary. I promised that if that ever happened I would make sure you reached her safely. Lucky for you my ship was in English waters when my spies told me the news.' He spat on the floor. 'I think that ends our conversation.'

'But you haven't explained everything to me,' Fleur protested. 'There's still so much I need to know.'

William pursed his lips and stared at her with such anger that she flinched. 'Don't push me, child. I've been kind to you. I only owe my brother, not his pathetic leftovers. Anger me further and you'll be sorry.'

With that, he went off to smoke his pipe alone.

Fleur watched him go and started to follow him, but someone yanked her back roughly. 'What are you doing?'

It was Tom. Fleur ignored him and tried to escape his bony grasp, but he clung onto her tightly.

'I warn you, Claw-cat, don't go after him. He's being kind to you at the moment, but his moods are as changeable as the sea itself. Don't anger him.'

Fleur stared at him accusingly. 'But he's going to bury my father without me. He's got no right to do that.'

The boy tossed his head back and laughed.

'What are you laughing at me for?' she snapped crossly.

'He can do whatever he likes,' he replied, then peered at her with eyes as blue and clear as rock pools on a sunny day. 'You don't know much about the cap'n, do you?'

'Of course not,' she snapped. 'I only just found out that he exists at all.'

Tom looked over at his captain with as much pride as fear. 'But his legend usually precedes him,' he replied, looking at her doubtfully.

'Well, it didn't precede him in my house,' she blazed back.

He stared at her with open surprise. 'But he's the most feared pirate in all the seas.'

Fleur raised her chin defiantly and nodded over in her uncle's direction. 'Well, he doesn't scare me!'

'You really are a stupid little girl,' the boy told her.

She spluttered indignantly. 'Don't talk to me like that.'

He smirked annoyingly and took a step closer to her. 'I can do what I like.'

'But you work for my uncle,' she pointed out.

He nodded. 'Aye, that's right. But I don't work for you. And who are you to start telling me what to do? You ain't welcome on our ship. The few of us that know about you hate you already. It's bad luck for women to be at sea.'

'Don't talk nonsense,' Fleur snapped. 'How can it be bad luck?'

Tom held the knife up to the light again, teasing her with it. 'There's many customs for those that live in the deep blue, and if you want to come with us you've to honour them.' He moved towards her with the blade and she flinched away.

'What are you doing?'

He reached out and grabbed a handful of the thick black curls that tumbled like a waterfall down her back.

'I'm cutting off your hair, Fleur. What kind of stupid name is that anyway? *Fleur.*'

She hopped away from him, but he snatched at her hair and pulled it painfully.

'You're not touching my hair. Get off me, you stupid boy.'

'Yes I am. And I'll make no bones about it,' he warned. 'There'll be mutiny on our ship if the crew thinks you be a dainty bit. The captain ordered me to cut it off and I'll tie you up if needs be.'

Fleur howled in frustration and snatched the knife away from him. Before he had a chance to move she had severed a huge tangle of hair from her head and was watching in shock as the wind stole it away. Then she went into a frenzied whir of activity and started hacking at her hair as if she were possessed.

'If anyone is to cut off my hair, it will be me,' she declared adamantly.

Soon all that was left was a jagged layer of short curls. She handed the knife back to Tom and pointed at the pile of clothes next to him. 'I take it they're for me?'

He nodded, clearly speechless.

'Well, I'd better put them on then, hadn't I?' She moved behind a rock and started throwing her clothes off furiously.

Tom watched her with a wry smile and muttered to himself, 'There might be hope for that girl yet.'

When Fleur had changed, he led her over to the captain and his men.

'By God, you look as I did when I was a boy,' William roared, much to the amusement of his men.

Fleur glanced down at her clothes and scowled. She wore a canvas doublet and breeches, a cotton waistcoat and drawers, stockings which itched, a linen shirt and horrible sea boots that were far too big for her. But despite her irritation at being forced to dress like a boy, she actually felt more comfortable than she did in her dresses and skirts.

Tom approached her with a sly grin. 'You forgot this.' He held out a red bandana. 'The cap'n says that you're to wear it all the time. Here, let me.' He spun her round roughly and tied the scrap of material about her head. He looked over at William. 'Is she good enough for you, Cap'n?'

William nodded. 'She'll do.' He turned to face his men. 'And if any of you speak a word of this, I'll carve out your gizzards and fry them for supper then chain what's left of you to the keel.'

The men turned to look at Fleur, their eyes full of hate.

'But isn't the keel underneath the ship?' she whispered to Tom uncomfortably.

He nodded. 'Their hands are tied to a rope which drags them under the ship,' he explained. 'If they're lucky they'll avoid the razor-sharp barnacles and lurking sharks – if they don't drown first, that is.'

Fleur looked away from the men's accusing glares while William searched the horizon with his telescope. He squinted and frowned suddenly, staring at a distant point, and then swiftly pocketed the telescope.

'We better be going. Our time here is up. Come on, men, we must be swift. The redcoats have long since heard of our landing and they're coming for me.'

The men jumped up and manoeuvred the coffin back onto their shoulders. William beckoned for Tom; the boy obediently dashed over to his captain, who muttered something in his ear. Tom nodded before running away, his feet kicking up loose sand in his wake. Without another word, the captain began walking away with the remainder of the small group filing after him.

Despite everything, Fleur couldn't help but feel excitement churn in her belly as she hurried along behind. It didn't matter to her that her uncle was a pirate. The important thing was that she had thought her whole family lost, and now *here he was*. As Henry had promised, she wasn't alone. And she was following in the steps of her beloved father and giving in to the call of the sea. He'd been right, it was in her blood. For years she had stood on the shore wishing to be in the heart-swell of the ocean. And her father *had* taught her well – he'd known that one day she would need to survive on a ship where no one would look after her, or even care if she lived or died. So he had prepared her for it without her even realizing it. She could survive; she *would* survive.

CHAPTER 4

When they reached the beach, Fleur caught sight of a magnificent ship lying in the bay. Her white sails fanned out like the wings of a giant butterfly. From a distance the crew looked like ants climbing all over her. As they approached, the ship's bell rang out, telling them the time.

'Know what sort of ship this is then, girl?' William snarled. It was obvious that he was just making a joke for his crew at her expense.

Fleur studied the ship, ignoring the jeers. She had two masts, with square rigging on the foremast and fore-and-aft rigging on the mainmast. She had oars as well as sails and the mainmast also had a gaff and boom. 'She's a brigantine,' she replied finally. 'Are we boarding her then?'

Tom looked at her in shock while William simply nodded.

'Well, well, the little bird is right. It seems you're more of a Hart than I thought. Yes, welcome to the *Libertine*.' He started to turn away. 'By the way, from now until you leave the ship, your name will be Finn.'

As they approached the *Libertine*, Fleur could see the crew clambering up the gangplank laden with food and water. A handful of chickens were trying to peck their way out of metal cages and a couple of skinny cows were tethered miserably. One of the crew dropped a sack full of dried beans and they fell into the water below. On seeing William, the man jumped straight in to rescue them. The fact that he couldn't swim wasn't as important as upsetting his captain! Fleur stared up at the magnificent ship floating gracefully on the water as if she was as light as air, and smiled to herself.

Suddenly a gunshot rang out, then another. Fleur turned to see a group of redcoats riding full tilt towards them, their scarlet tunics the colour of spilled blood. William drew his sword and shouted to his men to ready the ship to leave. The crew jumped into action. Tom appeared nearby; the captain turned to him and whispered, 'Make sure the girl gets aboard safely, Tom. If necessary, do all you can to protect her.'

Tom grabbed hold of Fleur, who was transfixed by the soldiers massing on the sand. He pushed her up the gangplank and they stood on the deck watching the scene below. All around them the pirate crew rushed to ready the ship as ordered. The anchor was raised and the sails trimmed. The beans were left bobbing in the shallows.

'So we meet again, William the Heartless!' bellowed the redcoat captain. 'Why don't you just give yourself up? You know we'll catch you in the end.'

The soldiers sat on their horses, facing the handful of pirates. A shiny colt reared up on its hind legs impatiently, only to be whipped sharply by its rider.

'You think I'm ready to dance the hempen jig, do you?' William roared back with a broad smile on his face.

'What's that?' Fleur hissed.

Tom was gazing down at the shore. She could tell he was itching to stand side by side with his captain.

'He means hanging.'

The redcoat captain nodded. He was a huge bear of

a man with long greasy hair tied back in a ponytail. 'I'd say it was overdue, yes,' he shouted over the sound of the crashing surf. 'Beelzebub himself could hardly desire better company.'

William took a few steps towards them, and as he did so, Fleur noticed that some forty members of his crew had been hiding in the sand dunes. They started crawling slowly towards the redcoats.

'What's happening?' she hissed to Tom.

'The captain saw the soldiers heading towards the ship so he organized a welcoming party,' he replied, his eyes gleaming with pride and excitement. 'Cap'n Hart never lets no one creep up on him.'

'You can't catch me, I lay my oath. I be untouchable!' William bellowed.

The redcoat captain began to raise his hand to give the order for his soldiers to attack.

'I wouldn't do that if I were you,' the pirate warned.

The captain laughed. 'And who will stop me – the woeful gaggle of men next to you? The rest of your crew are obviously drunk on stolen rum and cowering below deck.'

Fleur saw William give a slight nod in the direction of his hidden crew. 'Hold your whining – you've the eyes of a blind pup!' he roared. 'I'll devour you in a gulp.'

Suddenly a war cry sliced through Fleur like a blade of ice and, from the dunes, the pirates charged. Blades and axes were raised, pistols were fired. She watched her uncle and couldn't believe what she saw. He was an animal, hacking at horses, humans – anything that crossed his path. For the first time she fully understood why everyone was so scared of him. His men were as ruthless as their captain. They weren't as skilled, but made up for it with brutality. Blood soon stained the pale sand and screams echoed around the pretty little bay.

Fleur clung to the ship's rail as she watched in silent horror. The fight raged on until the remaining redcoats turned and fled, their captain leading the way. Bodies lined the beach.

William collected his men together, some of them bleeding, and led them back to the *Libertine*. As he went past, Fleur noticed blood splattered all over him. He called out to his crew.

'Shipmates, sail-ho and keep her steady. And for the hell of it, hoist the Jolly Roger.'

Fleur watched as they raised their pirate flag: a white skull and crossbones on a black field. It fluttered in the wind like a warning.

The captain caught her eye as he wiped his bloodied hand on his coat. 'As I said, welcome to the *Libertine*.'

CHAPTER 5

As the ship sailed away, Fleur stared back at Truro. The little cove they had left behind looked like a sad yellow smile. The aquamarine water frothed against the jagged rocks she had climbed with her father, and trailing into the distance was the path that would have led back home.

Home . . . She didn't know where that was any more. All her memories were anchored back on land and she had set sail knowing that she could never return. She almost felt thankful that William hadn't left her father there. She turned to face the open sea and drank in the scent of the brine swelling up and falling away beneath her. She closed her eyes – it felt right, almost as if she had woken from a dream.

The crew peered at her curiously. Fleur watched as a huge hulk of a pirate approached the captain. He was a striking albino man with hair as white as snow and eyes so red it looked as if they had been ripped out altogether, leaving nothing but bloodied hollows. His long wispy hair was tied back to reveal the heavy gold hoops in his ears and spidery tattoos on his neck. He was dressed just as flamboyantly as his captain – in fact his waistcoat was covered in gold trinkets.

'Ahoy, Captain,' he called out. 'Back just in time, I see. Did you get Henry's body?'

'Aye, Jack,' William replied. 'They're putting it in the bulkhead. A few of the crew are scared he'll haunt the ship, but a little fear ain't a bad thing. Is the rum cask ready for him?'

Jack nodded and a whisper of a smile brushed his thin lips. 'It is, Captain. Your brother'll soon be pickled in his favourite brew while we carry him to his final resting place.'

Fleur, who was eavesdropping, gasped in horror. 'What do you mean?' she said without thinking.

A few pirates looked over at her with open curiosity.

'Get here, *boy*, now,' the captain ordered her with a scowl.

Fleur shuffled forward reluctantly, with Tom hovering close behind.

William lowered his voice to a threatening hiss. 'Keep your questions to yourself,' he said. 'You'll give yourself away.'

Fleur looked from the captain to the albino man, Jack, who was staring at her with a cold, disdainful expression.

'But what are you doing with my father?' she asked quietly. 'I have a right to know.'

William glanced briefly at his companion, who immediately looked away. 'We're transferring his body from the coffin into a cask of rum,' he replied finally, 'because otherwise the rats'll smell his rotting flesh and start nibbling on him. Now get out of my sight before I pickle you with him.'

The albino tutted and shook his head at William. 'I told you that we'd hear nothing but nonsense from the sprat.' He spoke in a low growl so that he couldn't be heard by the crew. 'Why did you bother with the child, Captain? You know it makes me fearful. She'll bring us nothing but bad fortune.'

'Silence, man,' William ordered. 'Whose ship is this?'

Jack shrugged and glared at Fleur. 'Well, you know how I feel, Captain,' he replied. 'But I'll follow your orders.'

The captain patted him roughly on the shoulder and nodded. Then they moved away so that they could speak more privately.

'Who was that?' Fleur whispered to Tom.

He turned to her with a scowl. 'It's Jack, our second in command. He was part of the captain and your father's original crew.'

Jack glanced over just as she was studying him and their eyes met. His red eyes bored into her and she quickly turned away. 'He gives me the creeps,' she said. 'He looks undead.'

Tom rolled his eyes and sneered at her. 'It's just the way he is – folk come in all shapes and colours. Jack is a good man and a better pirate.'

Fleur reddened. 'I didn't mean to cause offence, I just ain't seen a living ghost before, that's all. And what about you?' she asked, quickly changing the subject. 'Where did you come from?'

He shrugged and peered down at the dolphins chasing the ship. They leaped in high arcs, bouncing across the waves as if it were a trampoline.

'I've been with the captain since I was eight. My

parents died and I stowed away in his ship. He found me and tried to throw me off, but I begged him to let me stay.' He looked at her warningly. 'I've had to earn my keep, I can tell you. I'm his cabin boy. I serve him and swab the decks, but I'm learning how to do everything so I can captain my own ship one day.'

'I think I'd like that too.' Fleur sighed wistfully.

'You?' he exclaimed. 'But you're only a girl. You can't be a pirate captain.'

'Yes I can,' she replied furiously. 'There's been female pirates before, and there will be again. I could already sail this ship alone.'

Tom laughed at her. 'You liar.'

She pursed her lips together and smacked her hand down hard on the ship's rail. 'I don't lie,' she hissed through her teeth. 'And I bet I know more about this ship than you do.'

He whipped round to face her. 'All right then – what's a backstaff?'

'Oh, come on,' she replied haughtily. 'That's easy. It's a navigation tool: you use it to measure the height of the sun at midday to calculate the latitude.'

That shut him up.

'Oh,' he responded. 'OK then – what's that called?' He pointed up to a platform at the top of the mainmast.

She sighed as if in boredom. 'Oh please! That's the crow's nest, used by the lookout to search for ships.'

He looked about the ship, frantically trying to find something else to ask her. 'OK, why don't you—?' he began.

'Tom, have you shown *Finn* where he will be sleeping yet?' the captain interrupted, reappearing behind them.

'No, Cap'n. Right, Cap'n.' And Tom led her away without another word.

The *Libertine* was a vast ship and carried just under one hundred pirates, who all scowled and grunted at Fleur as she passed by and teased her about the bow and arrows slung across her back. It seemed as if they came from every country that lay beneath the sun: Germans, Africans, West Indians, Irish . . . Henry had taught Fleur how to speak French and Spanish, but she had never heard so many other exotic languages and accents before.

The sun had started to sink towards the horizon and the sky was darkening, so lanterns bloomed light in the dark corners. The smell of rotten fish and human sweat clung to everything.

Tom raced ahead, pointing out things as they passed.

'That's where we keep the cannonballs, spare rope and sails,' he said as they hurried across the deck. 'Everything has to be stowed away safely. If the cargo started shifting around, the ship could capsize.'

A ginger cat leaped down from a nearby cannon and rubbed itself up against Tom's legs. He picked it up and sat it on his shoulder. 'Meet Parsley, the ship's cat.'

Fleur stroked the cat's head and it purred. It was a muscular animal, tatty and bald in places from fighting. 'Isn't it cruel to keep a cat on a ship?' she asked.

Tom shook his head. 'No. Parsley loves it. He's a tough cat and a good ratter. That's why we keep him on board.'

Fleur looked about her in disgust.

'There are plenty of stowaways aboard this ship, for we sail all the world over. Rats ain't the worst of it either – although when we get an infestation they'll gnaw through everything they can, including us.' Tom grinned at Fleur's expression. 'There's poisonous spiders, scorpions and fleas hiding in the cracks and the canvas. Now let's push on below decks.'

The smell grew worse the lower they went. Tom took her into the galley – the ship's kitchen. It was a dark room with a huge fireplace. The pungent scent of herbs and spices, cheese and fish filled the airless space.

Cauldrons bubbled over the flames and a pig was roasting on the spit.

'Hmm, that smells good.' Fleur sniffed hungrily.

Tom nodded. 'It might now, but a few weeks at sea and everything turns rotten. Hope you ain't squeamish?'

'What do you mean?' she asked.

He grinned wickedly. 'Nothing gets wasted so you'll be seeing a few maggots wriggling in your dinners soon.' He smacked his lips together. 'And when you're starving hungry they almost taste good.'

Fleur shuddered and looked over at the cook. He was busy salting joints of meat and fish to preserve them, and drinking straight from a bottle of rum. He was completely bald but his shiny skull sported a huge tattoo of an eagle.

'Got any hardtack, Sam?' Tom asked. 'I ain't eaten for hours and I'm starving.'

The burly man hacked the head off a huge fish. It fell to the floor and one dead, glassy eye stared up at the ceiling.

'Heaven's mercy, there'd be nothin' left for the crew to eat if I let you loose in my supplies. Take but a couple,' he slurred, and eyed Fleur suspiciously. 'Who's the new laddie?'

Tom helped himself to a couple of the long-lasting ship's biscuits made from water, flour and lard, and handed one to Fleur. She bit into it and almost broke a tooth.

'He's called Finn – we're taking him to the Caribbean.'

'Good – we can catch some nice juicy turtles for my pot there.' Sam took another swig of the rum and staggered into a table.

'He's always drunk,' Tom whispered as they watched him stumble around complaining that it was impossible to cook when the waves were so high. In actual fact the weather was calm and the sea was as flat as a pancake. Fleur sucked on a crumb of the tasteless biscuit and tried not to giggle. There was a lot of beer, ale, mead and rum onboard because it made the stale drinking water taste better and the rum helped kill the germs in it.

Tom led her aft – towards the rear of the ship. 'This is where the captain and Jack's cabins are. That's the tiller, powder store, rudder . . . ship's stores, ballast . . .'

Fleur had to run to catch up with him. 'And where do I sleep?' she asked.

Tom marched her down to the storage deck. Bulkheads – the ship's walls – had been taken down to create more space. Hammocks were strapped to every available post. Here it stank even more richly of sweat, sour rum and cigarette smoke, and a few pirates lay there, snoring loudly. Tom pointed to a couple of hammocks next to each other in a corner, hidden away slightly from everyone else.

'This is us. The captain wanted to make sure you got a little privacy.'

Fleur frowned.

'What maggot's burying under your periwig?' Tom teased.

'Do I really have to sleep in that?'

He eyed her slyly. 'You can sleep where you like. Most spaces are taken but I think there's room near the head.'

Fleur cringed. The head was just holes cut in a board at the bows of a ship. The sailors would simply sit on the holes and deposit their waste straight into the sea. There wasn't much privacy aboard a pirate ship.

'I don't think so,' she replied haughtily, then swung herself effortlessly up into her hammock and lay back. 'Actually it's not too bad. I thought the rope would dig into me.'

'We have to sleep in hammocks – well, except for the captain and Jack, who have proper beds. You can't fall out of a hammock easily, no matter how angry the weather.'

Fleur nodded. It made sense. Parsley jumped up, landed on her stomach and started nuzzling into her. Tom looked surprised.

'What?' she asked.

He shrugged. 'It's just that cat doesn't like many folk. The captain rescued him from drowning in a sack – he was a wild thing, clawing and scratching everyone in sight. But he broke him in.' He reached over and tickled Parsley under the chin. 'He doesn't like anyone apart from me and the captain.'

Fleur swung her legs over the side of the hammock and jumped down. 'Well, he's a good judge of character then.'

Tom stared at her for a while, saying nothing. 'You're not like a normal girl, are you?' he said finally.

'What do you mean?' Fleur snapped.

'I mean, you don't act all stupid.'

'Girls aren't stupid.'

Tom's face was blank. He still wasn't ready to be too friendly. 'That they are, acting like fluttering doves and the like. But not you. You're more like a boy. You're fearless.'

'Well, maybe you just haven't met the right kind of

girls,' Fleur muttered gruffly, though she was secretly pleased.

Tom swung himself into the other hammock and eyed Fleur thoughtfully.

'What?'

The boy shrugged casually and inspected his fingernails. 'I overheard you talking to the captain about the Hart staff, back in Cornwall.'

'And . . . ?' she asked, kicking a couple of cockroaches aside with her toe.

'Did you really see it?' Tom asked, his eyes widening.

Fleur leaned back against a wooden post and studied his face. There was a hungry glint in his eyes. 'Yes, I did,' she said. 'And it would make a good fishing pole if you strung a line on it.'

'You've got no idea how important that thing is, have you?' he sighed, flopping back into his hammock.

Fleur rolled her eyes and folded her arms defensively. 'Of course I haven't,' she grunted. 'I was trying to make a joke.'

Tom swung the hammock from side to side, making the wood around them creak loudly. 'It's the stuff of legends, that staff,' he blurted suddenly, unable to contain his excitement. 'I didn't really believe it existed, to be honest. Not entirely anyway. There's a prophecy, see? It says—'

'Hey, cabin boy,' came a man's voice from the other side of the room. Tom stopped talking and swinging immediately.

'You woke me up, you little sprat,' the man shouted. 'And who's the other laddie with you?'

Tom fell silent at once and the pair of them turned to see that one of the sleeping pirates had woken up. A huge silver cage sat next to the man's hammock: Fleur could just make out a pair of beady eyes inside it.

Tom tensed and gritted his teeth. 'That's Peg-leg,' he whispered. 'Jack met him and a few others in a tavern in Truro when we picked you up, and they joined the crew. Watch out for him – he's cocky, and nasty with it.'

'What's in that cage?' Fleur asked.

'An eagle,' Tom replied. 'And it's as cruel as its master.'

Peg-leg sat up in his hammock and let out a massive fart. Fleur squinted in the weak lantern light to try and see him clearly, but he was a blur of shadows in the gloom.

'Come on then, sea scum, who be the new boy?'

Tom scowled at him. 'It's the captain's business, not

yours. And anyhow, you're just as fresh to this crew as he is.'

Peg-leg prised a huge wad of soggy tobacco off the wall next to him, put it in his mouth and started to chew. He got down and hobbled over. Fleur heard a thump on the deck and realized it was the man's wooden leg. He approached them and prodded a finger into Tom's chest. 'That's all we need. More cannon fodder. Cap'n Hart must be going soft, picking up spindly waifs and strays from every port, while most red-blooded men pick up women. He'll have a crew of children soon. Lily-livered wimp. They call him William the Heartless, but seems to me he ain't heartless at all.'

'Don't speak about the captain like that,' Tom said hotly.

Peg-leg pushed him to the floor and spat tobacco juice at him. It landed on Tom's face in a big ball of spittle. 'Why? Will you be telling 'im?'

'I might,' Tom replied boldly.

Peg-leg reached out to grab him, but Tom darted out of the way. 'I'll wrap a marlinspike round your head, sonny,' the older pirate threatened, then got hold of Tom's leg and dragged him along roughly.

'Don't treat him like that,' Fleur raged indignantly. 'You're a bully!'

Tom looked at her with surprise, Peg-leg with contempt.

'A bully, am I?' He came over, bent down and stared into her eyes. Even in the darkness she could tell he was a hideous-looking man; his breath reeked and there was something about his raspy voice that struck fear into her very soul. 'And what are you going to do about it, sonny?' He pulled out a knife and held it to her throat. 'You're so new here no one would even notice if I cracked you like a flea.'

'*I* would.' A clear voice rang out.

Peg-leg went rigid and turned slowly to see the captain standing in the doorway. 'I was only teasing the laddies,' he said, cowering away. 'I didn't mean nothing by it.'

William stared at him before addressing him in an icy tone. 'You've a split tongue and I swear I'll hack your skull asunder if you dare disrespect your captain again.'

'I won't, Cap'n,' Peg-leg whined.

William slowly walked towards him. 'We have a choice: do you want an eternal swim in Davy Jones's locker or a flogging? You're not worth shiproom if you're going to be nothing but trouble – I'm only giving you the choice as you're a new matey on my ship.'

'Sir, don't throw me overboard,' Peg-leg whimpered.

'Yellow never was a pirate's colour, but a flogging it is then. That should trounce the devil from you.'

He forced Peg-leg up onto the deck; Tom and Fleur followed behind. The night had completely overtaken the day and the moon cast a beam of light onto the inky waves that stretched out like a carpet before them. Fresh from their battle, the crew were drunk and a fight had broken out among a small group of them. They were rolling around the deck, punching and clawing at each other like wildcats. The others were drinking grog and urging them on.

'Quiet, you scugs,' William roared.

The crew stopped immediately and turned to face their captain, who pushed Peg-leg forward. The man stumbled awkwardly onto his one remaining knee.

'Strap him up!' William roared.

Two of the men moved forward and dragged Peg-leg roughly back to his feet, then bound him tightly to some rigging with leather thongs.

'Thirty-nine lashes, Captain?' one of them asked.

'Aye, for he hasn't done much wrong to slur me,' William replied with a nod. 'This is a lesson, not a punishment. So, to all that have just joined us, watch and learn.'

Fleur dragged Tom away as Peg-leg stared at them with all the hate he could muster.

'I can't watch,' she whispered to him. 'It's so brutal.'

'It's the way it is at sea,' Tom replied. 'It's not for the faint-hearted.' He looked down at his grubby bare feet and pivoted awkwardly on his heel. 'I . . . um . . . thanks for what you said to Peg-leg by the way. There's not many that would stand up for the likes of me.'

'Well, I will, if you do the same for me.'

Tom shrugged. 'Maybe,' he agreed reluctantly. 'But you're still a girl and I still think it's bad luck for you to be on this ship.'

The flogging had started. There was a crack of a whip and Peg-leg cried out in pain.

'Why thirty-nine lashes?' Fleur asked, wincing as the whip rang out a second time.

'It's called Moses's Law,' Tom explained. 'The law itself means forty lashes – it's from the Bible. Forty lashes are enough to kill a man, so thirty-nine are what you can give a man without wanting him to die. But that number of lashes usually makes a man pass out or die anyway.'

He nodded towards Peg-leg, who looked close to collapse – only the binds were keeping him standing.

'Look, he's a trickster. I bet he's going to pretend to faint, the chicken-hearted wimp.'

Sure enough, they watched him sink into a further swoon, flicking his eyes open briefly to make sure the captain was watching.

'I reckon a man like that probably cut off his own leg for the eight hundred pieces of eight you're paid for losing a limb aboard a pirate ship,' Tom muttered.

Parsley padded up to them and nuzzled his nose into the backs of Fleur's knees. She bent over to pick him up and scratched his neck. A deep purr vibrated from the cat's warm belly. Fleur frowned in concentration as she watched William order his men to cut Peg-leg down: there was something about the one-legged pirate that chilled her to the bone.

'Now, you lazy swabs, stir yourselves and shake out a reef. Starboard the helm and let's make some speed. Look alive, lads,' roared their captain. 'We've a fair distance to travel and a ripe body rotting in the bowels of this brigantine.'

As he disappeared below decks with Jack, Fleur turned to see Peg-leg open his eyes.

He shuffled into a sitting position and winced as his raw back rubbed against a splintered piece of wood. He searched the crowd for a face and smiled cruelly to himself when he found hers, raising an eyebrow and miming a blade across his throat. Someone moved a lantern nearer him and she saw him clearly for the first time. As Fleur slowly raised her eyes to meet his, he mouthed four words that made her flesh crawl:

'I'm coming for you.'

CHAPTER 6

'William? William? Are you in there?' Fleur whispered urgently, banging on his cabin door. She checked to see if anyone was coming and knocked again. '*William?*'

The door was flung open and her uncle stood there, seething with rage. He narrowed his eyes at her and dragged her into the room. 'Get in here now,' he hissed. 'Quick's the word.'

She stumbled forward and stared at the sumptuous surroundings with wide eyes. The huge double bed was covered in dusky-coloured silks and black sheepskins. Papers and navigational charts covered a small wooden table, and the walls were decorated with maps, oil paintings and a crude sketch of the Hart staff. A battered old sea chest bursting with belongings sat in a corner; the well-polished brass telescope pointed out of a porthole in the direction of the stars.

'And don't call me *William*!' Fleur's uncle added. 'I'm Captain to you.' He slammed the door shut behind her.

'Ouch!' she yelped. 'That hurt.'

'Quieten down, child, or I'm likely to cut your tongue out.' He pushed her into a chair and stepped back to glower at her. 'You need to be invisible on this ship, Fleur,' he warned. 'My crew are wild things – the dregs left over when all that is good and true is gone. They're killers: that's why they sail with me. If they found out about you, I would not be able to guarantee your safety. A pirate captain's murder is only a mutiny away, and I ain't wanting to join my brother yet.'

Fleur pointed over at the sketch of the Hart staff. 'Why didn't you tell me that thing had a prophecy attached to it?' she asked.

Her uncle glanced at the drawing. 'What business is that of yours?'

'I'm a Hart, ain't I?'

He folded his arms. 'In name, yes. Now, is that all you came to ask me? If so, go away.'

'But I have something to tell you,' Fleur said urgently.

William poured himself a large glass of rum and sat down, rocking back in his chair and throwing his feet up on the table; dried mud dropped off his battered sea boots.

'Speak, child.'

Fleur sat forward. 'Peg-leg threatened me. He's out to get me.'

Her uncle didn't say a word. Instead he downed his glass of rum in one and started loading his pipe with tobacco. Silence burned between them as he lit it. The tobacco crackled and glowed red as smoke poured out. He took a puff and breathed out slowly. Fleur could barely contain herself, but finally he spoke.

'So what do you want me to do about it?' he asked. 'Throw him in the brig to rot until we reach the Caribbean? I've already had him whipped.'

Fleur's eyes widened with thoughts of revenge. 'No, make him walk the plank,' she spat.

William roared with mirth. 'You know we seldom do that, my bloodthirsty little duck. There are far better ways to sink and burn a man.'

'So what are we going to do then?'

He scowled at her presumption. '*We? We* won't be doing anything.'

'Well, if you won't do anything, I'll . . . I'll confront him.'

The laughter stopped immediately. 'You will not,' he roared.

'But, Uncle—'

He threw his hands up in the air with frustration. 'I will not have a slip of a girl causing trouble on my ship. And I said, do *not* call me Uncle. I care nothing for your feelings as long as you remain in one skinny piece. And I will not reprimand a man for despising you. This is life on a pirate ship, girl, and if you can't handle it, you're welcome to leave at any point.' He scowled at her. 'There is no place in my world for children or family. Now get out before my blood boils. You've no more brains than a sea turtle.'

'But Peg-leg's trouble,' Fleur persisted. 'There's something about him I don't trust, Unc— I mean, Captain.'

William was suddenly right in front of her. He bent down so that his face was inches from hers. She could smell the foul reek of his breath and see right into the hell furnaces burning in his eyes.

'I am the captain of the *Libertine*. And while you sail on her, you do as I say. Now get out or I'll use you for musket practice.'

Fleur backed away slowly, then spun round and dashed from the room. She climbed up to the deck and leaned against a mast, trying to calm her breathing. A chill seeped into her bones as she realized that she'd just stared right into a darkness that scared her more than anything she had ever known.

Fleur ignored the calls for dinner that night and went straight to bed. The crew had gradually filtered into their sleeping quarters, each man drunker than the last, singing sea shanties well into the night. At one point she was aware of someone standing at the foot of her hammock, watching her. As he walked away she heard the sound of a peg leg thumping and scraping across the floor.

In the grey dawn Tom silently led Fleur onto the deck and they helped haul on the ropes that set the sails aloft. A cool wind blew above the waves and the rigging creaked as the sails lifted, straightened and filled with the breeze. Fleur stood with the rope running through her hands and drank in the morning. At that moment the sun broke on the horizon and light flooded down onto the world, as if someone had turned the colour up. The sea glowed indigo and seagulls began to mew and soar above them.

Tom sighed with contentment as he stared out over

the rolling waves. 'It's the best thing ever, ain't it?' he said, without the usual barbed spike to his voice.

Fleur looked at him with surprise and nodded. It was true, the sea burned in her like a fever.

After more early morning chores they breakfasted on salt fish, ship's biscuits and water. The cook asked Fleur to fetch some tea leaves, so she picked her way through a flock of hens pecking away on the deck and climbed down into the airless hold. It was stacked high with bales of cotton, spices, silk, tobacco and tea; the pungent stink of the cargo made Fleur feel dizzy. Strange shadows flitted among the spaces between the towering piles; all was quiet except for the persistent scratch of rat claws. Fleur was aware that her father's body lay somewhere in the belly of the huge ship, and there was some strange comfort there. She wasn't sure what happened to people's souls after they had died, but she was certain he'd be watching over her, if he could. As she reached up for a bag of tea, the door at the top of the stairs swung open and light flooded the gloom.

'Who's there?' she called out.

The door closed and there was silence.

'Hello?' she asked again.

More silence. Then she heard a foot at the top of the steps, followed by a sound that froze her to the spot: the thump of a wooden leg and a raspy breath. Panic constricted her chest so that she could barely breathe and she looked around wildly to see if there was some place to hide. But Peg-leg was coming steadily down the stairs and had her locked in his sight.

'Go away,' she begged.

'Or what?' he asked slyly.

Fleur backed into a corner. There was something about this ugly man that sent shivers of fear down her spine. She felt as if she knew him – but from where?

'I'll tell the captain,' she said.

Peg-leg laughed and looked around theatrically. 'He won't hear your cries from here, *dearie*.'

She went cold. 'What did you just say?'

He raised an eyebrow. 'There be rumours on board this ship that you're a girl in borrowed breeches.'

'A girl on a ship?' she replied. 'It's bad luck. William would never allow it.'

Peg-leg spat on the floor. '*William*, is it? Not Captain? He would if he had a good enough reason to carry you. I'm reckoning you're worth a fair bit of gold that he ain't sharing.'

He drew out a knife and Fleur withdrew further into the corner. She looked about her but there was nowhere to go. Peg-leg ran the knife through his fingers playfully.

'And if he ain't sharing, I don't see the point of you bringing bad fortune to us all.' He was only inches away and the blade swung dangerously in the silence. Fleur bit her lip and the metallic taste of blood seeped into her mouth. If only she had a weapon to hand, at least then she'd have more of a chance against this bully. Instead, she scuttled along into another corner, but Peg-leg was blocking the exit so she was trapped. He swished the knife as if trying to slice through the air, then began hobbling towards her. Fleur shrank into a tight ball and closed her eyes. Her father had trained her for moments such as this. She knew that she might have a chance if she defended herself against the man. But fear clouded everything she had learned.

'Get up, sea sprat.'

Fleur snapped her eyes open as his words sliced through her: his strangely familiar voice filled her with pure panic.

The ugly pirate grinned at her cruelly. 'I ain't going to kill you,' he taunted. 'Not now at least. I don't want to earn meself any more lashes because of you.' He nodded towards the stairs. 'Get up there now – the crew need some entertainment.'

Fleur dashed up towards the pale sunlight that filtered through the door before he changed his mind. Peg-leg hurried after her, stumbling up the stairs in his haste. He pushed her aside roughly as he reached the top and walked out onto the deck first.

When she emerged, he was standing with a small group of sailors a few feet away. Her entire body began to tremble violently, but she refused to look away and stood her ground. She saw Peg-leg's eagle circling above them, but now it swooped down to alight on his arm. Fleur hadn't seen the bird in daylight before. It looked vicious: its powerful hooked beak was still bloody from the flesh of its recent prey. Peg-leg stroked its head and it hopped up onto his shoulder to watch the proceedings. Tom had appeared and was sitting on the deck, staring over with open curiosity. Fleur bit her lip nervously.

'If you're a proper sailor boy, you need to prove it.' Peg-leg looked about the ship, searching for a way to test her.

'Let's just use the child for pistol practice,' one of his cronies taunted.

'Or we could fire him from a cannon,' someone else suggested.

Laughter rippled around the small group and Peg-leg caught sight of Tom. 'Hey there, cabin boy, what say you?'

'I ain't got nothing to say on the matter,' he said quietly, his eyes cast down. 'You can do with him what you want.'

Fleur's mouth dropped open in shock but Tom just shrugged.

'But, Tom,' she cried out, 'I thought you said . . . I thought . . .' Her voice trailed away.

Peg-leg watched with interest. 'See, even your little friend won't help you.'

Tom spat on the deck. 'It's each man for himself out here,' he replied matter-of-factly – although his eye twitched nervously. 'Sorry, Finn, but it's the only way to survive.'

'Let's strap Finn to the mainmast and let the gulls peck at him,' a squat little pirate suggested.

Peg-leg nodded and moved forward, grabbing roughly at Fleur's arm. 'Aye, that'll test him all right.'

At that moment Jack strode into the crowd wearing a furious expression. 'What the hell is going on here, you filthy drunks?' he demanded, staring directly at Peg-leg.

'I've heard the rumours.' The one-legged pirate pointed towards Fleur. 'There's talk about Finn here. They're saying he might be a bitch pup in hiding.'

Jack glared at him in disgust. 'And why would the

captain bring bad luck upon the *Libertine* by allowing this?'

Peg-leg's eyes bulged with greed. 'For treasure. He's carrying the child for nobility, mark my words, and he's probably lying to you too.'

Jack took a step forward and Peg-leg scuttled away like a rat. There was a force about the lieutenant that wasn't just about his huge muscular frame. Even though he appeared calm, something in his steady gaze made men fear him: pure fury simmered within him like lava.

'You're a fool if you believe them whispers,' he said, his eyes resting on Fleur as he spoke. 'Finn is a boy and there's nothing more to discuss. If anyone wants to check for themselves, go ahead. But when my word's affirmed you'll earn a good thrashing for not trusting your captain.'

Fleur's body went rigid as the pirates looked her up and down suspiciously. It was a risky game that Jack was playing. Fortunately for both of them it worked, and the men gathered around, grunting their acceptance.

'Anyhow,' Jack continued, 'Captain Hart wouldn't risk the crew for his own gain.'

The crew's murmurs revealed a split. Some of them agreed with Jack wholeheartedly; others clearly sided with Peg-leg. It was the disgruntled grumblings of the second group that were gradually growing more disruptive. The situation was becoming dangerous.

The loud crack of a pistol silenced the rising mob at once. The captain stood a few feet away, staring at them blackly, one arm held high, the pistol still smoking in his hand.

Jack nodded to him grimly. 'Captain, they're goading the new laddie again. I told you nothing good would come of carrying young Finn.'

William frowned at his lieutenant. Jack tensed, biting his lower lip. He could barely contain himself, and stared into Fleur's eyes with obvious contempt before spinning on his heel and striding away. Fleur leaned against one of the masts, wiping her sweaty palms on her baggy old sailor's slops. Her mere presence on board seemed to be causing her uncle trouble.

'Tell me, men,' the captain asked, setting aside his weapon. 'Do you honestly think a girl could survive the life we've chosen, eh? Do you think she would want to?' He laughed heartily and, slowly at first, his audience began to join in. 'Brothers, we are the stuff of nightmares. The scum from hell's plughole.' He glanced over at Fleur. 'I would never let a woman join my crew. Why, I'd rather eat my own hat. No fluttering dove could survive a life on the crest of these waves.'

Anger pulsed through Fleur and she glowered at her uncle as the crowd erupted into wild cheering. He was wrong, Fleur knew it. And she would prove it to him.

'Get to work *now*,' William roared. He pointed directly at Peg-leg. 'I'm watching you.'

The crowd dispersed quickly, leaving Fleur trembling in her uncle's shadow.

'Like I said, *Finn*, be invisible,' he muttered, before storming off.

Fleur blew air from her cheeks with relief and noticed Tom was still sitting nearby. He sighed and rose to his feet wearily.

'You said you'd look out for me,' she said accusingly.

'I didn't promise anything,' he replied with a shrug. 'Sorry, but I don't want you here. Like I said, you ain't nothing but a girl. And like Cap'n Hart said, you don't belong on this ship. I'm only putting up with you because I was ordered to.'

Fleur thrust her hands on her hips and fumed. 'I've got as much right to be here as you. In fact I've got more right because it's in my blood. You're just a castaway.'

'Shut up!' Tom shouted, his cheeks flushed with anger. 'I earned my right to be on this ship. You're only a passenger.'

'I can do anything you can do!' Fleur shouted back furiously.

Tom looked around desperately and then grinned. He pointed up at the mainmast. 'All right then. If you're so capable, you should be able to climb up that mast to the crow's nest like a jungle cat,' he said, pointing upwards. 'I'll climb another one and we'll see who gets to the top first.'

Fleur looked from Tom to the tip of the mast and began to panic. It was *so* high − much taller than the biggest tree she had ever climbed. Tom leaned against the rail and folded his arms, staring at her with a challenging, taunting look. She looked up again at the small perch at the top of the mainmast and her throat constricted with fear. It was just too high: the gulls that dipped and dived around it looked tiny. But she remembered what her father had told her when he taught her how to climb: *Just throw yourself up to the heavens like it's your right to be there. Don't look down because it will only remind you that you are earthbound.* She took a deep breath, and then, without another word, kicked her boots off. She had to prove herself to Tom. She needed someone on her side, and if this was what it took, so be it. Tom looked surprised, but without a further word moved across to the mizzenmast and nodded for them to begin their ascent.

Fleur's fury gave her the energy and confidence she needed. The wood of the mast was worn and smooth and she clung on tightly with her legs. She could feel the weight of Tom's stare, but she didn't look back. Her hands were sticky with sweat and every now and again she slipped. Her limbs began to tremble and her palms stung. Soon all she could hear was the hush of the wind and the waves and the cawing of the gulls. She glanced over at the other mast and a thrill of excitement ran through her: Tom was behind her and she could hear the murmur of the pirates below. Up, further and further she climbed, barely resting, until finally she reached the top. She swung herself onto the platform effortlessly and finally let herself look down, brimming with pride and confidence. Tom had not yet reached the top of his mast, and she registered his shocked expression before turning away triumphantly. She had won and surely proved herself to Tom.

Instead of climbing down, Fleur turned to stare out at the sunny morning. The sea was azure blue and melted into the cloudless sky. A strong wind blew and the sails strained and billowed. The breeze whipped against her skin and she licked her salty lips and laughed out loud. She had never felt so free, or so close to her father. Fleur squeezed her eyes shut and imagined Henry standing beside her as they charged across the rolling waves. *See, my girl*, she could hear him say. *This is what we were born for.* And she realized then that she didn't really need to visit a grave on Ile aux Forbans, because while she was close to the sea Henry was all around her.

Fleur opened her eyes, and as she gazed at the horizon, she noticed a tiny speck in the distance. She squinted against the sun and for a moment she thought she saw a ship sailing behind them. But then a wave blinked and it was gone. She breathed in deeply and closed her eyes. She could have stayed up there for ever – or at least until they had reached St Kitts safely. While Peg-leg was on the *Libertine*, the threat of discovery was only a raspy breath away.

CHAPTER 7

After the mast-climbing competition Tom's attitude towards Fleur changed. She had beaten him to the top, hands down, and had proved herself to him fair and square; he couldn't help but show her a new respect. Fleur saw the change and glowed with pride. Respect meant everything out here on the ocean. If she was to become a pirate and one day captain her own ship, she would need to be able to win over the most stubborn shipmate. And besides, she was pleased to know that Tom actually sought out her company now. She certainly enjoyed being with him.

Days quickly turned to weeks aboard the *Libertine*,

and Fleur took William's advice and made herself as invisible as possible. Her brooding uncle refused to acknowledge her at all. The pirate crew ignored her too, mostly, so it was easy to disappear into corners and hide. She was used to such company: she had often helped her father serve the rowdy drunks in the Pandora Inn. It was only when they were the worse for wear that the pirates really picked on her. But then they did the same to Tom. The proud cabin boy pretended that it didn't bother him, but it was obvious that it did: his cheeks would redden and he'd start chewing on his fingernails. They were a surly, violent bunch of men, prone to boredom and squabbling. William kept them under control with threats and punishment, but they were like a sleeping volcano, ready to erupt and spew forth at any moment. Fleur decided that if she ever became a pirate captain, she would pick her crew with care.

Everyone on the *Libertine* worked hard, and Fleur set about her tasks with a will. Days were long – sometimes the crew would be working for sixteen hours straight – but it was better than the idle boredom of inactivity. To pass the time and to help them with their chores they sang sea shanties; their voices bounced over the waves as steadily as the ship itself. There were short drag shanties for shortening or unfurling the sails, long drag shanties for heavier duties. There were capstan shanties for raising the anchor and other repetitive tasks, and then the forecast shanties saved for the evening, when all the work was done. When the sun dipped low they would sit in clusters, drinking their grog by lantern light, and their songs would tell stories from all the lands they had seen.

Fleur was exhausted. A sailor's life wasn't easy. Her bones ached from all the physical duties, and bruises and cuts covered her sunburned flesh. Her lips had blistered from the salty air and her hands were raw and bloody.

Tom helped her with her duties as much as possible, but all the while she knew that Peg-leg was out to get her. He was a bully by nature, and he obviously had it in for her. Whenever he was bored or grumpy, which was most of the time, he made a point of tormenting her. He often appeared when Fleur was alone, creeping up and leering at her. She was convinced that she'd come across him before. Still, she couldn't put her finger on the why or the where of it – though she wondered whether he might have visited her father's inn. It was impossible to know, and she wasn't about to ask.

Whatever the truth, Peg-leg's presence chilled her to the bone. Sometimes he would simply stare at her. Other times he would aim a pistol at her or pretend to slit his own throat. His fierce eagle would brush past her on the deck, or when she was climbing the rigging or the masts; and she knew that Peg-leg was somewhere watching and laughing at her. Night times were the worst. She slept with a small knife hidden nearby, just in case she woke to see his yellowed eyes peering down upon her.

'Hey, Claw-cat,' Tom called out as he clambered down from the mast one evening. He was frowning.

Fleur walked over to him, sipping from her skin of water. The rain swirled around them in a fine mist, slowly soaking them. 'Hoa, Tom,' she said in reply. 'What's wrong?'

'I'm not sure,' said Tom, swiping the skin from her and taking a large swig. 'Have you seen anything odd from the crow's nest today?'

'Like what?' she asked.

Tom handed back Fleur's water, and his frown deepened. 'Like a ship skirting the horizon.'

'I knew it!' she gasped. 'The first time I climbed the mast I thought I was imagining it. But I thought it was there yesterday, almost too far to see.' She thought for a moment. 'Then, this morning, it seemed to be there again, but was gone before I could be sure.'

Tom looked grave as they leaned against the ship's rail

and stared out at the empty sea. Cats' paws of wind played along its surface, rippling the water.

'It's like seeing the idea of something,' he said. 'But nothing ever actually appears.'

Fleur nodded. 'Maybe we're just imagining it. The water's always playing tricks on me. I thought I saw a new island the other day, but it turned out to be the shadow of a storm cloud.'

'Hmmm, maybe,' Tom muttered. 'Maybe it ain't a *real* ship exactly.'

Parsley appeared, rubbing around their ankles and purring loudly. Tom bent down to pick him up and the cat's purrs grew ever louder as he presented his ginger scruff for a scratch.

'What do you think it is then,' Fleur asked him, leaning over to tickle Parsley's belly, 'if it's not a ship?'

Tom shuddered and looked back out to sea with a fearful expression.

'What is it?' Fleur was intrigued. 'Come on, I promise I won't be scared.'

'All right, I'll tell you,' snapped Tom, glancing at her crossly. 'And don't start thinking I'm crazed, because I ain't the only one that fears things that go bump in the night.' He paused dramatically.

'Oh come on, get to it,' urged Fleur. 'I promise I won't

think you're crazed.' She twirled one finger at her temple and stuck out her tongue.

Tom's face softened, then grew stern again. 'I think it could be a ghost,' he replied earnestly.

Fleur snorted incredulously and Tom glared at her.

'Sorry,' she said, trying to straighten out her smile. 'It's just, well . . . a ghost ship? You're not serious?'

'You said you wouldn't think I was crazed,' said Tom sulkily, wrapping the purring Parsley around his shoulders like a scarf.

'That was before you announced that we're being pursued by spirits. Woooo!' she wailed, laughing.

Tom turned to leave, but Fleur reached out to stop him, conquering her giggles.

'Don't go, Tom. Tell me what you know. I'm sorry I teased you. I promise I'll be serious.'

Tom shrugged her away and sighed with exasperation. 'All right,' he said, eyeing her cautiously. 'But if you start, I'm off.'

'Cross my heart,' said Fleur. 'Tell me.'

'Well,' said Tom, 'I've heard the stories about the cursed *Flying Dutchman* since I was a young 'un. 'Tis said she's doomed to sail the seas for ever.'

The ship lurched suddenly as a wave slapped down hard onto the deck, covering them with spray. Parsley leaped off Tom's shoulders in disgust and shook the excess water from his scrawny body before darting below.

'Why?' Fleur asked, beginning to feel nervous in spite of herself. 'Why can't the *Dutchman* ever go home?'

'The captain made a pact with the devil and in doing so brought a terrible curse on his ship and crew. She's usually seen from afar,' Tom said, swallowing uncomfortably. His voice dropped to a whisper. 'It's thought that anyone who sees the *Flying Dutchman* will have great misfortune brought upon them. 'Tis an omen of doom that none can escape.'

Fleur swallowed hard and searched the horizon for the phantom ship. What if there *was* something in the tale? If Tom was right about this, they were surely doomed.

'This ain't a good voyage we're on,' he murmured, more to himself than to her. 'I can feel it. It's not just that we started on a Friday, which always means bad luck; it's more than that.' He shook his head thoughtfully. 'I might be young but I know when trouble's coming.'

'And is it?' asked Fleur seriously.

Tom turned towards her and she saw that his eyes were wide with fear. 'Oh yes,' he said shakily. 'It's coming fast.'

★

In the days that followed, Fleur began to notice whisperings that she strongly suspected were about her. The split in William's crew was getting worse. Someone had been stoking the fire of gossip and suspicion and now a storm was brewing. There were those who, having sailed with him for years, were enamoured of his cut-throat legend and would always admire and fear their captain. But there were plenty whose loyalty was less strong, and they were beginning to question him – though not, of course, to his face. They made certain that he didn't hear their whispers. But slowly, their boldness was growing.

It was the same rebellious crew members who muttered about Fleur each time she passed by. Their sudden silence whenever she approached made it quite obvious, although the handful of Frenchmen and Spaniards didn't even bother to lower their voices, unaware that she could understand every vile, mutinous word they said. Those who believed the rumours that she was a girl were convinced she was unlucky. Others claimed she was a prince that William had agreed to transport and were furious that he wasn't sharing the fee with them. The rest couldn't quite put their finger on what unnerved them about their skinny new shipmate.

William stayed out of her way, but Jack pushed her to the very limit. Fleur wondered why he was hard on her. After all, he had sailed with her father and knew exactly who she was. She would have liked to question him about Henry, but it was obvious that the subject was closed. Jack would tolerate no sign of weakness from her and criticized her relentlessly.

Fleur quickly found her feet as part of the crew. In fact she was a natural sailor. She worked harder than anyone, even Tom, to prove herself equal to the others. She swabbed the decks and took orders without complaint, stepping in to help anyone who would let her. The ship's carpenter, a jolly red-faced man with a kind smile, accepted any offer to lighten his workload, so she often accompanied him on his inspection rounds, checking the hull, placing oakum between the seams of the planks and stuffing wooden plugs into leaks to keep the vessel tight. Fleur would tag along with the bosun as he checked the sails and rigging for damage or dropped and weighed the anchor. The master gunner showed her how to keep the weapons in good order, and she accompanied the riggers up towering masts to unfurl the broad sails, conquering her fear of slipping from a spar high above the rolling deck and breaking her neck. She slept less than anyone else, yet never complained.

With everything her father had taught her, Fleur might easily have steered and navigated the ship herself. And while she worked she often daydreamed about what it might have been like to take the wheel beside Henry, instead of his troubled twin. But however easily she took to life at sea, nothing could have fully prepared her for her life amongst William's pirate crew. It was like living with bad-tempered, foul-smelling wild dogs. And the snarling, ever-present Peg-leg was the worst. Fleur had a feeling that his bite, when it came, would be worse than his bark.

One afternoon Fleur was helping the sailmaker mend tears in the ship's vast sails. A ripe sun burned fiercely down on them and salty beads of sweat ran into her eyes and blurred her vision. The tips of her fingers were tender and bloody from the sharp needle, which kept slipping from her grasp as she tried to pierce the heavy canvas. It had been yet another busy day for all aboard the *Libertine*, and when a lengthy shanty finally ended, the silence left behind was filled with tension.

'Ouch!' Fleur exclaimed as the needle slipped again and more of her blood stained the sail.

The sailmaker stared at her and scowled. He'd drunk too much cheap rum the night before and his queasy stomach was still grumbling. He muttered something incoherent and staggered off to vomit over the side. As Fleur looked down at her handiwork, something moved in front of the sun and cast a shadow. She glanced back up to see a thuggish-looking rigger with a huge beard that reached down to his belly, a cruel smile on his dark face. Suddenly he lurched forward and pretended to stumble. He crashed down on top of her, shouting and swearing that she'd tripped him on purpose. As she stared up at his oily face, she realized she'd seen him in Peg-leg's group.

'You little piece of sea scum!' he shouted in a thick Italian accent. 'Why did you do that?' He drew a knife from his pocket and held the cold blade to her neck; his face was so close she could smell his sour, sweaty skin.

'I . . . I didn't do anything,' she stuttered, and backed away from him.

As he staggered to his feet, he lunged forward and ripped the locket from Fleur's neck. She froze in silent shock as the world seemed to fall away from her. Then, as the truth sank in, rage took over.

'Give that back!' she yelled, balling her hands into tight fists and swiping at him. 'It belonged to my mother.'

'*Si*,' the pirate replied as spittle flew from his rubbery lips. 'And it's a girl's piece for sure.'

Fleur saw him exchange a wink with Peg-leg and realized immediately that the whole scene had been planned.

'Does that mean *you're* a girl?' the Italian boomed with a knowing expression. 'Or maybe this little trinket is a royal heirloom, and worth a few pieces of gold?'

Fleur reached up and tried to grab the precious locket, but the man dangled it out of reach and roared with laughter.

'You'll have to prove yourself to get this back, *boy*,' he spat.

'Give it back *now*,' Fleur demanded, showering his stomach with punches. 'I've proved myself enough.'

The pirate looked down at her small fists and laughed. He grabbed her wrists with one of his hands and pushed her away. Tom appeared from below decks and fought his way through the swelling, jeering crowd.

'What's going on?' he called over to Fleur.

She pointed to the pirate, who was backing away from her as if to throw the locket overboard.

Tom threw down the bucket he was carrying and

stormed over to them. 'That belongs to Finn,' he said indignantly.

'Well, he'll have to earn it back then, won't he, clam-brain,' Peg-leg replied, turning to the other pirates. 'Brothers, you want to see the new laddie prove her mettle again, don't you?'

They nodded in agreement and their mutterings grew. Life in the middle of the ocean was boring, so fights were welcome breaks, and Peg-leg always seemed to be stirring up trouble. As the jeers grew louder, Tom tried to grab the locket but the Italian pushed him roughly to the floor. The boy scrambled to his feet and threw himself at the solid wall of muscle. But again the bully hurled him to the deck with ease. Blood started seeping from Tom's nose; he wiped it away and tried to stand again.

Fleur stepped forward, motioning for Tom to stay back. 'Get off him,' she told the pirate. 'This has nothing to do with Tom,' but the tremble in her voice betrayed her.

The man glared at her. 'Or what?'

'Or . . . or . . .' she stuttered hopelessly. Her voice trailed into silence.

The men around her immediately broke into laughter and Fleur hung her head in defeat. Peg-leg hobbled over eagerly, clearly enjoying the show-down he'd been waiting for. He pointed to a small piece of rigging high up on the mainmast.

'If you can shoot clean through that rope, you can have your locket back, *laddie*.'

Fleur gazed up at a taut rope high above the deck. 'I don't have anything to shoot it with,' she replied, trying to keep her voice steady.

Peg-leg moved forward and handed her a large, ornate gun. The handle was made of solid silver and it was so heavy that she had to hold it with both hands.

'Well, go on then,' one of Peg-leg's cronies urged.

'Quick as you like,' he sneered. 'You get two shots.'

Fleur studied the gun and her heart sank because she knew at once that she'd been set up. Peg-leg had handed her a musketoon, which had a short barrel, meaning it was only accurate at close quarters; she didn't have a chance of hitting the distant target that had been set for her.

She looked up at Peg-leg. 'This won't reach it. I'll need something like a flintlock musket for that.'

'Sweet merciful heavens, Finn knows his guns, lads,' Peg-leg teased, holding out his arm as his eagle swooped down. It hopped up to his shoulder to watch the proceedings. 'Does anyone happen to have another gun on them perchance?' he added slyly.

The pirates shook their heads, just as Fleur had expected. The Italian was grinning as he swung her locket over the side of the ship like a pendulum. She raised her chin defiantly. So, they wanted her to prove herself again, did they? Well, she'd show them. Fleur raised the butt of the gun to her shoulder, just as her father had taught her, and aimed at the rope, squinting against the sunlight. All around, the sailors jeered and taunted her, but she blanked them out and concentrated on her breathing. *In through the nose, out through the mouth*, her father had once told her. *Make the gun an extension of your arm, then* fire!

Fleur pulled the trigger. The shot rang out, the sound ricocheting around, and she was blown backwards with the force. There was a shriek as one of the seven seagulls that had been sitting on the spar fell to the deck with a small thud; the other six moved to a higher crosspiece, where they stared down accusingly. The eagle, obviously more used to gunfire, hadn't even flinched. Howls of laughter erupted all around Fleur, but Tom dashed over and helped her up.

'You don't have to do this,' he hissed as she pushed him away.

Fleur looked over at her mother's locket and cold

determination gripped her. 'Yes I do,' she replied firmly without even looking at Tom.

'One more try,' someone cried out.

At that moment the captain and his lieutenant appeared on the deck; Jack's gaudy jewellery glinted in the sunlight.

'What the hell is going on here?' William roared, glancing at the smoking gun in Fleur's trembling hands.

The crowd backed away.

'You heard your captain,' Jack demanded. 'Speak up.'

'Finn still needs to prove himself to the lads,' Peg-leg replied, turning back to egg on his silent cronies. 'We need to see if he's worth his food rations, don't we, brothers?'

William and Jack exchanged glances.

'And whose orders is the boy following, man?' the captain spat icily.

Peg-leg waved a hand in the direction of the crowd. 'Your crew's, Cap'n.'

'I see.' William eyed the men with contempt. 'But hasn't the boy proved himself enough with his work among you?'

Peg-leg shook his head. 'We ain't convinced that this child is seaworthy at all, sir, and it's making us all uneasy. We need to know that your judgement ain't skewed.' He smiled, showing a row of broken yellow teeth. 'I'm only speaking on behalf of the men here, Cap'n Hart, sir.'

A series of angry 'Aye's erupted from the crowd and the mood turned darker.

Fleur's face burned crimson as she stared at the contorted faces all around her. She understood that William couldn't be seen to stick up for her too much without seeming weak. But Peg-leg was winning and she knew that she needed to prove herself yet again. The Italian was swinging her precious locket precariously from his little finger above the churning grey waters below.

Suddenly an idea came to her. 'Wait a minute,' she said, and disappeared below decks, ignoring the jeers that followed her.

'Spineless coward!' Peg-leg shouted after her. 'Are you ready to give up yet?'

'Go on, titbit, hide below deck like the other vermin,' someone else added.

However, silence fell when Fleur reappeared moments later carrying her father's bow and the leather quiver full of arrows. It was a beautiful weapon, made from the hardy trunk of a yew tree for extra strength, and looked way too big for the plucky girl carrying it. William looked from the bow to Fleur with a strange thoughtful expression and nodded discreetly. Jack noticed the exchange but said nothing.

'And what are you going to do with that?' Peg-leg taunted. 'Archery practice?'

'No, I'm going to shoot through that rope,' Fleur replied calmly.

Peg-leg let out a wail of protest. 'But it's not a gun!'

'Silence, man!' the captain bellowed so loudly that a stunned hush fell at once. He made his way over to the cringing Peg-leg and stared at him menacingly for a long minute.

'I'm growing sick and tired of your squealing, little pig,' he said in a low, threatening voice. 'I am your captain, by God, and you will bow to my orders without objection or face the most painful consequences. I'm letting this little' – he waved a hand dismissively – '*charade* play out for my own sport. If you spoil my fun, no one will eat tonight. Do I make myself clear?'

With rations low, a missed meal would have left the men ravenous and looking for someone to blame. Peg-leg nodded his head frantically, unwilling to face the wrath of hungry shipmates. He let out his breath as William straightened up and nodded to Fleur, urging her to continue.

Fleur swallowed nervously and reached back into her

quiver for an arrow, mentally blocking out everything around her. The arrow's length was the distance from her nose to the tip of her middle finger to allow for maximum draw on the bowstring. With practised ease she nocked the arrow, smoothly pulling back on the bowstring. The weapon felt more natural in her hands than any gun. She closed one eye so that she could focus on the target. She loved the feeling just before the arrow flew.

'It's *not* a gun,' Peg-leg repeated under his breath.

'You didn't say it had to be a gun,' Fleur replied.

Peg-leg began to protest but the crowd around them began urging her on, assuming she'd miss.

Fleur squinted at the target, aimed and fired. The arrow shot from the bow and soared clean through the rope. A few of the friendlier crew cheered, but most started grumbling that they'd have to replace it. William and Jack didn't react at all, but Fleur could sense their relief as they murmured quietly to each other. Tom grinned over at her with a look of pure joy.

With only a glance in Peg-leg's direction, Fleur marched over to the Italian thief and held out her hand. 'Give it to me.'

The man shook his head. 'No.'

Fleur tried to grab her locket from him but he held it out of reach. 'Jump for it like a monkey,' he taunted.

She stared at him, then spat at his feet. The man's jaw dropped in surprise and he threw a punch in her direction. All at once her father's training came back to her and instinct took over. She moved fast, stepping back and thrusting out both fists, left above right. Deflecting the punch, she grabbed his outstretched arm with her left hand, then got hold of his fist with her right hand, hopped gracefully to one side and, flipping his arm round, threw him to the floor. The man lay motionless as the crowd looked on in shocked silence.

'Give the locket back to the lad now, Mario,' the captain roared authoritatively. He frowned at Fleur. 'What did I say about trouble? No one eats tonight!'

Mutters of complaint swept across the deck but no one dared protest out loud: William was not to be challenged. The crowd dispersed and the Italian rose to his feet and gave the locket back to Fleur, who grabbed it eagerly.

Mario started to walk away, but William stopped him. 'Where do you think you're going?' he demanded.

'To get on with my work, sir,' Mario replied quickly.

The captain shook his head, then turned to Jack. 'Tie him to the mainmast, his arms and legs extended, and leave him there until I say otherwise.'

Mario opened his mouth to protest but Jack's look silenced him immediately.

'We was just having a bit of fun with the new laddie,' Peg-leg said meekly as William approached, his sea boots clomping on the deck.

'Keep your barbed tongue behind your teeth, man. It seems to me that you've got it in for Finn.'

Peg-leg scowled over at Fleur. 'That's because I don't fully trust him, sir,' he said. 'And I reckon he'll bring us nothing but bad luck. He's got that look about him.'

'And you've got the look of a cold dead fish, but I'm not gutting you tonight,' William snapped, staring at Peg-leg's weasel face. 'Now shut your gab and go and mend that rope.'

'But I didn't shoot through it,' the pirate grunted.

William glowered at him. 'Well, you should have thought about that before. Do it. *Now!*'

Peg-leg disappeared, swearing under his breath.

The captain turned to Fleur. 'A word, laddie, if you please.'

He led her into a quiet corner where no one could hear them. Fleur turned to him excitedly: she'd proved herself to Tom and now to the rest of the crew. William was bound to be pleased with her.

'Thank you,' she began, 'that was really—'

'Hold your gab,' he snapped in return and gripped her arm hard. 'You're going to have to be more careful or they'll discover you.'

Fleur stood in shocked silence, her mouth agape like a landed fish. Her uncle's eyes flashed with rage as he yanked her over to the ship's rail. She'd been expecting congratulations, not an attack. She tried to push him off, but he held onto her firmly, his strong fingers bruising her skin.

'How did you do that, girl?' he demanded.

She met his searching gaze. 'My father taught me.'

He blew air from his cheeks and shook his head. 'You're bringing attention to yourself. A child as young as you shouldn't have such knowledge. Why, *I* don't even know how you did that.'

'But they were testing me again. They're always getting me to prove myself, sir. I'm telling you, they know I'm a girl.'

The captain bent down and peered into her face. His breath was heavy with rum. 'And you ain't helping by making an exhibition of yourself, child. I thought I told you to lie low,' he hissed.

'But they were about to throw my locket into the sea,' she argued. 'It's the only thing I have of my mother's.' She choked with emotion and her voice faltered as hot tears welled up in her eyes. She looked away, embarrassed, roughly wiping at the traitorous tears with the back of her hand.

William stared down at Fleur with a startled expression and immediately released her arm. He addressed her in a kinder tone and smiled awkwardly, revealing teeth like a series of broken gravestones.

'Rose was a good woman' – he cleared his throat – 'from what I've heard. And her daughter deserves to wear her locket,' he said in a gruff voice. 'But you must understand that them men would've thrown it overboard anyhow – they was just riling you. They want to catch you out, and if they do, all hell'll break loose and I'll not be able to protect you. Do you understand that?'

'Aye, sir, I do.'

William's smile faded as he straightened and looked around. 'I've made no bones about the fact that I don't want you here, girl. You're trouble, and bad luck at that, but I will keep an eye on you out of respect for Henry, and I will be civil to you until we reach the Caribbean. But don't expect no favours and no kindness from me and we'll get along all right.'

Fleur nodded at him, but her heart ached with sadness. He really didn't care about her at all. Their conversation over, William turned on his heel, but then paused and looked back at Fleur.

'I'm warning you now, watch out for yourself because I won't always be there to help you. Our life ain't a bed of roses, and there are always the hellish, crafty sprats on board a ship that will be looking for any excuse to cause mayhem. Let's not give it to 'em.'

As Fleur watched him leave, she wondered if it was already too late for that.

CHAPTER 8

As the evening drew on, heavy clouds blanketed the sky and the sun choked and vanished. The sea grew bleak and troubled, and suddenly the *Libertine* felt very small to Fleur. That night a grey fog descended, swallowing everything up in its chill grip until all that could be seen in the murk was the weak golden glow from a lantern tethered to the mainmast. The men's shanty rode the wind, a dirge that was at once monotonous and intense.

'Keep her steady and slow, laddies,' the captain instructed. 'We're coming to the Devil's Web and I won't have us dashed on its teeth.'

Fleur turned to Tom, who looked unusually pale and

anxious. 'What's the Devil's Web?' she asked him.

The boy opened his mouth to reply but at that moment William saw them and marched over.

'Get up the mast, boy,' he barked at Tom. 'I need your eyes. Although I doubt you'll see much in this gloom.'

'Aye, aye, Cap'n.' Tom started climbing the mainmast immediately, although he turned briefly to reply to Fleur: 'The Devil's Web be a maze of islands that sprang up from hell itself.'

'But why a web?' Fleur shouted after him. 'Tom? *Tom?*'

But Tom had already disappeared up into the dense, drifting fog. Suddenly the captain was right beside her, his voice low and heavy in her ear.

'Because if they get you, you're trapped there for ever. Now get below, child – you've too many enemies lurking in this fog.'

'But—'

'Now.'

At that moment there was a horrible raking crunch beneath them as something ripped into the bottom of the ship. The fat sailing master, Carlton Bart, appeared through the gloom and William forgot all about his niece's safety.

'Why are we running aground, man?' he asked him. 'Aren't we heading north?'

The rotund man wiped at the beads of sweat glistening on his brow and nodded. He was a good man, kind to Fleur and loyal to William. He was usually as calm as the summer tides, but at that moment he was bursting at the seams with stress and panic.

'Aye, Captain. The compass is pointing directly north. We shouldn't be hitting the Nest.'

The ship tripped over the waves as more sharp rock scraped beneath them. The two men looked at one another in confusion.

'We *are* meant to be going north, aren't we?' William asked.

Carlton nodded. 'Aye. I've checked the charts and 'tis the only way through.'

At that moment the ship's bell rang out. Along with telling them the time, the crew also used it to work out the watches. There were eight bells – one for each half-hour of a four-hour watch. The sound of the bell was eerie in the dank mist but also reassuringly human. Out there, in the still silence of the vast ocean, with nothing to see but strange vapoury shadows and nothing to hear but the slap of the tide and the groan of the rigging, it was all too easy to believe that you had become a ghost.

Just as Fleur was about to slip below decks, the opaque clouds above parted momentarily, revealing a patch of deep black sky bursting with luminous stars. As she stared up, Fleur realized that something wasn't right. Blooming amongst all the others sat the huge North Star, bold and fierce in the vast galaxy. Fleur frowned in thought: if they were supposed to be heading directly north, they should be heading *towards* the North Star. So why was the star to their right? It didn't make any sense. All around her, figures dashed about like phantoms in the soupy fog. Who could she tell?

'Didn't the captain order you to go below decks?'

Fleur whipped round and saw Jack standing behind her. He was captured in a soft halo of light cast from his lantern and his white hair was damp and frizzy from the mist. At that moment the ship lurched forward again, grazing the rocks, and they stumbled into one another.

'We're going the wrong way,' Fleur blurted out.

Jack steadied her. 'What do you mean?'

She pointed up at the sky, but the clouds had knitted themselves together again and there was nothing to see but the swirling fog. 'The North Star is about ten degrees west of us. I thought we were supposed to be heading north?'

Jack nodded and frowned. 'But we are, child. The compass is pointing that way.'

Fleur shook her head adamantly. 'It has to be wrong. I'm telling you, we're going the wrong way.'

Once again the rocks raked the belly of the poor *Libertine*; Jack looked about him wildly.

'Please, Jack. We've got to change course.'

He looked irritated and opened his mouth to argue, but then someone called him away. He slipped away through the wall of mist without even giving Fleur a glance. She stamped her foot hard on the deck. Why wouldn't anyone ever *listen* to her? She knew she was right. She picked her way through the fog to the poop deck, where she could just make out the figures of the captain and Carlton Bart. As she approached, Peg-leg dashed past, bumping into her and cursing loudly as he hurried away into the swirling void.

William turned, his face twisting with fury as he spotted her. 'You little fool. Do you want to be tossed overboard?'

Fleur swallowed back the fear that rose like bile in her throat and approached them cautiously. 'We're not heading north, Captain,' she said as clearly and calmly as possible. 'We're heading west of it. I saw the North Star and we're not sailing towards it.'

Carlton Bart scowled at her and spat onto the floor as if what she had told them had left a bitter taste in his mouth. 'We *are* going north. Look at the compass.'

Fleur stared at the huge brass compass lying nearby. The arrow was pointing directly north. She shook her head in confusion. 'I'm telling you both, that can't be right.'

Again the ship pitched forward as the hull ground against more rocks. William and Carlton Bart turned away and peered over the side.

'There are rocks everywhere. Are you sure about this, Bart?' asked the captain urgently.

The man nodded. 'As sure as I am about anything, Cap'n.'

'But we shouldn't be running aground . . .'

As the two men argued, Fleur stood by the compass hopelessly: they were about to die and there was nothing she could do. Again the clouds above thinned and the North Star pierced the gloom. Her heart soared: she had proof.

'Captain, Carlton Bart – look! The North Star!' she cried out.

But both men ignored her and her stomach clenched with frustration. Veiled by the swirling mist, Fleur crept up onto the poop deck and stared down at the compass.

By her calculations they were definitely still heading ten degrees west of north. She frowned with concentration. *What could be wrong?* Then she saw it: someone had left a gun lying nearby. The gun was magnetic and had spun the compass into confusion, leading them off-course. Again the ship scraped past a jagged monolith that rose from the sea like a clawed finger and Fleur heard the wood splintering. *They were running out of time.* Glancing back up at the North Star, Fleur decided to act fast. She leaped forward, sweeping the gun aside with a loud clatter and spinning the wheel hard so that the ship veered sharply to starboard.

'What are you doing?' William shouted, and dashed over to where Fleur was standing. He grasped her by the scruff of the neck and threw her away from the wheel.

'Wait!' Fleur shouted, scrambling to her feet. 'Look at the compass.'

William looked down at the compass and then spotted the gun lying on the deck: his furious expression changed to one of surprise. 'But . . . ?' he began.

There was a grinding, jerking bump; then suddenly they were skimming smoothly over the waves as if nothing had happened. Fleur flopped against the mast and breathed a deep sigh of relief.

The captain merely glanced at her before turning to

confront the sailing master. 'Was that your gun, Bart?'

The man shook his head in confusion. 'No, Cap'n.'

William rocked back on his heels, his hands clasped behind him. 'Can you explain to me why it is that a child can navigate my ship better than you?'

Carlton Bart stared over at Fleur with a bewildered expression and she looked back at him apologetically.

'There wasn't no gun there, Captain, I swear to you. I wouldn't be so careless.' His tone was fearful; he seemed devastated. 'I'd say someone else put it there – I can't think of any other explanation. But it wasn't me.'

William walked towards him slowly and the look on his face was pure venom. 'For God's sake, man, any more foolish slips like this and I'll wring your fat head from your body. Do you hear me?'

Carlton Bart lowered his head and nodded feebly. 'Aye, Captain.'

William shook his head in disgust and dismissed the man with the back of his hand. 'Get out of my sight and make sure the crew are dealing with the damage done by the Nest.'

The sailing master nodded obediently and staggered blindly off into the fog. The captain walked over to Fleur, who stared up at him nervously, her legs trembling with fear.

DREAD PIRATE FLEUR & THE RUBY HEART

'You disobeyed me, child.'

She looked down at her feet. 'Yes,' she whispered. Terror had stolen her voice.

William bent down and reached out to raise her chin so that his eyes were level with hers. By now her entire body was shaking.

'You did well, child.'

It took Fleur a moment to realize what he had just said. 'I . . . I did well?'

Her uncle looked at her with pleased surprise. 'So Henry really *did* teach you how to navigate a ship then?'

Fleur nodded enthusiastically. 'He did, sir. He made sure I learned my letters so that I can understand the charts. He also taught me how to use navigational instruments and how to work out where we are by looking at the sun, the moon and the stars.' Her heart burned with both sadness and pride as she remembered her father.

William peered at her as if she was some strange creature he had just discovered. 'And did he teach you how to fight and protect yourself?' he asked.

'Since I was old enough to walk, sir,' Fleur replied.

Her uncle straightened suddenly and she slipped behind the mast, wary of his erratic moods. He rolled his eyes with impatience, reached into a wide pocket and brought out a thin brass ring about six inches in diameter. He held it out to her. 'Do you know what this is?'

Fleur took a step forward and stared at the instrument in his rough hands. It had three engraved nautical scales running around it and a sighting vane attached to the centre. 'It's an astrolabe, Captain.'

William nodded and handed it to her to examine further. 'And can you tell me what it's used for, lassie?'

Fleur turned the heavy object over in her hands. 'To measure the height of the sun or a star above the horizon. Knowing the height of the sun at noon, or of the Pole Star at night, tells us our latitude, which is our position north or south on the earth.'

William chuckled to himself and scratched at the coarse bristles that itched his chin. 'Well, ain't you the sea dog? Henry did school you well. Tell me, do you like it out here in the deep blue?'

Fleur nodded, still amazed that he was being so pleasant to her. 'More than anything, sir.'

Her uncle cocked his head to the side thoughtfully as he considered her words. 'Even on a ship such as this?'

Fleur met his steady gaze with her own. 'Aye, even on a pirate ship . . .' She paused. 'I think I was born for it.'

He looked at her so intensely that it unnerved her.

And then he smiled, suddenly and awkwardly. 'Maybe you were, child.'

There was a pause, and then with a swish of his heavy velvet coat he turned to leave.

'But, Captain,' Fleur said, holding out the navigation tool, 'you've forgotten this.'

'Keep it,' he replied, nodding over his shoulder at her. 'You might need it to save us again.'

'Thank you,' she said, hugging it to her chest with pride.

'You've earned it. It was your grandfather's,' he added, 'so keep it safe. 'Tis only to be handled by those who have the sense to use it properly.' His face hardened and the moment was gone. 'Now get below decks as I ordered.' The captain puffed out his chest, and with the tiniest of smiles he doffed his hat to her and strode away purposefully. Fleur stared happily down at her grandfather's astrolabe. Her first real pirate treasure.

As the ship plunged through the ocean over the next week, storm clouds gathered above them. A chill wind rode upon the waves, licking them with its spiky tongue. The pirate crew cursed the wail of the rising wind and looked out nervously. The sea darkened and the waves thrashed hard against the ship. Peg-leg's eagle was kept in its cage, which was tethered firmly to the deck. It spent its time yelping like a puppy and hissing at anyone who dared approach it.

'Danger's heading our way,' Tom warned Fleur one evening.

They'd been trying to sleep for a while, but their hammocks were pitching them about. Fleur never seemed to get seasick, but now her belly churned like the troubled sea below them.

'Danger?' she asked. 'Have you seen the *Flying Dutchman* again?'

Tom tried to sit up, but the ship jerked and he fell back into his stringy bed. 'There's a storm coming and we're in the belly of the sea. We'll just have to hope it shows us mercy.'

'Will we be all right, Tom?'

He shrugged. 'It depends how high the waves rise. We'll know soon enough.'

In the early hours the ship started tipping and lurching about like it had an itch. Every man was called out on deck. The bilges were flooding and the foul water was being pumped out furiously before it rose too far and rotted the ship from beneath. Rain hammered down like musket balls and enormous waves sent water thundering over the deck. Most of the chickens had been swept out to sea before the remaining few were scooped up and hidden in the ship's stores. The ship's cook was already in there, sitting on the floor drinking from a bottle of rum and muttering prayers. Up on deck the crew were dashing about, trying to keep the ship from capsizing. A torn sail flapped among the rigging and a stray rope whipped anybody who approached it.

Amongst it all the captain stood as sturdily as he would have upon dry land. His black hair was drenched and stuck to his face in soggy tendrils. He was an island of calm in the chaos, shouting as loudly as the wind roared, 'Keep her trimmed by the head and man the braces!'

Jack stood at the prow, equally magnificent and equally terrifying, clinging to the wheel with all his might, making sure they maintained their course despite the intent of the raging sea. And then the deck tipped and bucked and the storm went mad. Lightning clawed at the sky and thunder boomed and echoed above them. Waves climbed higher than the mainmast and rocked the ship to its bones. Fleur stared into the towers of black water and realized that she wasn't scared at all. In fact, to her surprise, she felt exhilarated. Water fell on her like a thousand punches and she stood firm.

Suddenly her uncle caught sight of her. 'Finn, Tom, get below decks now.'

Tom scowled but the captain immediately raised an eyebrow. It was enough for Tom to grab Fleur by the wrist and drag her down into the hold. They sat on the tilting floor near a bulkhead and hung onto anything that kept them steady.

'We have to stay here,' Tom said sullenly. 'The captain wants me to babysit you.'

Fleur tried not to smile, for she knew that William would have sent Tom down there alone.

The storm raged for hours, until everyone on deck was worn out by the relentless assault of the huge swells. But they managed to stay upright. Finally the water stopped churning and the sky calmed. Tom and Fleur stepped out and stood upon the battered deck and Fleur wondered if she'd ever see the ocean that wild and beautiful and angry again. The crew were slumped all around them, exhausted. Some were bleeding; three men had been swept overboard and lost to the sea. Peg-leg, however, was standing to one side of the ship, apparently searching the waters for something, and the captain was standing on the poop deck studying the seas ahead with his pocket telescope; he looked like a magnificent sea god. Fleur and Tom grinned at each other with relief.

Then, from nowhere, a blue flame appeared at the top of the ship's masts. The strange light broke up and danced along the yardarms like falling stars. It brushed the *Libertine* with its glowing tongue, but didn't appear to be hot. When it travelled down the mast and surrounded William, he didn't even notice its luminous radiance. Fleur took a couple of steps towards him and the light stretched out and held her too. She reached out with her fingertips, but then it was gone. The crew nudged each other and whispered.

Fleur turned back to Tom. 'What was that?' she asked.

'St Elmo's Fire,' Tom explained. 'Some folk say it's a good omen – the fingers of God reaching down to protect us. Some think it's to do with the power of a storm.' His expression darkened.

'What is it, Tom?' Fleur asked, suddenly fearful.

He was staring nervously over at the captain. 'There are also those who believe that when it is seen around a sailor's head, they will soon be dead.'

Fleur gazed up where the light had been and a sudden chill crept through her.

★

The ship was in a sorry state but she was sturdy enough to continue her voyage. The captain ordered his crew to make minor repairs but would allow nothing to slow him down. Both the storm and the scrape with the Devil's Web had caused more friction aboard the *Libertine*. There were whispers that the voyage was doomed, and William's leadership was again questioned by the rebels. Fights exploded on a daily basis and men had taken to sleeping with a knife beneath them. But their course was re-plotted and on they raced, as quickly as the weather would allow.

CHAPTER 9

One particularly balmy night, Fleur stole outside while most of the pirates were sleeping. Their snores were keeping her awake. The sky was as black as nothing as stray storm clouds sailed over the moon and stars and stole their light. The only sounds were the creak of the rigging and the crashing of the waves. Parsley appeared and wound himself around her legs. She picked him up to press her face into his soft warm fur. A breeze carried voices towards her and she heard the word 'Finn' among the whispers. In the faint glow of a lantern she saw a dozen or so burly pirates huddled together near the stern and crept stealthily towards them.

'A girl, ye say?' came a shocked voice.

'Aye' – unmistakably Peg-leg – 'and Finn ain't her name, I'd bet my good leg on it.'

Fleur froze, the panic rising in her throat. It looked like the jig might be up with her disguise, but there was more to her sudden shock than that. Something was connecting in her mind and, in a tumble of memories, she at last recalled precisely where she had heard that rasping voice – Peg-leg's voice – before: the knowledge of it made her blood run cold. *How had she not realized it before?*

Another man spoke with a thick Spanish accent: '*Si, amigo*, that much is clear, but hold your tongue and let's focus on what is important here. Our complaints have turned a good many of Hart's precious crew. The loyalty of more is wavering. The time for mutiny is almost at hand.'

Fleur crouched down as low as possible, straining to hear. Her breath came short and sharp and her heart pounded so loudly in her ears that she feared the sound of it would give her away: then her fate would surely be sealed, for now she knew with horrible certainty that Peg-leg, who had made her life on the *Libertine* so difficult, had been there that terrible night at the inn; he had helped to snuff out her darling father's life with a cowardly blast from his musket. She hadn't noticed his wooden leg then, but a good look at the tattoos on his back would confirm his identity. And here he was again – her nemesis – planning a mutiny on her uncle's ship. It was too strange to be a coincidence. Who was this one-legged man really? She cupped her ears with her hands and listened on.

'I disagree about Finn,' somebody muttered. 'He ain't no girl, and I don't need to strip the lad down to his birthday suit to know it neither. Ain't you seen him climb the mast? No lass could shimmy up a pole like that. Still, all them rumours about him are helping us no doubt – it's making them who're still loyal to the captain doubt him all the more.'

'What do you mean?' asked the Spaniard.

'Isn't it obvious?' came the reply. 'The gods are with us plotters: we've been fortunate enough to run into some bad luck for the ship. Thanks to our rumours and tattle-talk, half the crew thinks the boy Finn has cursed us and the *Libertine*'s voyage is damned. They see that their captain is blind to it and that he's losing his edge.' The pirate laughed darkly. 'And they won't sail into hell without a fight.'

'Good. It's all going to plan,' Peg-leg said. 'Jack didn't doubt us for a moment when we met him in Cornwall and asked to come aboard.'

'No,' someone sneered. 'After a few ales he was easy enough to sway.'

Fleur wanted to jump to her feet and bolt for her uncle's cabin to warn him. The mounting tension aboard the *Libertine* made sense to her now. From the moment Peg-leg and his men had joined the crew they had been working to topple the captain from the helm.

'Aye.' Peg-leg laughed. 'Captain Blood will pay us well for this. He follows close behind in the *Revenge* – and we'll all have our revenge soon enough, boys.'

There was a haunting shriek as Peg-leg's eagle suddenly took flight with a broad sweep of its huge wings.

'Blood won't take the ship until the crew have turned against their beloved Captain Hart and he is weakened. His humiliation will be so much crueller then,' Peg-leg growled. 'Captain Blood is no fool: he knows there is no point attacking until the rot has set in. I'll send him the sign when the time is right.'

Fleur stifled a gasp. So *this* was the ghost ship that both she and Tom had made out from the crow's nest. She had been scared at the thought of the ghostly *Flying Dutchman* tearing towards them, but that was as nothing compared to the absolute terror she felt now. She wondered what Peg-leg meant by 'the sign'.

'And are we almost ready?' the Spaniard grunted.

There were a series of muttered 'aye's.

'I think we know those who are with us now,' Peg-leg replied. 'I tried to turn Carlton Bart – he's a good sailing master and we could use him – but the fool is too loyal.'

'What did you do?' someone asked.

'I left a gun near his precious compass. I thought that if the captain doubted his abilities and turned on him, Bart's loyalty would weaken. But no such luck.'

'A risky move, brother,' someone growled. 'You could have sunk us all.'

'It was worth it, for the cause,' Peg-leg spat. 'I'm sure Blood wouldn't have cared about his plan too much if William Hart had been tangled and ripped upon the Nest's teeth.'

'I think we should try and convince his cabin boy. He's feisty and strong and Blood could use him,' the man replied. 'And I reckon there's still a few of the others we could turn too. Let's create a few problems and make them doubt their precious captain even more.'

'Aye,' Peg-leg agreed. 'And keep spreading them whispers that Finn is a girl and a jinx to the ship. We need 'em to keep questioning Hart's loyalties.'

'Can't we just swing them all from the yardarm by

their thumbs and quarter the captain with a fish knife? I'm bored of waiting,' one pirate muttered.

'I want to kill William Hart with my own hands,' the Spaniard mumbled darkly.

There was a thump as a fist hit the deck and Fleur recoiled, hugging her knees to her chest.

'No,' barked Peg-leg. 'Captain Blood wants to deal with William the Heartless himself. It's personal. Hart will be marooned; a far worse punishment than a quick death for a man such as him.'

'Aye, and while he waits to die he can think about Blood possessing the Hart staff.' One of the conspirators chuckled.

'After murdering his brother,' the Spaniard added.

They all laughed heartily at that and Fleur balled her hands into fists.

'To think that fool probably still believes in the legend of the staff!' Peg-leg scoffed. 'He'll soon learn. No one can beat our Captain Blood. Not when he's sailing with the devil himself at the wheel.'

Fleur hugged Parsley to her and felt truly scared. She had to warn William before the sign was sent. She stood to leave, but as she did so, her arm caught on something and a lantern clattered to the deck. She froze in panic and stared down at the extinguished candle, still smoking guiltily. There were a few moments' silence and then the group scrambled to their feet.

'What was that?' one of them hissed. 'Is someone there?'

Fleur thought quickly. She threw Parsley down next to the lantern and then slid into a small dark space beside a cannon. It was lucky she was small because even the blackest shadow couldn't have hidden her on the deck. Parsley stretched and padded over to sniff at a stray fish head. The men turned the corner and spied the cat nibbling at its prize, the shattered lamp next to him.

'Just the stupid cat,' Peg-leg muttered. He threw an empty bottle at Parsley, missing him by inches. Fleur held her breath.

'Plague-ridden flea-ride. As soon as I have the chance, I'll skin it and feed it to the eagle.'

When the group finally dispersed, Fleur slipped silently below decks. She knocked quietly on William's door. It opened and he scowled down at her.

'What is it this time?' he demanded.

His shirt was unbuttoned to the stomach. Fleur noticed an angry scar running over his broad, hairy chest and wondered if someone had once tried to rip out his heart. Burning candles flowered behind him and a leather-bound book lay open on the table; its pages were as thin and yellowed as ancient skin.

'Can I come in?' she whispered.

He rolled his eyes but nodded silently and stood back to usher her into the room. He indicated that she should sit down. 'Well?' he asked briskly.

Fleur pulled out a chair and perched on the edge. 'Peg-leg . . . it's him . . . he's the one . . .' She was struggling to get the words out, such was the force of her emotions.

'Spit it out, girl,' barked the captain. 'I have more important things to do than listen to your stammerings.'

Eyes brimming with angry tears, Fleur finally explained, 'That scum is the man who shot my father!'

Now Fleur had her uncle's full attention. He didn't speak but his eyes widened in sudden shock and he waited for her to go on.

'I was hiding, so I couldn't see everything. But I heard everything, sir. I recognized his voice – it's been frustrating me for weeks. I knew I'd heard it before. And he has these tattoos of gallows on his back – if I can get a look at them, I'll know for sure it's him.'

William looked at her scornfully. 'A voice is not proof enough, girl. And you're telling me you ain't even seen what he's got drawn on his back?' He shook his head dismissively. 'Even if you had, there's lots of sailors that have the same tattoos of the fate they're hoping to dodge. How can you say for sure that he's the very same man?'

Fleur fidgeted and squirmed in her seat with impatience. 'It *is* him. I'm sure of it. Those evil pictures on his flesh haunt my dreams. I will know them immediately. And he talked about the legend of the staff again, sir. What does he mean?'

'I don't know,' he replied quickly, avoiding her probing stare.

Fleur blew air from her cheeks in exasperation; she knew he was hiding something. 'Well, what are you going to do about Peg-leg then?'

The captain rose to his feet and walked over to stare out of the porthole. The waves sparkled beneath and beyond as if all the stars from the sky had fallen into its depths. 'Nothing,' he replied calmly.

Fury raged through Fleur and she jumped to her feet. 'Nothing?' she exclaimed. 'But he killed your brother. We have to avenge him.'

'Again I say to you: you've got no proof.'

'My own ears and memory are all the proof I need,' Fleur stormed, her eyes dancing with fury. 'But it's more than that. Please listen, sir, I'm trying to help you. Peg-leg's planning a mutiny.'

'Well now,' said her uncle, 'it's true enough that there's

often talk of mutiny aboard a ship, but it seldom comes to anything.'

Fleur gripped the sides of her seat with impatience. 'Peg-leg and others on this ship are part of the crew of Alexander Blood – he's the one who ordered my father's murder, isn't he?'

William nodded briefly and waited for her to go on.

'Well, they joined you in Cornwall so that they could stir up trouble. Blood is following behind and he's going to take this ship soon. Peg-leg and his men have been turning your own crew against you. I just overheard them talking.' She spoke quickly and the words blurred into one another. 'Peg-leg's going to send him a sign somehow. And soon too.'

William had turned away from the porthole and was playing with a gold coin, deftly flicking it between his fingers. His face revealed nothing. 'And you heard this with your own ears, child?'

Fleur nodded. 'Aye, that I did, sir. They're planning your end, 'tis beyond doubt.'

At that, his expression began to darken. It was as if every star in a cold black sky was vanishing one by one. He seemed to be drawing everything around him into the raging furnace of hate simmering within. Fleur could barely breathe.

'Did they say when Blood was planning his attack?' he snarled after a while.

'Any day, sir. Peg-leg has stirred up some of your men and is still trying to turn more against you . . .' She paused. 'They're going to try and turn Tom too.'

William arched an eyebrow at Fleur thoughtfully. 'Tell me, why do you think Blood hasn't attacked us in all these weeks at sea, girl?'

Fleur raked a hand through her hair impatiently. 'I reckon he knows that you're too strong for him with your crew in place. That's why he's waiting for a mutiny. They're cowards – they haven't the guts to take you on unless you are damaged in some way,' she told him passionately. 'They want to humiliate you, Uncle – I mean, Captain. They said something about marooning you, rather than killing you outright – what do they mean? How can that be worse than murder?'

Her uncle was silent for a few moments as he took this in. 'So they're planning to maroon me, are they? 'Tis a cruel pirate's punishment, girl. A marooned man is left behind on an inhospitable island, sometimes no more than a sand bar. All he is given is a bottle of water and a loaded pistol to kill himself with.'

Fleur gasped in horror.

'Look, thank you, child,' he went on, his tone warmer

than ever before. 'Your loyalty and keen ears will help me a great deal now.'

Fleur glowed with pride. 'So what are you going to do?' she asked him.

'Nothing at the moment,' he replied calmly. 'I knew there was trouble brewing, and you've helped me with that, but I *will* manage it in good time.'

She stood up and the chair scraped back loudly. 'You won't be able to. They'll storm this ship and bring hell with it. I heard them, sir.'

William shook his head firmly. 'Now is not the time to act. Sometimes the mouse has to play with the cat.'

'What do you mean?' Fleur demanded, her eyes shining with frustrated tears.

He narrowed his eyes and clenched his teeth. 'Alexander Blood isn't the only one determined to win our war. Let him come to us and we'll make sure we're ready.'

'There's not enough time,' Fleur said.

'Fleur, we've spoken of this before. Unless I am mistook, I am your captain and you must leave me to make my plans. You are to be quiet and behave yourself.'

'But—'

'No!' he shouted. 'I will not have you defy me.'

Fleur could barely keep the tremor from her voice. 'I'm trying to help you. I . . . I . . . don't want you to die too.'

For an instant she saw his face soften and a light flickered in his dark, dead eyes.

'I'm not planning on dying. Now, go away, lassie. It's time for you to sleep and I need to think.'

'But, Captain, you won't be able to—'

Anger flashed on his face and the warmth in his eyes had all but gone. 'Do I have to warn you again?'

She backed away, shaking her head. 'No.'

But as she turned to walk out he spoke again, quietly and sadly. ''Tis true, you're as brave and bold as your father.'

CHAPTER 10

There was a flurry of activity the next morning. Carlton Bart was scanning the navigation charts and the captain was shouting orders to his crew as if a sea serpent were on their tail.

'Make fast there,' he boomed. 'Hands aloft to loosen the sail and draw on every rag of canvas the yard will hold. We're changing course for Ile aux Forbans.'

The *Libertine* skipped across the waves and the wind hurled them forward with all its might. Fleur grabbed at Tom as he dashed past and asked him what was happening.

'The captain has decided that we should bury your

father first — he said something about picking up silk from Madagascar to trade for tobacco in the Caribbean. So you'll be with us a good deal longer than intended.' He grinned. 'Hope that's all right with you, Finn?'

Fleur nodded, speechless, and quickly turned away to wipe at the sudden tears that swam in her eyes. It was what she had longed for: a chance to say goodbye to her father properly. But she was aware that William's change of course had nothing to do with pandering to her grief. As Tom turned to go, a thought struck her and she grabbed his arm again.

'There's silk and tobacco in the hold already,' she stated simply.

'I've seen it — I know what cargo we carry.' Tom shrugged and his eyes twinkled with mischief. 'It ain't for me to question the captain. Perhaps we need more.'

They grinned at each other knowingly, for Fleur had told Tom all that she had overheard the night before. But her smile faded as she stared at her friend more thoughtfully. Tom in turn frowned back at her.

'What's with you?' he asked self-consciously. 'Am I dribbling or something?'

'What do you know about the Hart staff, Tom?' she asked directly.

Tom looked at her in surprise. Then he checked

around to make sure that no one was nearby. When he was satisfied, he leaned in towards her. 'Like what?' he whispered.

'Like the prophecy.'

Tom rubbed his chin as he thought. 'Well,' he began, 'it's been passed down through generations of pirates, the tales muddied and embroidered some, but I can tell you what an old sea dog told me.' He fell silent as Carlton Bart bustled past with a large map rolled underneath one arm, then ushered Fleur into a quieter corner.

'Cap'n Hart don't like us talking about it,' he continued in hushed tones. 'From what I've heard though, the Hart staff has some sort of power.'

'What? Magic?' scoffed Fleur.

'Aye, magic,' said Tom defensively. 'And maybe you'll be quicker to accept such things when you've lived longer at sea and seen . . .' He trailed off, lowering his eyes.

Fleur's eyes bulged at the mystery of it all. 'Go on,' she urged. 'The staff . . . ?'

'Yeah, well, it's magic, like I said,' grunted Tom. 'And 'tis said that someone from the Hart family will be able to free its power somehow, and rule the oceans or something.'

'Free its power somehow?' teased Fleur. 'To rule the

oceans or something?' She punched Tom playfully on the shoulder. 'What do you actually know about the prophecy, Tom?' she asked.

He shrugged and put a finger to his lips to shush her. 'I told you. There's a hundred different stories about the staff. Some folks say that whoever fulfils the prophecy will be able to speak the language of whales and fishes. Others say that the Hart who frees the power will become a mighty god of the sea.'

Fleur hummed thoughtfully.

'Whatever the case,' Tom continued, 'all pirates know about it and no one, especially Blood, wants the Harts to have the staff – just in case.'

Fleur stared at her friend in amazement as the world seemed to slow down around her. She was remembering her encounter with the staff. 'You know, I think I felt it, Tom,' she said breathlessly, recalling how the ruby had somehow sought her out. 'The power from it, I mean. The night my father was murdered. It was as if the staff was connected to me somehow.'

Tom frowned, but a small smile at the corners of his mouth betrayed his true thoughts. 'Really?' he asked.

Fleur tutted at him. 'You reckon it can't be me in the prophecy because I'm a girl,' she spat irritably.

Tom grinned. 'As if I'd ever dare to even think that?'

He turned to leave but Fleur stopped him. 'What?' he asked defensively. 'I was only joking.'

'You'd never betray the captain, would you?' she asked.

Tom glared at Fleur scornfully. His bright blue eyes were unswervingly clear and honest. 'Don't be a fool,' he told her sternly. 'I owe him everything.'

Tom darted away, and as she watched him go, Fleur noticed Peg-leg squinting into the frothing foam of the *Libertine*'s wake. No doubt he was searching the horizon for a sign of Captain Blood's ship. Fleur sighed hopelessly: she still needed to see those tattoos if she was to prove to herself once and for all that Peg-leg had killed her father. But how? She scanned the deck, searching desperately for inspiration, until her eyes rested on a large cauldron of water. The cook had filled it, ready to carry below and boil the rabbits for dinner. Now he was merrily chatting to a couple of riggers.

Fleur marched over to offer her services. 'Do you want me to take this down to the galley for you?' she asked.

The cook nodded without turning away from his conversation. So Fleur heaved the weighty cauldron into her arms and staggered away clumsily, slopping water over the sides as she struggled across the deck. Soon she was right next to Peg-leg.

'Whoops,' she shouted theatrically, feigning a skid on the slippery boards. As she toppled over, she made sure to send the cauldron in Peg-leg's direction. The large iron pot bounced against the side of the ship and clattered loudly to the deck. Water arced through the air in a transparent sheet, drenching the pirate before he could react to Fleur's cry.

'What the——!' Peg-leg shouted as he stumbled backwards in shock, soaked from head to toe. He saw Fleur scrambling to her feet and his face turned the exact colour of boiled beetroot. 'You . . . I . . . Just you wait, you stringy little piece of hen gristle.'

He struggled out of his wet shirt and threw it to the floor angrily. The cook stormed over, demanding an explanation.

'Sorry,' chirped Fleur innocently. 'I slipped.'

Peg-leg inched towards her with his fists clenched before deciding she was not worth the effort, and hobbled away instead, grumbling. As he left the scene, Fleur's knees buckled beneath her and she had to grasp the ship's rail to keep herself upright. There they were: the same grim gallows and skulls tattooed on the pirate's back. The marks she had sworn she would never forget. So Peg-leg had helped murder her father on Blood's behalf. He was part of Blood's crew, and her sworn enemy.

Fleur grasped the strong timbers of the *Libertine* and stared at the bustling crew moving in and out of the morning mist. Instead of feeling angry, she felt vulnerable and alone. She had all the proof she needed now, but what was one young girl going to do with all the proof in the world? Tears welled in her eyes, and for the first time since Cornwall she felt like giving up. Then she noticed something that fired her with hope and strength: as he went about his business, William kept glancing over in Peg-leg's direction too. The captain's expression was strange and intense, like a hawk watching a rabbit from high above. He suddenly noticed his niece and threw her a meaningful look, before returning to his study of the one-legged pirate. And that was all Fleur needed. Her heart swelled warmly as she realized that however things fell out in the end, she wouldn't be facing anyone alone. She leaned back and smiled secretly to herself. For the time being, all she had to do was be patient and trust in William.

The weeks passed and they rounded the Cape of Good Hope and headed north. Fleur had never seen anywhere but Cornwall and couldn't help staring in awe as they passed the clusters of islands on entering the waters of the Indian Ocean. All around them, beaches with sand as white as snow led into rolling, lush green jungles. The palm trees lining the shores were strange spindly things that looked like giant dandelions from a distance. The sea became sapphire, and when the breeze paused for breath, she could feel the hot dry heat burning her skin.

But then the winds started to abandon them altogether and the sails hung limp and lifeless from the masts. The mood on the *Libertine* was already rotten where Peg-leg and his men had stirred trouble. But the boredom of inactivity made it even worse. Fleur tried to stay out of the way, although she could barely contain herself whenever she saw Peg-leg. But William had asked her to be quiet and behave, so she gritted her teeth and did as she was told.

Fights between the men broke out constantly now, and Fleur could tell that more of them were turning against their captain. They were hostile and drunk most of the time, and their mutinous whispers were growing louder. It didn't help that they appeared to have run into more very bad luck. First the drinking water started making them all sick, almost as if someone had poisoned it. Then a fire broke out in the hold, destroying half their food and cargo. The remaining livestock simply disappeared one night, as did the musical instruments and most of the rum. The mood was becoming very black indeed and the captain was losing control.

After a few days becalmed the pirate crew started whistling for the wind and a stolen piece of wood was fastened to the keel for luck; someone even threw their sea boots into the glassy ocean as an offering to the weather gods. But still the winds refused to blow. William was like a caged animal, staring out behind them with his telescope and poring over his maps.

One listless afternoon shouts pierced the quiet tension: 'Damn and blast. Damn. Blast!'

They had anchored to catch some fish in a wide basin of water near a row of tiny islands. The noise echoed and bounced over the smooth surface, scaring away the flock of sooty terns that had been bobbing on the water nearby. Fleur scurried towards the racket and found Jack hunched over the side of the *Libertine*, groaning. It was a strange sight – he was normally so composed.

'Those pearls are worth more than all the rest of the world's oysters could ever hope to produce,' he moaned, staring down into the still water below.

A small group had gathered around him. Tom looked up when he saw Fleur and pulled a silly face.

Jack narrowed his eyes at the boy. 'I'll throw you in there after them, laddie, if you be smirking at me.'

Tom's smile disappeared immediately. 'Jack's lost his black pearl bracelet,' he explained to Fleur.

She glanced at the jewellery that jangled on Jack's muscular, tattooed forearms. She had never known anyone to be so fond of such things! Fleur joined the men peering over the side of the ship into the clear water below.

'Can't someone jump in there and get them?' she asked after a while. 'It's not that deep.'

Jack glanced at her with a look of exasperation. 'Don't be a fool, Finn. None of us can swim,' he told her.

The crowd around them nodded and muttered in agreement and Fleur looked at them all in amazement. 'But you're sailors. Aren't you worried you might fall in and drown?'

Jack tutted at her, then returned to gazing down into the water where his pearls had fallen.

'Most of us come to sailing one way or another, and we learn the skills we need to get by. But swimming ain't one of 'em,' Tom explained.

'Them pearls meant more to me than my own mother,' Jack mourned loudly for all to hear.

'Can't he get more?' Fleur hissed quietly to Tom. 'He is a pirate after all.'

Tom shook his head and rolled his eyes. 'Doubt it. He

took 'em from a Tahitian king as payment for marrying his pig of a daughter.'

Fleur looked over at Jack in amazement. What a dark horse he was. 'And *did* he marry her?' she asked.

Tom looked at her scornfully. 'What do you think? Jack only uses women for his own gain. He's not the type to have ever known love.'

Suddenly the crowd scattered as the captain thundered across the deck like a storm cloud. 'Look ho, lads, we need to pull up the anchor and set sail. The wind is finally picking up and we've wasted too much time here already.'

Jack let out a fresh wail.

'What's wrong with you?' William snapped at his lieutenant impatiently.

Jack replied without turning away from the water. 'I've lost my pearls to the sea, Captain.'

William glanced down at the water. 'But they've only returned where they once came from, Jack,' he replied.

Jack waggled his right wrist in the air. 'This is their home, Cap'n.' He slapped the ship's rail hard. 'Blow me down, them pearls were going to look after me in old age.'

The captain frowned at him in warning. 'Jack,' he said in a low voice, 'you know as well as I do that we can't waste any more time. We've got to move as soon as we can.'

'Yes, Cap'n,' Jack muttered. 'If I could swim I'd throw myself in right now to retrieve 'em, and we would have wasted but a few moments.'

Fleur fidgeted beside them. She admired Jack and wished she had his esteem: maybe this was her chance. 'I can swim,' she blurted out quickly.

Both William and Jack turned to look at her.

'What did you say, child?' the lieutenant asked with interest.

'I can swim. I could jump in and get them for you. Like you say, it would take but a few moments. By the time you've set the sails I'll be back.'

Jack began nodding in enthusiastic agreement but the captain frowned as he looked down into the water. 'No, Finn, it might be deeper than it looks. And who knows what's lurking beneath?'

Fleur kicked off her boots. They slipped off easily as they were at least three sizes too big. 'But, Captain, please, I'm a strong swimmer.'

Jack looked at William desperately. 'See, Captain, Finn's a strong swimmer.' He pointed down into the sea. 'Look, it's not that deep at all. It wouldn't take the laddie any time at all to fetch them.'

The captain scowled at him. 'If it's not that deep, why aren't you jumping in there yourself, Jack? Stay out of this, man, I'm warning you. And as I said, we must be moving on.'

Jack backed away a few steps, waving his arms as if he'd given up.

'I really am a good swimmer, Captain,' Fleur said quietly. She cast her mind back to happy days spent diving for sea bass and crabs on the Cornish coast. She'd been faster than any of the local boys and hardy enough to swim right out where the tide's pull was strong.

Her uncle glared at her with cold eyes. 'I care not whether you can swim or not, *boy*, only that you swab my decks and do as I ask until we reach your destination.'

Fleur turned to Jack hopefully, but he looked as if someone had just wiped out his entire family. He remained silent, kicking the deck in anguished defeat.

'But, Captain, I could actually be of use. I—' Fleur began.

'Silence!' he shouted. 'You'll do as I say or I'll tie you to the anchor myself.' His dark eyes fringed with coal-black lashes met hers, and again resentment bubbled up in her belly.

As he turned to leave, Fleur took her chance. She

knew that she could swim down to the sea bed without any trouble, and no one was going to tell her otherwise. With a single smooth movement she threw herself over the side of the ship and dropped into the water below. There was a loud splash, then complete silence. It was cool and still, and sunlight sparkled on the surface like diamonds. Fleur took a deep breath, held her nose, then flipped over and dived. The water became chillier and darker the further down she swam, but as her eyes grew accustomed to it, she marvelled at the life that teemed around her. Tropical fish dashed past in shimmering shoals of iridescent colour while sea turtles bobbed about beside her, flapping their flippers like wings. Large buttresses of coral rose sheer from the sandy sea floor like the battlements of a castle, and lobsters, eels and stingrays slipped through its honeycomb crevices to hide. It was a vast, silent kingdom where everything existed in perfect harmony. Fleur had always felt most at peace when she was splashing around in the sea. Like her father had said, being on land only stripped her of her fins.

On the sea bed, the sand was coarse and gritty under her bare feet. Sea grass tickled her ankles, waving about as if caught in a meadow breeze. The heavy sand rose up and muddied the clear water around her as she searched around desperately, blindly, her lungs almost bursting with the strain. *Where were those pearls? She had to find them.* But she needed air and her chest burned and her head throbbed with the pressure. She kicked her legs hard and swam back to the surface, where she burst through, gasping for breath.

'Don't swim away with the mer-folk,' Tom shouted down at her.

'Come back up here at once, you little devil!' the captain commanded. 'Someone throw down a rope.'

'Did you find my pearls?' Jack bellowed from above.

'Not yet,' Fleur shouted up to him, choking in the salty water.

'Damn you, Jack,' William growled. 'Them pearls have been nothing but trouble since you nicked them. Thanks to you we can never return to Tahiti, and there's good trade to be had there too.'

Fleur splashed around, desperate to return to the depths – and not just to find the pearls. She wanted to stay on the sea bed for a while longer, far away from Peg-leg and the filth and violence waiting for her on the *Libertine*. Without waiting for any more orders from her uncle, Fleur took a few deep breaths and dived back down amongst the coral spires. This time she floated above the ocean floor, scanning it for the heavy pearls. An octopus crawled along nearby, pulling and pushing with the clingy suckers that ran along its eight boneless arms. As it approached Fleur, it suddenly drew six of its arms around itself and pushed itself away with the backmost pair. It pulsed through the water, its colour changing from orange to peacock-blue as it camouflaged itself against the matching coral. Fleur had never seen anything like it and for a moment she allowed herself to watch the octopus light-show in wonder before resuming her search. *She had to find those pearls.*

Something stirred and glided out of a dark cave nearby, but Fleur ignored it – she was running out of breath again: panic was setting in and her lungs felt as if they were about to burst from the pressure. She didn't want to fail in her task; to face Jack's disappointment and the jeers of the other pirates. She teased back the sea grass with her fingers, hunting desperately for the bracelet. And then she saw it, glowing like a pile of tiny moons, and a slow smile spread across her face. She reached down and picked it up eagerly, but when she turned to swim to the surface, her joy was replaced by terror. A huge dark form slid out from the shadows, its fearsome mouth slashed in a sinister smile. A few precious bubbles of oxygen escaped as Fleur gasped in panic and started backing away.

The shark peered at her with eyes like little black

cannonballs. Light from the surface caught the rough texture of its body, reflecting off it like silver war-paint. It looked ancient, cruel and deadly. Fear held Fleur to the spot as they faced one another through a scattering school of terrified clown fish. The creature was gigantic – probably three times as long as Fleur was tall. She shut her eyes tight as it started swimming towards her. She didn't have a chance. It would swallow her in one bite. Fleur waited for the end . . .

Then, when it didn't come, she opened her eyes again. To her surprise, the shark was simply swimming around her in slow circles, eyeing her calmly. Fleur stared back, treading water cautiously, and felt its rough sandpaper skin brushing against her legs. She didn't dare break for the surface in case the shark decided it had seen enough and was ready for its meal. But she couldn't stay there for ever – as every bubble that escaped her lips reminded her. Her head felt fuzzy and blood rushed in her ears as she searched her mind desperately for her next step.

Then, slowly, the gigantic shark opened its deadly jaws . . . and sang – at least, that was the only word Fleur could find that even came close to describing the sound she heard. Sharks aren't known for their singing, but there you have it. The shark sang a long, low note that resonated across the ocean floor and found an echo, as if every creature of the ocean – everything with fins or gills or a shell or a blow-hole – was joining in. Fleur heard them all around her, but beneath the chorus of ocean life was a deeper song, at once soothing and deafening.

It startled her so badly that she let out all the breath she had left and had to kick out desperately for the surface. There was nothing for it but to swim with all the strength she could muster; her life depended on it. It felt as if she were moving through lead, each stroke upwards a battle; and every moment she feared that the shark would bite off her legs.

Fleur's mind suddenly flashed back to a sunny day on the beach with her father:

'Listen carefully, girl,' Henry had said, crouching to be level with her. 'What do you hear?'

'Gulls, Daddy,' said little Fleur. 'And the waves on the beach.'

'Listen closer,' said her father gently. 'That low note beneath all else, child. The song that calls you to the sea. That's the song of the ocean itself, my girl, and once it's in your head, you'll never shake it.'

Fleur burst out into the warm, fresh air and gulped at it greedily. The shark was nowhere to be seen and all was silent. She'd made it!

The captain leaned over the side of the ship and scowled down at her. 'Don't you ever ignore my orders again.'

'There was a shark,' she managed to croak. 'I got away.'

A rope had been thrown down for her and it dangled into the water like a limp arm.

'Obviously,' Jack bellowed. 'Now, did you get my pearls or not?'

She nodded and waved them in the air, still panting with exhaustion and shaken to the core. 'Aye. I did, sir.'

A broad smile broke out on Jack's face and he clapped his hands together. 'Good work,' he hollered, shaking his head in surprise. 'Well, well. It seems I was wrong about Finn. Seems to me the lad *can* hold his own around this brigantine.'

He exchanged a glance with William, then peered back down at Fleur. 'Now hurry up here, laddie – we're about to set sail as the captain said. And make sure you don't drop 'em on the way.'

As Fleur had hoped, Jack's attitude towards her shifted the moment she stepped back aboard the *Libertine*. He wasn't particularly nice to her – that wasn't his style – but at least he started to treat like part of the crew. And that was good enough for her.

William, on the other hand, was furious that she had defied him and set her the mind-numbing task of sifting the gunpowder. It was a necessary chore on any pirate ship, ensuring the gunpowder stayed dry and preventing the explosive ingredients from separating. But it was incredibly boring, so nobody was expected to work at it for more than a day at a time.

'Three weeks!' barked William as he dumped the first load of powder at her feet.

Fleur sighed, changed quickly into some dry slops and plonked herself down at the prow of the ship. The large barrel of gunpowder sat waiting to be sifted, but she was lost in thought.

'Hoa, Claw-cat,' Tom said, nudging her out of her daydreams. 'What's on your mind?' He handed her a biscuit, which she accepted gratefully.

'Nothing that would make any sense to you, Tom,' she answered.

He pulled a face. 'Oh, girl's stuff then?'

Fleur laughed. 'No, silly.' She sighed and stared out at the glittering water. 'Promise you won't think I'm losing my mind if I tell you?'

Now it was Tom's turn to laugh. 'Fleur, we all lose our minds out here. It comes with the job.'

They grinned at each other and Parsley padded out

of the shadows to nestle down between them.

'Come on, tell me,' Tom urged, poking her gently in the ribs.

Fleur shifted on the sun-warmed deck and scratched at Parsley's neck absent-mindedly. 'Something strange happened to me when I was in the water. Remember I said I saw a shark?'

Tom nodded encouragingly, nibbling on the edge of his stale biscuit.

'It came at me as if it was going to attack. Only it didn't. It just stared at me – like we had an understanding.' She frowned, trying to recall the peculiar incident. 'I know I sound mad, but there's something else too. A sound. A song. It was so noisy down there, Tom. As if every living thing in the sea was trying to talk to me at once. And then there was this other sound that I can't even begin to describe. But it felt like I was inside a giant beast and could hear its heartbeat. I think it was the song of the ocean.'

Tom looked at her doubtfully and Fleur flopped back onto the deck with frustration. 'You don't believe me, do you?'

He shrugged and shifted slightly to keep the sun out of his eyes. 'I think our minds can conjure up all sorts of odd things, Fleur,' he began. 'And maybe I'm speaking out of turn here, but perhaps your wanting to be the one to fulfil the Hart prophecy led you to fantasize a little when it looked like your number had come up.'

Fleur tutted and sat up straight, scowling at her friend. 'What? You think I'm making this up because you told me the chosen Hart would be able to talk to the fish?'

Tom shrugged again apologetically. 'Maybe.'

Fleur thought about it, but it didn't make sense. 'No,' she decided. 'You don't know what I heard down there. It was real.'

'Fleur, lack of air and the pressure from the water can play tricks on your ears,' Tom said. 'There's been plenty that have complained about the burning roar when they dive down to the bottom of the sea. I'm just saying that there might be a different explanation for it, that's all.'

Fleur's scowl grew deeper, and for a moment she looked very like her uncle. 'So what about the shark?' she asked eventually. 'Why didn't it eat me?'

'Maybe it doesn't like skinny girls?' Tom suggested.

Fleur couldn't help but laugh at that. She grinned at Tom and turned back out to sea, their conversation over. No one could possibly understand what had happened to her under the waves. She'd just have to puzzle it out for herself.

★

The breeze was fitful at first, playing with the men's hopes, but sure enough, it soon picked up and the *Libertine* was on her way again. Time rolled past, as did the sea miles, and before long thvey were approaching their destination. William wanted to stop at a small island to pick up some provisions a day or two from Ile aux Forbans and so the anchor was dropped in a lagoon next to the island's tiny beach.

But by this time the atmosphere on the ship had become toxic.

CHAPTER 11

'Hey there, laddies,' Jack called out to Fleur and Tom, who were slumped on the main deck, exhausted from their morning duties. 'Captain Hart wants to see you in his cabin *immediately*. Look lively.'

They exchanged puzzled glances. The captain rarely invited lowly crew members to his cabin.

'Jump to it!' Jack barked, clapping his hands.

They scrambled to their feet and scampered after him to the captain's cabin, where Jack left them abruptly. A few moments later they were sitting at the table in the quiet sanctum of William's private quarters. He poured them each a nip of rum and rocked back in his chair to study them both over the lip of his cup. Neither of them dared say anything.

'I'm sure Fleur has told you what she overheard above decks, Tom,' said William finally.

'If you mean about the mutiny and ... and Alexander Blood,' Tom replied hesitantly, 'then, aye, sir, she has.'

The captain looked satisfied. 'Good,' he said. 'Less for me to explain.' He left his chair to stare out of a porthole, his eyes searching from east to west across the rolling waves. 'I knew Blood was coming, and Fleur here helped me piece the details together.' He nodded over at his niece, and Fleur was filled with pride.

'I reckon they'll be planning to attack us soon,' he went on. 'But I don't like surprises. So' – he turned back to them, downing his rum in one gulp and slamming the empty cup on the table with gusto – 'I have a plan.'

'Do you want our help, sir?' Tom asked eagerly.

William shook his head. 'It's all in hand, lad, but I wanted to warn you that something is going to happen soon.'

'What?' asked Fleur, intrigued.

William only arched an eyebrow knowingly. 'I'll spare you the details, so you don't have to pretend at being surprised when it all plays out. Alexander Blood is a wily sea dog and he'll know if you're hiding something. Better to stay in the dark for now than to know too much and wear it like a beacon on your bonce.'

'But, sir,' said Fleur, beseechingly, 'like you said, it was my eyes and ears that helped you. I swear I wouldn't give you away.'

'I've made my decision. We'll leave it at that,' her uncle growled.

Fleur ignored Tom's warning nudge and protested again. 'But—' she began.

'Silence!' he demanded, slamming his palm down onto the table so hard that his empty cup bounced off and crashed to the floor. 'Do not push me, child. I'm not in a good mood, you know: in case you hadn't heard, there's a mutiny underway on my own bleedin' ship.'

Fleur dropped her head and stared down at her lap, hoping to hide her burning cheeks. She could feel her uncle's piercing black eyes on the top of her head.

He tutted impatiently and cursed under his breath. 'You'll know all soon enough,' he sighed wearily. 'In the meantime, remember this. Sometimes you have to lose all to gain all. Don't be shocked at what you might see, girl – you must trust your uncle to be trickier and more cunning than the Bloods. Whatever happens, mark you: I'll have it in hand. Now go,' he said, shooing Fleur away with a flick of his hands. 'Tom, stay – I want words.'

Fleur opened her mouth to protest again, but a glance from the captain silenced her at once. Tom shrugged at her apologetically as she stomped out of the room. It was only when she was outside that she realized she was still holding her tin cup of rum. She threw it to the floor. It clattered loudly and the rum spilled out and soaked into the wood of the ship. *It just wasn't fair.* What on earth did William mean with his riddle about losing all and gaining all? What a load of rubbish. And why was Tom allowed to know more about the plan than her, when she was the one who so desperately wanted to avenge her father's death? It was bad enough that she had to share a ship with the repulsive Peg-leg, foot-soldier to Blood, who seemed hell-bent on wiping out her entire family.

How often Fleur had fantasized about meeting the enemy pirate captain – not hiding in a cupboard like a frightened mouse, but staring into his cold, arrogant face while she gave him her name and the point of her dagger. She was a true Hart, damn it, however much William ignored the fact, and the same passion and fury ran through their veins. But as she listened to the dull murmur of their voices behind the heavy door, Fleur thought – not for the first time – that if only she had been born a boy things would have been different. She kicked the cup out of her path and stormed off into the bowels of the ship.

A little while later, Fleur was helping the cook to make bone soup. They'd run out of meat, and aside from a few scraggy birds and a meagre catch of fish, they had little left to eat. Fleur hated it – the stink of old animal carcasses and fish bones simmering in a watery broth clung to her nose and throat and made her feel sick. But in some ways she preferred working down here, out of Peg-leg's sight. As she worked, she became aware that someone was shouting on the deck above her. A gunshot rang out, then other voices joined in and the language became much more colourful. There was a brief scuffle and then more shouting. The cook had passed out with his bottle of grog so she crept up on deck to find out what was going on.

To her surprise and shock she found that it was the captain shouting at Jack. A small group of scowling pirates were standing behind the lieutenant, all holding knifes and guns as if about to attack.

'You're a dead man, Jack!' William shouted.

Jack raised his cutlass. 'On my soul's salvation, you're the dead one, Heartless.'

William shook his head and closed his eyes as if it

hurt to look at him. 'Of everyone I know, I trusted you the most, Jack. You'll rue the day your mother ever spawned you for this betrayal.' He turned to the other men. 'I took some of you in as if you were my own blood, and this is how you thank me. Bones is what you'll be if I ever see a scrap of any of you again.'

'What's happening?' Fleur asked the nearest man urgently.

He scowled but answered her, his eyes blazing with glee. 'The captain has found out his lieutenant was planning a mutiny with a handful of his favoured crew. He's kicking them off the ship. And they're lucky that's all he's doing to 'em.'

'But . . .' Fleur's words trailed away. Was this really her uncle's plan? Or was Jack actually fighting with his captain? There had been so much tension aboard the ship that it was hard to remember who was on whose side. Peg-leg was the one planning the mutiny though – she'd heard him with her own ears. And these men standing against her uncle now were surely his allies, the only crew he trusted. She stared over at the men in Jack's group – the only pirates who had ever shown her any kindness at all. These were the men who had known and sailed with her father all those years ago. Their betrayal would have cut *her* deeply, let alone William.

She searched the deck for Tom, desperate to hear him confirm that this was all staged; an elaborate part of William's so-called plan. But Tom was nowhere to be found. The argument roared on until Jack stormed off the ship. His followers filed behind him defiantly and a chorus of jeers accompanied their departure. Fleur noticed that Peg-leg was watching the drama unfold with a mixture of twisted delight and utter confusion. But she wasn't sure who was play-acting any more. If this mutiny was real, the captain's only true allies had gone, and Blood's attack was closer than ever before.

Without a further word, the captain disappeared into his cabin, leaving his rebellious crew to drown themselves in drink. Fleur searched the decks again for Tom. When she finally saw him, her flesh turned cold. He was standing with Parsley curled around his neck, talking to Peg-leg and the nasty Mario. The three figures were huddled together conspiratorially. Tom was smiling and nodding and Peg-leg slung a heavy hand over the cabin boy's shoulder. They looked like old friends. Then the one-legged pirate handed Tom a heavy-looking bag.

As Fleur stared over at them, rooted to the spot in shock, Peg-leg caught sight of her and pointed in her direction. Tom met her quizzical gaze with a look she had not seen before. The boy she thought she knew was gone, and she could barely recognize the surly Tom-shaped stranger standing in his place.

Rage surged up inside her and she clenched her fists hard. Was it possible that he had been lying to her and her uncle? Or had he just switched allegiance to the highest bidder? How dare he pretend friendship? Fleur fumed. She remembered asking him if he could ever betray his captain. He had convinced her then that he never could. What a fool she had been. He wasn't a friend to her at all. Tom was just another pirate with a soul as dark as Alexander Blood's.

She glared at him with as much steel as she could muster until he turned away. Then she slipped below decks and sat in silent shock. Now she was truly alone. Not even Parsley was around to give her comfort. For the first time on the long voyage she actually longed to reach St Kitts.

CHAPTER 12

That night, with the captain remaining below deck, the crew got horribly drunk. Fleur hid away from them wherever she could. Music and raucous merriment rang out into the early hours and the deck was awash with broken glass and drunken men who had passed out in their own vomit. She waited until most had fallen asleep before creeping into the sleeping quarters, and when she glanced over at Tom's empty hammock, tears stung her eyes.

Mario stirred as she passed by. 'You've got no one to protect you no more. The boy is with us and the lieutenant has shown his true colours.' He sat up to peer at her in the gloom. 'Soon I'm going to snap you across my knee.'

She fled the room and spent the rest of the night cowering in the shadows on deck.

The next morning was hot and the air was dead. After only a few hours William ordered his crew to drop anchor at a nearby island, ready to haul it up onto its side. Fleur understood that this was for careening – scraping and burning the barnacles from the ship's bottom and replacing worm-infested planks and any other necessary repairs. If it wasn't done regularly the ship was slowed down and was in danger of rotting and sinking. The *Libertine* was pulled into a safe haven because all the rigging and cannons had to be removed, leaving her vulnerable to attack.

Fleur understood why her uncle had wanted to leave the island where Jack and the others had mutinied, but thought it strange that he should choose to land in such an inhospitable place only a few days away from Ile aux Forbans. But who was Fleur to question William's motives or doubt his plan? The crew were doubtful too, and there were mutters and groans, although they followed their captain's orders. It took a long while to navigate a channel through to the island, as the waters were shallow, yet busy with rocks and powerful undercurrents.

As they approached the island, shouting broke out among the crew. Fleur wearily crawled out of her hiding place and made her way towards the new commotion. The captain was staring out to sea through his telescope and cursing loudly.

'Damn that stupid boy!'

Fleur noticed Peg-leg lurking nearby, watching closely.

'What is it, Captain?' she asked.

William didn't take the glass from his eye as he answered. 'Young Tom has left us,' he growled. 'In the ship's rowing boat, with everything of value that the greedy-fingered pup could lay his hands on. Bah!'

Fleur reeled backwards, confused. What on earth was going on now? *Was* Tom in league with Peg-leg or had he run away alone? She had no idea what the truth was any more. She eyed William doubtfully. *Could she even trust him?* Fleur glanced around nervously and saw Peg-leg beckoning a couple of his cronies to join him. They huddled together like pilgrims at an altar and fell into a heated conversation.

'What has he taken, sir?' Fleur asked, turning back to her uncle.

He snapped his eyeglass shut and slipped it into his pocket. 'He must have crept into my quarters – several of my personal belongings are gone. I spotted a stray arrow where the rowing boat was kept, so I'd check your things – oh, and he took Parsley too, I'm afraid.' He grunted. 'Lord knows why. He's probably planning to eat the wretched beast.'

Fleur leaned towards him and lowered her voice. 'Please, sir, was this part of your plan?'

Her uncle's eyes flitted over to Peg-leg and then back to her. 'People choose their own paths. I failed to plan for that. Now go and check your belongings.'

She turned, her eyes wet with tears, and ran blindly down to the empty sleeping quarters. Sure enough, her most precious things had gone, including her father's bow and quiver and her grandfather's astrolabe. Tom had known how important those treasures were to her, but he had stolen them anyway.

Fleur was crying over the bitter betrayal when the door to the hold was thrown back and light flooded the room. Peg-leg peered in with cruel grin.

'So he did the dirty on you too, did he?' he sniggered. 'I always did like that boy.'

'Go away!' Fleur snapped at him.

But the pirate only laughed. 'You should do that

yourself. Flee this ship while you can.'

'Never!' she said, getting to her feet. She stared at him defiantly. Hatred burned through her like boiling oil. 'I'm not leaving my captain.'

'Your captain is a dead man,' Peg-leg told her, then turned and hobbled away, leaving the door swinging open.

A loud wrenching sob tore from Fleur as she sank to the floor again and stared around the dingy room with blurry eyes. Tom had betrayed them. He had betrayed *her*! How stupid she had been to trust him. Now she felt hollow, as if someone had scooped out her insides and stitched her up again. Self-pity and loneliness began to engulf her like a python swallowing its prey.

Fleur sat in the silent gloom for ages, staring at nothing. A rat brushed her foot and she watched it scuttle off to nibble the fallen scraps from the eagle's cage. That's when she noticed it: the door of the cage was open and a small capsule was lying inside; the sort that might carry a message tied to the leg of a carrier pigeon – or an eagle. She stood up and strode purposefully over to the cage. With trembling fingers she picked up the capsule and prised it open to find a tiny piece of carefully folded parchment. She unfurled the note carefully and began to read:

Message received. Good work, brother.

If all goes to plan I shall expect you to send my bird

to me tomorrow for the final time. We shall attack

upon its return.

Captain Alexander Blood

Her heart skipped a beat as the realization sank in. So the eagle was Blood's. Which meant that Peg-leg had been able to send messages back and forth to his captain at will. She would have liked to wring the scrawny bird's neck, but it was too late for that. The bird was gone. Which meant that Blood's attack was not far behind.

Fleur ran straight to William's cabin and handed him the note without a word. He read it quickly and nodded sternly, but said nothing. What was there to say, after all? Better to spend their remaining time sharpening their swords and cleaning their pistols.

The atmosphere on the island was eerie. Fleur wished she had someone to talk to: the strange whispers that came from the dense jungle beyond the beach scared her; but there was no one now. She watched her uncle stride about, barking orders, but it was clear to all that his heart wasn't in it. His crew were now openly ignoring him. The tide rose and fell against the *Libertine*'s hull, but the repairs were forgotten.

The captain looked tired and strained, a ghost of the demon Fleur had first clapped eyes on. Dark crescent moons hung beneath his sunken eyes and the fire within him seemed to have burned out. He looked as if he was carrying the weight of the world on his shoulders. Fleur wanted to let him know that she was still on his side; that all would be well if they were together. But she knew that he would probably just shoo her away. After all, she was a mere child, and a girl at that.

At last the wind picked up from the north; there was a chill in its fevered bluster. Every now and then William would stare out to sea with his telescope, searching the horizon for something. And then it came.

The ship raced towards the island, white foam churning behind her like the spittle of a rabid dog. The black flag bore the red image of a skeleton stabbing a heart with a spiked blade.

William came to stand next to Fleur.

'It's him, isn't it?' she asked quietly. 'That's his ship.'

'Aye,' he replied. 'That's the *Revenge*.'

Fear ran through Fleur like a blade. The last time she'd

seen Alexander Blood he had been covered in her father's blood.

'Yes,' her uncle went on. 'It's time.'

She opened her mouth to question him further but Peg-leg interrupted. The crew, now armed to the teeth, had shuffled up to surround their captain.

'Your course is run, William the Heartless,' Peg-leg sneered. 'Alexander Blood is upon you.'

The captain turned to stare at the rodent before him but remained silent. He left Fleur fidgeting nervously and walked among the crowd of turncoats, snarling, 'You'll all go down with the tide. Mark my words. You'll pay for this betrayal.'

None of the cowards could meet his accusing gaze. Fleur watched in terror as the *Revenge* weighed anchor and a small rowing boat was lowered. Blood appeared on deck and raised a telescope to his good eye. His wild red hair hung down his back like crackling flames and his eagle sat haughtily on his shoulder. He climbed into the rowing boat with one other man, who rowed him speedily over to the island.

William came to stand next to Fleur again. He remained ramrod straight and didn't move a muscle, but Fleur noticed his fingernails digging into his palms. She stood beside him, suppressing the urge to run, but shaking with fear and rage as the pirate captain approached. This was the moment she had been waiting for. She reached for the small knife in her belt, but her uncle stopped her.

'No, child,' he said, his large hand briefly covering hers.

Fleur looked up at him pleadingly, her heart pounding. 'But he killed my father, sir.' Her voice was hoarse. 'This might be my only chance.'

William shook his head slightly and his scowl softened. 'No, trust me, Fleur. This won't be your only chance. Stand with me now, girl. Don't betray yourself. If we play this right, we'll have our revenge.' He winked at her and lowered his voice to a bare whisper. 'Remember who you are.'

Fleur nodded and stared over at Alexander Blood, who was now striding towards them. She recognized him at once, and memories of that terrible evening came rushing back to her. Her heart pounded and her knees almost gave way beneath her as she watched him walk towards them through the shallows.

'William Hart,' Blood bellowed, glancing briefly at Fleur. 'We meet again.'

'Curse your blood, Alexander.' William's low voice simmered with fury. 'I know you had your spies watching the waters for me. You couldn't catch me without help. Why, I believe you're even working with the redcoats, you filthy traitor to the brotherhood.'

The pirate captain threw his head back and addressed the crowd gathered around him. 'I'm not the only one who wants you out of the way, William. But to tell the truth, I knew that you would turn up once I'd killed your brother. Once I'd found him it was easy. You're not the ghost you think you are, Heartless. I always knew I could creep up on you in the end.'

'Coward!' William spat.

'Scum,' Blood retorted.

'No he's not,' Fleur blurted out without thinking. She immediately covered her runaway mouth with a hand and pressed her lips together.

The pirate slowly swivelled his head to stare at her with his one good eye. 'What did you say, brat?'

Fleur looked from William to his enemy and suddenly felt wildly reckless. After all, if she was going to die, maybe it was best to get it over and done with.

'I said, *no he's not*,' she repeated firmly, although she couldn't hide the tremor to her voice. 'He's the greatest captain to sail the seven seas.'

Blood laughed scornfully. 'Oh, is he now?' he mocked. 'Well, you be the only one left standing who thinks so.'

'Leave the boy alone,' William muttered darkly. 'Either take him or kill him, but don't toy with him, for I haven't the patience.'

Fleur whipped round to face her uncle in hurt shock. 'But—' she began.

'Well, blister me, Heartless he is indeed.' Blood laughed, sneering down at Fleur. 'Perhaps you should have switched your loyalties when you had the chance, boy. It seems your great captain here cares little for you.' He looked Fleur up and down critically. 'And I have no place for this little scrap of bone among my crew.' He thought for a moment, then stepped back to address his men. 'Tie 'em both up.'

A few of them moved forward and snatched at Fleur, but they hesitated before laying hands on William. He glared at them venomously and they faltered beneath his cold gaze.

'You betrayed me, men,' he spat. 'Dead or alive, I will haunt every waking moment and kill you in your dreams. I vow we'll meet again.'

They edged away, but at a snarl from their new captain they crept closer again. Fleur and William's hands were tied roughly behind their backs and they were thrown onto the beach. Blood strode over to them and stared down at William with contempt.

'Behold, men, the great William Hart. Bound to a runt and waiting to die.' He paced around Fleur and her uncle in a tight circle. 'And if I remember rightly, Captain Hart,' he taunted, 'you vowed to murder me the next time we met. Well, so much for that!'

William spat at his captor's feet. 'To see you die will one day be my pleasure.'

The one-eyed pirate bent down so close to him that their faces were almost touching. 'As it was mine to murder those you loved dear,' he retorted in a hideous sing-song voice.

Fleur felt William's limbs tense against her, but he kept control of his temper.

Blood rose to his feet and started to walk away. 'It has been a bloody feud between our families,' he called out gleefully over his shoulder. 'I will almost be sad to see the sport end. Don't you think, *William*?'

'Where's my staff?' William growled, ignoring the taunts.

His enemy swivelled slowly in the sand. 'What? Did you expect me to bring it to you?' he replied scornfully. 'Now, we both know I'd never do that. I know how tricky you can be and I don't want you anywhere near it. Not that there's anything in that old Hart prophecy, I'm sure.' He pretended to swish an imaginary staff in the air. 'And besides, you've held it in your hands, have you not, William, and I ain't noticed anything that special about you.' He turned to his men. 'Any of you think he looks like a living god of the sea?'

He roared with laughter and his men joined in, though they kept a good distance from Captain Hart. The pirate narrowed his one good eye and smiled cruelly. 'The prophecy weren't nothing but an old wives' tale – probably started by Jacob Hart in the hope of scaring us off for good. Pah! No chance. You're the last of the line, and you're not long for this world.'

'Where's my damned staff, Blood?' William repeated icily. 'I'm starting to think you ain't got it after all.'

Blood nodded over at one of his crew; the man fired a shot into the air without a word. 'Look,' he said, pointing over at the *Revenge*.

Both Fleur and William stared over at the ship. They could see one of Blood's men standing on the binnacle with the Hart staff on a rope, which he was spinning around his head. They could see the ruby heart glowing like fire as the sun caught it.

William could no longer contain his fury. He started struggling furiously against his bonds, shaking the unfortunate Fleur around like a rag doll. All she could do was stare at the ruby as it twirled through the air. There was no denying it this time: even from a distance she could feel its mighty pull. A powerful desire flooded through her. All she wanted was to possess the staff.

Blood's mocking voice snapped her back to the beach. 'It's quite useful to have around actually,' he said mockingly. 'We use it to harpoon rats.'

'You're an idiot, Blood,' William said, collapsing against his bonds.

'And you're dead, Hart,' came the reply.

They watched as the staff was lowered out of sight. Fleur felt its absence like a missing limb.

The one-eyed captain turned to Peg-leg. 'Is the *Libertine* ready to sail?'

Peg-leg nodded. 'Aye, Captain. We made sure she was ready for your arrival.'

Blood looked back at the brooding darkness beyond the beach. Ink-black spaces welled up in the dense wall of trees; eerie shrieks echoed from its heart. The place throbbed with dark energy.

'This island promises nothing but death. There'll be wild cats and monsters hiding in that jungle, ready to swallow you whole.' He walked over and peered at Fleur with his bloodshot eye. 'I'm leaving you and this boy here until bones is what you'll be. You'll never get off it alive.'

Peg-leg hobbled over to them awkwardly in the fine sand. 'There be rumours the child be a prince, or even a lassie.'

The captain rolled his one eye. 'Don't be ridiculous, man. If the child was a prince, William would have hidden him better. And how could a little girl survive on a pirate ship?'

Fleur fidgeted self-consciously, relieved that her bandana was hiding her growing curls. Blood beckoned to a surly African brute, who handed him a pistol. 'I'm marooning you, William, to face the monsters in that jungle. As you die, you'll see the ghosts of my ancestors waiting to avenge you in hell. There be two shots in that pistol. I suggest you use it before something else gets you.'

He hurled the pistol and water to the floor. The bottle smashed against a conch shell and the dirty water seeped into the sand. Alexander laughed heartily; the men around him joined in. William's hand flexed near his sword but he didn't move.

'Come, men. Let's leave them to their death!'

The two pirate captains glared at each other.

'Alexander Blood, I swear the death you face will make men's blood run cold for all eternity!' William bellowed.

The pirate captain laughed and his eye danced with glee. 'Aye, William, I'm sure it will, although it won't be at your hands.' He turned away and started wading through the shallows to the rowing boat.

William could barely contain himself but held back, muttering, 'Oh, it will. 'Tis fate. I'll blast you to kingdom come.'

Fleur and William sat on the beach in awkward silence, watching Alexander's swollen crew board both the *Revenge* and the *Libertine*. They sat there until the ships had sailed away and the horizon was empty. Then William shook a small knife out of his sleeve and hacked away at their bonds until they were free. When he turned to Fleur, she saw to her surprise that his eyes were sparkling.

'Are you happy that we are about to die, sir?' she asked, looking fearfully into the trees.

'Did you honestly think I'd let that happen, child? You have me mistaken.' The captain scanned the trees and frowned. 'Why, everything has gone exactly as I planned.'

'Really?' she replied moodily.

He nodded emphatically.

'Hmmmph.' Fleur turned away.

'What's prickling you, girl? You should be happy Alexander left you alive.'

Fleur whipped round again and scowled. 'No thanks to you, *sir*,' she replied. 'You would have let them kill me if they had so desired.'

'It was a gamble that paid off,' he replied impatiently. 'I know how Alexander thinks, child,' he added, tapping the side of his head with a finger. 'I hoped you might stand up for me and I also knew that if I made it apparent that I thought nothing of you, Blood would leave you here to rile me in my final days.'

Fleur nodded. 'I suppose that makes sense,' she replied, 'but it mightn't have worked.'

'True,' William replied brightly. '*All* of my plan mightn't have worked.'

Fleur scowled at him again. 'And *do* you think nothing of me?' she asked curiously.

Her uncle ignored the question and started scanning the trees again.

'*Sir?*' Fleur asked.

He turned away from her and rose to his feet. Frustration and rage poured through Fleur.

'Now then,' her uncle began briskly, determined to ignore her, 'what we need is—'

But Fleur had reached boiling point and she wasn't

going to let him avoid another question. She lunged across the sand and grabbed his forearm, pulling him back down to the ground.

'I've had enough of this!' she snapped. 'William Hart, you are a horrible, horrible man and I hate you.'

William looked down at the little hand wrapped around his meaty forearm. He couldn't suppress a bemused smile. No one had dared to talk to him like that since . . . well, not since Henry. Fleur pulled her hand away, realizing she had crossed a line, and sank back into the sand, frowning.

'Well now, my little lioness,' he teased. 'You hate me, do you?'

Frustrated, Fleur punched a fist down into the soft sand. 'Yes I do!' she declared, folding her arms in front of her chest. 'Why can't you ever just answer a simple question with a simple answer?'

'Some questions shouldn't be asked,' her uncle replied without hesitation. 'And some answers are far from simple.'

'Argggh!' Fleur bellowed so loudly that the birds on the beach took flight. 'Well, why can't you – oh, I don't know – try actually being nice to me for once. Because whether you like it or not, I am your niece, you know!'

They stared defiantly at each other, neither wanting to be the first to look away.

'I'm aware of that, young 'un,' William said more gently. 'But as you know, I ain't used to having family around me – or to being nice, for that matter. I'm out of practice.'

Fleur sighed in exasperation. 'So what? If I can learn how to be a pirate, you can learn how to be an uncle, can't you?' Her words were tripping over each other now. 'I was so happy when you showed up because then I wasn't alone any more. But all you ever do is put me down – if you're not ignoring me completely, that is. You make me feel like I'll never be good enough to be a true Hart – when I know in my bones that I am and I always have been.' Her eyes flashed with anger. 'And another thing: I don't hate you, I ... I ...' she stammered. 'But you wouldn't care how I feel anyway. You don't give a damn about anything!'

William winced as she swore. He opened his mouth to speak, but she cut across him with the next wave of her tirade.

'I haven't finished yet,' she snapped fiercely. 'I don't care if you never tell me about the Hart prophecy because I'll find out anyway. I know there's something strange about that ruby heart, whatever you may say.'

Her uncle opened his mouth again but Fleur charged on. 'I am not scared of you any more, *Uncle*. I don't care if you kill me with your bare hands right now, because at least then I'd be back with my father, who actually loved me.' Hot tears pricked at her eyes and she slumped back, suddenly exhausted.

Her uncle stared at her in astonishment; then a broad smile crept slowly over his craggy face and his eyes twinkled like starlight in the desert.

'My God, Fleur' – he laughed warmly, which wrong-footed her completely – 'you are so like your father I can barely look at you.' He swallowed before continuing, 'You are a Hart through and through, child. I knew that from the first moment I met you and I'm sorry if I've ever made you feel otherwise. And I will tell you the truth about the family staff, but not now. Don't rush to know all, girl – some truths are hard to understand.'

Fleur wiped her eyes with the back of her hand and looked at him. William rubbed his temples as if he had a headache coming on and sighed, but a newfound respect showed on his face as he considered his niece carefully. He reached a hand out towards hers, then pulled it away again abruptly.

'In truth, Fleur, I sealed up my heart a long time ago.

I never wanted to feel anything again. Then you came along, and it was easier to ignore you.'

'So you *do* care about me.' Fleur sniffed hopefully.

'One way or another, you bother me as much as your father did, that much is true. But you're more fiery, and I'm not sure whether that's my blood or your mother's in your veins.'

They smiled at each other, acknowledging that something had changed between them.

'Can I ask you something?' Fleur said. 'And promise you'll answer truthfully.'

Her uncle frowned. 'Let's see what you're asking first?'

She rubbed at her wrists where the ropes had chafed. 'Do you remember when we first met, and I asked you whether you knew my mother?'

'Aye.'

'Were you lying when you said you didn't?'

William nodded. 'Aye, I was lying,' he admitted. 'I did know her.'

'I knew it!' Fleur exclaimed. 'What was she like?' she whispered, her throat suddenly dry. Her fingers fluttered automatically to the locket about her neck.

Henry had told Fleur all about her mother, repeating favourite details again and again, but she was always hungry to learn more.

Her uncle looked about the beach impatiently, then sighed and gave in to the moment. 'I only knew Rose for a short while,' he began, allowing himself a small smile at the memory, 'but she wasn't one you could easily forget.' He sighed. 'She was beautiful, Fleur, with long auburn hair and eyes that could swallow you whole. She was sweet as a kitten but strong as an ox – like you, girl. And as fiery as a hellcat.'

Fleur blushed. 'Were you there when she met my father?' she asked.

'I was,' William replied. 'She was a farmer's daughter, you know?'

Fleur nodded eagerly as her uncle settled down on the sand next to her.

'Well, Henry and I were hungry, having been so long at sea and our supplies running low. We landed on the west coast of Ireland, and we saw your grandfather's farm and decided that he'd have more than enough to share a little. What we didn't count on was Rose.' He chuckled to himself. 'She saw us coming and was firing her pistols at our feet before we knew what was happening. She was all alone on the farm that day and most women would have hidden away from sight, but not Rose. She was furious.'

'Tell me what happened,' Fleur begged.

William rolled his eyes but he was warming to his theme. It was actually quite pleasant to cast his mind back to happier times.

'Well, Henry fell in love the moment he clapped eyes on her, I reckon. He saw her standing there like an angel, her hair the colour of molten gold and those eyes flashing like lightning—'

'And then she shot him,' Fleur finished.

William's burst of laughter took her by surprise. It was as warm and promising as a barrel of rum.

'Aye, child, that she did. You do know the story then?'

'I do,' she replied, 'but hearing about her makes it feel more real somehow.'

A strange expression passed over her uncle's face, and when he spoke again his voice was gentle. 'So, yes, she shot him in the thigh, and Rose, being Rose, felt terrible – she was always taking in poorly creatures and dying birds and the like. Anyhow, we ended up staying on the farm until Henry could walk, and by the time we left she was as smitten with him as he was with her, despite the wound in his leg.'

'And were they always happy together?' asked Fleur. 'And what about you? Are you sure I haven't got any cousins you've been keeping secret?'

William's face hardened and the laughter lines that had creased around his eyes abruptly vanished. He stood up, shaking the fine sand from his breeches.

'Uncle?' Fleur asked, frowning. She had so many more questions to ask.

But the mood had turned and William had shut his heart again. 'Enough,' he grunted. 'Remember not to be too familiar, girl, when we're back with the crew. Don't you get into the habit of calling me Uncle. When you sail with me, I will always be your captain.

'Now,' he muttered, 'let's see — my throat is parched.'

Suddenly he strode across to the trees and tore at a thicket of tangled undergrowth. Fleur followed him. His mood swing had left her dazed.

'What are you looking for, sir? Aren't there dangerous beasts in there?' she asked.

'No, child — that's what Alexander believed, but there's nothing to threaten us here. Now, let's see . . .'

He searched until he spied something that resembled a palm tree. Its fan-shaped leaves formed flat half-moons, and its clusters of spiky yellow and green flowers looked like birds of paradise. William reached for his pocket knife and hacked away at one of its stems. 'Here.' He held it out to Fleur. 'Thirsty?'

She nodded and took it from him cautiously. It was

the most exotic thing she had ever seen and might as well have fallen from the heavens. 'But what's that?' she asked. 'I don't want to drink tree sap. It'll surely be poison.'

He put the bottom of the stem to his mouth and took a few thirsty gulps. 'See, 'tis fine. This be a traveller's tree. It stores water in its trunk. Drink, child.'

It was more of an order than a request and Fleur reached out for it timidly and took a sip. To her delight, the water was cold and pure and she drank it down greedily. The ship's water supply quickly went stale, but this tasted as sweet as nectar to her. She smacked her lips and wiped away the water that had dribbled down her chin.

'It's good,' she said. 'They don't have these in Cornwall.'

William raised a brow and cut them both another stem. 'No, I reckon there'll be a lot that you've not seen before' – he motioned for her to sit down beside him – 'and I suppose you'll be needing to know what's been going on.'

'Aye,' she replied, settling herself next to him on the warm silky sand. She scooped up a handful and let it slide through her fingers.

'I had my spies on the *Libertine* so I *knew* Alexander

was tailing us before you confirmed it to me. I'd heard talk on the ship that a mutiny was coming and I knew who was willing to turn on me for money. I decided it was best to let Alexander take 'em than try and win them back. A captain is only as good as the crew he sails with, and there be plenty of others out there willing to give their lives to the sea.'

'But what of Jack?' she asked frantically. 'And why did you let Alexander maroon you?'

''Twas also part of the plan,' he replied. 'When you told me his intentions, I was able to make my own plans. I changed course and made sure he caught up with us exactly where I wanted him to rather than being attacked without the support of a proper crew.'

Fleur looked about her apprehensively. 'But we're stranded on this island with a jungle of things that will surely want to eat us.'

William roared with laughter and threw his head back to pour the remains of the water down his throat. He threw the stem into a thicket and burped. 'I'll admit, I actually know this island well and things ain't what they seem here,' he told her. 'It has secrets.'

'So what happened to Jack and Tom and the others?' she asked impatiently. 'And what do you mean by *secrets*?'

Her uncle glared at her. 'Don't deafen me with your questions, girl. It's bad enough that I'm trapped here with you at all, and now I have to contend with your mindless jabbering.'

Fleur's eyes widened as she looked at him, hurt.

He rolled his eyes and smacked his forehead with the palm of his hand. 'You see, this is why women don't travel on ships.'

They sat in uncomfortable silence for a while. William picked at his sea boots and Fleur pursed her lips, her cheeks burning with indignation. Every now and again her uncle would stare around the island with his telescope, like he was waiting for something to appear. The sun was a ball of white heat above them so they edged into some shade. Pink and white shells, driftwood dotted with insect tunnels, and twisted slithers of seaweed were strewn about them like litter.

'Jack and the others are waiting for us on Ile aux Forbans,' William explained finally. 'They're gathering together a trustworthy crew for me' – he looked at Fleur out of the corner of his eye – 'and you'll discover this island's secrets all in good time, lassie.'

'Thank you.' She nodded and swallowed nervously. 'Um . . . will Tom be there?'

He ignored her question, and instead looked over her

shoulder and squinted into the distance.

'Captain . . . ?' she asked, turning to look behind her.

Someone was walking towards them along the strip of burned white sand. A smile broke out on William's stern face and he stood up. 'No, Fleur, Tom isn't with the others,' he told her. 'I needed him elsewhere.'

Fleur jumped to her feet and stared hard at the approaching figure. When she realized that it was Tom, she had to stop herself from sprinting over to him. Parsley was sitting on one of his broad shoulders, tail coiling about his neck. Tom was concealing his delight at seeing Fleur. However, Parsley wasn't so coy: he leaped down and padded straight over to her. Fleur picked him up and tickled him under the chin as he licked her hand with his rough little tongue, purring happily.

'Hoa, Cap'n,' Tom said, his gaze flicking towards Fleur. 'Hello, Claw-cat.'

'Hello,' she replied and bit back a huge smile.

William stepped forward and patted Tom on the back. 'Did you manage to bring all that I asked you, boy?'

Tom nodded and pointed back towards the tracks he had made in the sand. 'Aye, Cap'n. Everything is hidden over there with the rowing boat and the cask is safe in the shallows nearby.'

Fleur exclaimed and slapped a hand to her mouth.

Of course, her father's body. In all the excitement she had forgotten he had been pickled in the bowels of the *Libertine*.

William looked at her with scorn. 'You think I'd have left him behind, Fleur?'

She shook her head quickly. No, it seemed that William had thought of everything – except for a ship to sail in, that is.

Tom grinned over at her. 'Don't worry, Captain Hart asked me to bring your things too. I thought I'd catch myself something to eat with your bow, but all I got was branches.'

They both laughed. Tom unhooked a small bag from his belt. Fleur recognized it as the one Peg-leg had given him. It clinked as he held it out to William.

'They gave me this to turn on you, Cap'n. 'Tis only right you should have it.'

But the captain shook his head. 'No, laddie, 'tis yours. You've earned it,' he replied. 'You're a good cabin boy and a trusted member of my crew. Call it a thank you.'

Tom proudly clipped the bag back onto his belt.

'Now show me my things, Tom,' William said, staring up at the sun. 'We have a journey to make before the end of day.'

Tom led them back along the beach, then into an

opening in the dense jungle. It was cold and dark out of the sunshine and the treetops whispered in the slight breeze. Tom pulled back a blanket of tangled thorny bushes to reveal William's battered chest of belongings, along with some supplies, a few weapons and Fleur's treasures. Fleur knelt down at once, eagerly reaching for her beloved bow and quiver of arrows, and the leather pouch carrying her astrolabe. William flung open the lid of his chest and started rummaging though it.

Clutching her treasures, Fleur went to sit on the beach with Tom. ''Tis good to see you, Tom,' she said after a while.

He nodded at her and replied huskily, 'I should say so.'

Her eyes sought out his. 'I thought you'd abandoned us,' she stated quietly.

He sighed and nodded over at William. 'I wanted to say something, but I swore not to just in case. I'd *never* leave my captain.' He looked down at his toes and shrugged. 'Probably not you either.'

Fleur reached out and touched his hand briefly. They smiled at each other with real warmth; nothing further needed to be said. Fleur slumped back in the warm sand, suddenly exhausted, and looked out to sea with a secret smile. Tom hadn't betrayed William after all; he hadn't betrayed *her*. She realized then how much she had missed him and hugged herself with joy. Yes, she was delighted to see her friend again.

Suddenly William's shadow loomed over them.

'So will Jack be coming to get us soon?' Fleur asked him, sitting up a little.

He shook his head. 'No, we'll be sailing to meet him and the new crew members he's finding.'

'On what?' she dared.

Her uncle grinned and pointed through the trees. 'Come on. I'll show you.'

He led Fleur and Tom further into the jungle. It was dark and cool under the thick, whispering tunnel of leaves knitted above them, but it was anything but quiet. All around them monkeys jabbered and shrieked, and biliously coloured parakeets squawked and fled into the canopy. Fleur had never seen so many shades of green: at times the humid jungle seemed to close in all around them like some deadly green trap. The dappled stems of gigantic trees dripping with clinging vines stood around them like a living curtain. The sticky wet heat swarmed with flies and mosquitoes, all but choking her as she slogged along. But it was such a beautiful paint box of contrasting, clashing colours that Fleur could barely take it all in. At times the floor was a writhing carpet of plants and insects: strange hissing cockroaches; shiny millipedes; grasshoppers and cicadas chirping loudly; oily black beetles scuttling over their toes; and armies of ants marching in never-ending lines.

'Mind the snake!' William shouted back at Fleur as a huge python slunk across just in front of her toes.

They came to a clearing where light was able to seep through and Fleur stopped to marvel at her surroundings. A rainbow of butterflies flapped lazily in the spaces where light poured in and the sweet scent of jasmine hung in the sultry air, the waxy petals glowing like pearls in the undergrowth. Everything was imbued with a vibrant, abundant energy and at times Fleur felt like she was dreaming.

'Keep up, child,' William hollered as she fell behind to stare at a goggle-eyed amphibian stuck to the branch of a huge monkey-bread tree. It was the most curious thing she'd ever clapped eyes on.

'Tree frog,' he bellowed back to her, without missing a stride.

The three of them walked on until the trees thinned out and the red earth grew hot and dry. They halted while William cracked open a few coconuts with his knife, and drank the milk, digging slabs of the fruit out with their teeth. Then they shared a bunch of sweet bananas that were tiny enough to eat whole. Fleur had never seen or tasted such exotic fruits and devoured the delicious meal rapidly.

The moment they had finished eating William stood up. 'Not long now,' he said, wiping sweat from his brow.

He set off again at a cracking pace, with Tom at his heels and Fleur slipping and stumbling behind, impeded by her bow. He showed his young charges no mercy, ignoring the fact their strides were half the size of his own. They dropped down through the lunar landscape of a volcano, where all was quiet and still, then climbed up over the spine of a grassy plateau where pollen danced in the pure, clear air. When they reached its summit, both Fleur and Tom gasped at what lay beneath them. There was a lagoon of aquamarine water so clear you could see shoals of fish darting about even from such a height. A waterfall frothed and churned into a deep, emerald pool of fresh water nearby. Trees and bushes were stooped and bowed like old men, carrying their burden of sun-ripened fruit. And all this lay hidden, invisible from the sea.

Anchored at the edge of the lagoon, in a channel that led out to the open sea, Fleur saw a huge, strange-looking ship.

'Ain't she bonny?' the captain said proudly.

Fleur and Tom nodded speechlessly, still panting for breath. Fleur's father had told her about the sturdy flat-bottomed junks that sailed the eastern oceans, but this ship was like nothing she had ever set eyes on. She was as ugly as she was beautiful; a strange exotic insect crouching on the water, her sails resembling skeletal bat-like wings. For all her size and weight, she looked as if she might leap out of the water at any moment.

'She's called the *Black Dragon*,' William told them, 'and she's as old as time itself. Course, she's had some improvements over the years. Generations of sailors from every corner of the world have owned and loved her, and every one of 'em has left his mark – and perhaps a little of his soul too. She's a fine ship. A legend. And now it's finally time for me to claim her.'

'How did she get here, Cap'n?' Tom asked, standing on tiptoe as he tried to gauge the point where the lagoon met the open sea.

'She was dashed against the rocks in a storm,' William explained with a wave of his hand. 'When we found her, the hull was crammed with chests of opium and the bones of Chinamen.'

Fleur shivered and gestured at the four sails. 'They curve as if the wind were in them,' she said, following the arc of the foresail with a finger in the air. 'And yet there's no wind.'

'And where are all the ropes?' added Tom. 'She's a little short on rigging.'

William raised his eyebrows and studied them, impressed. 'The sails are curved with battens of wood called bamboo,' he explained. 'There's less need for rigging and you can position all four to catch every last puff of wind and profit from its force.'

Fleur was gazing intently at the strange mechanism of the sails. Eventually she said: 'I reckon if you turned them right, you could sail straight into the wind.'

'Aye, girl,' said William. 'You could sail this ship into the mouth of hell.' He nodded over at her. 'Henry really did teach thee well, didn't he?'

Fleur couldn't help but think of the cask left behind. 'We will be burying him soon, won't we?' she asked.

Her uncle nodded, his face expressionless, then started to lead the way down to the lagoon. 'Aye, as soon as she's ready to sail we're on our way. There's a bit of work to be done with her first, and I'll be counting on all your sailing skills. Do you think you can help me?'

Tom agreed eagerly.

'Yes, sir . . .' Fleur paused. 'Please, may I ask – who did you mean by "we" when you found the ship?' She spoke politely: she didn't want him turning on her yet again.

''Twas your father and me, child.'

Fleur stopped dead and stared at the ship bobbing gently in the water. *He might have walked this very pathway.* 'My father?'

William halted for a moment and turned to nod at her. This time he was actually smiling. 'Aye, that's what I said. And once we've settled aboard I promise to tell you a few things about the past and the family you came from.' He winked at her. 'I reckon you've earned it.'

Then he raced away again, almost sprinting down to his beloved *Black Dragon*, leaving Fleur and Tom to stumble behind as quickly as their tired legs could carry them.

CHAPTER 13

The *Black Dragon* lay serenely in the aquamarine water. Tropical birds with flamboyant plumage perched along the rigging; they cawed noisily as the strangers approached, as if passing judgement.

'Looks like she's already got a crew,' said Fleur. A nimble spider monkey sent the birds scattering as it climbed a mast. 'Sir?'

But William seemed to have forgotten that his young charges were even there; he hurried towards his beloved ship, lost in memory.

The waters of the lagoon were warm and silky and dotted with shoals of tiny iridescent fish that tickled their ankles as they waded out towards the ship. Once aboard, Fleur and Tom started exploring the sun-baked deck while the captain dashed about checking every available inch of ship.

'There's still work to be done,' he grumbled as he swept past, 'but she's in good shape, God bless her. The tools we stashed in the ship's hold are still there. A few weeks and we'll be able to raise anchor.'

The *Black Dragon*, her name also painted on the side in Chinese characters, William told them, was indeed a formidable ship. Weather-beaten as she was, and littered with animal droppings and other debris, there was still a majesty about her. She was high-sterned, her proud projecting prow clad in bronze. The four bamboo masts held oddly curved sails. Each sail could be spread or pulled up like a Venetian blind. Silk flags hung down from the masts: the images they carried – of birds, dragons and fanged demon gods – were sun-bleached and tattered almost beyond recognition. At the stern was a huge wooden rudder – far too big to be manned by a single sailor. Large guns and swivel cannons lined the deck on either side; the hold was covered by the tatty remnants of a bamboo roof. The space below decks was split into multiple compartments accessed by separate hatches and ladders. There were a few large cabins – some even had lavatories – but most of the crew had obviously slept in hammocks strung up in the vast hold.

Fleur soon managed to find the cabin that had been her father's all those years ago. In his hurry to leave, he had left behind a few clothes, now mouldy and moth-eaten, as well as a knife with a pretty mother-of-pearl handle. Perhaps it was this knife he'd used to scratch his name into the walnut headboard of his bed. Fleur traced the H and closed her eyes tight, remembering her father.

Just before sunset, William left Fleur and Tom on the *Black Dragon* and took the ship's tiny rowing boat around the curved hip of the cove to collect his sea chest and his brother's body. The sun burned low and heavy on the horizon and the moon sailed high in the darkening sky as they watched the captain's powerful strokes. They could still hear his raucous singing long after the little boat was out of sight. For a while they each wandered around separately, content to be alone. Solitude was a luxury aboard a ship, pirate or otherwise. Fleur ran her hands over the *Black Dragon*'s smooth timbers and imagined her father and William as young men, labouring together on the broken vessel.

However, as the last light vanished and the silence of the night overwhelmed her, Fleur began to grow anxious.

Where was her uncle? She paced the long deck of the empty ship, watching strange shadows unfold in every dark corner, and couldn't help imagining all the sailors' blood that had stained the decks. What if William didn't come back? she wondered. After all, he'd made no bones about the fact that she was a nuisance to him. What if Alexander Blood changed his mind and returned to kill them both?

A sudden animal shriek from the depths of the jungle left her shaking uncontrollably and she felt the burning of beady eyes upon her. Was somebody watching from the shadows? She called Tom's name, but there was no reply, and then the panic really began to set in. Fleur squinted into the gloom and took a tentative step forwards. There was a frantic rustle of leaves and the loud crack of a branch snapping along the shore; she scrambled back against the warm wood of the ship, her heart pounding.

At that moment Tom emerged from the hold.

'Where were you?' she demanded. Seeing Tom had filled her with relief, although she wasn't planning on admitting that to him.

He raked a hand through his hair and yawned. 'Sorry, I fell asleep,' he mumbled apologetically.

Fleur thrust her hands on her hips. 'While I guard the ship, I suppose!' she exclaimed.

Tom laughed, and stifled another yawn. 'From what? Birds or monkeys?'

She stalked away from him and leaned over the side of the ship, peering into the darkness.

'How long has the captain been gone?' Tom asked, sidling up next to her.

'Too long,' she replied quietly.

Time ran away; just as they were about to despair completely, Fleur heard the slap of oars in the water and a swinging speck of light appeared.

'Ahoy, Cap'n, ahoy,' Tom shouted eagerly.

A sudden breeze whipped Fleur's hair, carrying the scent of coconuts and flowers. William looked up, saw them on the deck and waved. Relief poured over Fleur like honey. For the first time since her father's death, she felt at home. It seemed that, for better or worse, home from now on meant wherever her uncle was.

He tutted and huffed when he saw Fleur's flustered appearance.

'I – I didn't think you'd come back for me, Captain,' she stammered, her face hot. 'I was worried for you,' she added quietly.

William's expression softened a little at that. He reached out falteringly and patted her on the shoulder

– hard enough to make her resolve to check for bruises later.

'I was set on spending a little time with him again,' he explained. 'I needed to say goodbye, child, and make my peace with him. I haven't seen my brother in a long while . . . Do ye understand?'

Fleur nodded and her brow furrowed. 'Yes, only too well. I've had little chance myself for a real farewell.'

William resumed his painful pats. 'You'll get your chance, girl, soon. On Ile aux Forbans. We'll make sure he gets a proper send-off.'

Fleur nodded and smiled up at her uncle hopefully. She was unused to kindness from him, but maybe, just maybe, he did care about her after all. 'I'm glad you came back,' she said, thinking aloud.

William nodded back absent-mindedly and looked up at the starry sky. He sighed happily and stamped on the deck. 'Of course I came back, young 'un. Why would I leave the *Black Dragon*?'

With much swearing and grunting, they all managed to drag and roll Henry's rum barrel into the hold and carried the captain's belongings to the grandest cabin. Only after some serious nagging from Fleur did William ask Tom to leave them for a while so that they could have the family history lesson he had promised her. The flickering glow of a lantern softened his scarred and weather-beaten features, and for a moment he looked so much like his brother that Fleur had to stop herself from reaching out to hold him. At first the only sounds were the creaking timbers of the *Black Dragon* and the slap of water below.

'We come from a long line of seafaring fortune seekers, Fleur,' William began. 'Your father and I were the last of the Harts – or so I thought.' He smiled over at her with real warmth. 'Some of us were more . . . well, more morally flexible than others, you could say. Some were outright lunatics, if truth be told – but all family nevertheless. Now, your grandfather, my old dad, Robert, he was one of the more creatively vicious rogues to carry the name, and I dare say he probably deserved his death at the point of Ben Blood's sword.

'That's what sent our old family feud spiralling though. Ben killed Pa, I killed Ben's brother Patrick, then I killed Ben, then Alexander got involved and . . . well . . . I'm sorry for the mess we brought to your door, girl. Anyway, for a time your father and I sailed together. Henry – born first by a cat's whisker, and never let me forget it – was the captain; a gentleman pirate, as I've said before – if such a thing exists. He led us with a certain flair at least, and a sense of boundaries that is uncommon in the pirating game. Me, though' – William's face hardened suddenly – 'I was always my father's boy deep down.'

The intensity of her uncle's gaze made Fleur shiver. She recovered herself and ventured a question, although her voice shook slightly. 'So how did the pair of you find yourself on this island?'

William filled and lit his pipe as he continued to talk. 'Our ship was taken in battle and we were forced to jump overboard. We'd already ordered Jack to take the ship's rowing boat to escape with the survivors, so there was nothing else for it. We were in the water for ages, trying to reach this island, but the current kept pushing us back out to sea. Finally, both exhausted, we let ourselves be captured by the tide, which eventually swept us into the lagoon leading to this hiding place. It was Henry who first spotted the prow of the *Black Dragon*. It was blind luck, girl; that or divine providence.' He laughed long and hard at his last comment. Finally he wiped his eyes and carried on.

'We were stranded for six months, and the *Black Dragon* was all but ready. But we never got to sail her out of here.'

'Why?' Fleur asked, intrigued.

William sighed deeply. 'We'd left our pirate flag fluttering on the beach – the one that Alexander just marooned us on. We knew any survivors from our ship were bound to revisit these dangerous waters to try and find us. And they did.' His expression darkened. 'We saw 'em coming from afar and recognized their flag, so we made ourselves known. It was Jack and the rest of our men on a borrowed ship. They'd made it to Ile aux Forbans, where they'd heard a terrible rumour.'

'What was it?' Fleur whispered.

William flinched as he recalled the day. 'As soon as Jack had the gossip confirmed, he turned round and came back to these waters. They'd been travelling for weeks, but this island is hard to locate. Jack didn't even know for sure whether we'd survived the previous battle, but he was determined to find us, dead or alive. You see, Alexander had struck again.' He paused, clenching his teeth. 'He'd killed my wife and son, a babe in arms.'

Fleur gasped in shock and horror. She hadn't imagined for a moment that her uncle had a family of his own. She just couldn't picture him gazing tenderly down at his own new-born child. Yet here he was now, in anguish. She remembered their first meeting: his face had darkened when she'd clumsily asked him whether she had any cousins. How that must have pained him. Fleur wondered what the monstrous pirate captain had been like before he'd lost those he loved. It might all have been different had fate not turned him against the world. But William had given up, closed off his heart and lost himself to the sea.

'I'm sorry, sir,' Fleur said softly, biting back her tears. She watched her uncle's shoulders rise and fall as he gained control.

'Aye, a son. I named him Robert, after his grandfather. He was a bonny little thing.'

'And your wife?' Fleur asked.

William allowed himself a small smile and stared into the flickering flame of the lantern. 'Anna was beautiful,' he told Fleur, 'and far too good for the likes of me. I'll never see her kind again.' His face darkened, and he coughed, composed himself and carried on with the story. 'Anyhow, I won't go into too much detail here, because it all got darker than it should have, but the Hart brothers were finished and Henry turned his back on the sea for good. After what happened, he took Rose, who was pregnant with you, lassie, and hid the lot of you away. 'Twasn't cowardice, mind, even though I thought that at the time. He gave up something he was born to do to save those he loved most. But a Hart without the pirate life is like a violin without strings, or a night sky without moon and stars. It was always going to catch up with him eventually.'

Fleur swallowed uncomfortably at that. 'And you?' she asked.

'I slid further into the cruel ways I'd learned from your grandfather. And I never set foot on this island again, till we arrived together.'

They sat in silence for a while, both lost in their own thoughts. Then William straightened and stared directly at his niece.

'Your father gave you a measure of readiness for this life, child,' he told her seriously. 'You understand that, don't you?'

'Fighting and stuff, you mean?' asked Fleur, thinking back to happier times, when she and Henry had sparred playfully in the yard of the inn. 'Aye, I reckon he did.'

'You hold back though. I've seen it myself,' said William. 'Scared of what you might do?'

Fleur fidgeted uncomfortably. 'A little,' she admitted. 'Father taught me a lot. Eastern stuff, from his travels in the Orient. He wouldn't let me fight the drunks when there was trouble at the inn. Said it was for *their* protection, not mine. I always thought he was joking and, you know, trying to keep me from harm. But . . .'

'But now you're not so sure?' asked her uncle. 'Aye, well,' he continued. 'If you thought it was a joke, 'twas best he kept you from the fray. Like as not, he kept you from the gallows too.'

Fleur gasped. 'What do you mean?'

'You underestimate yourself,' he said gruffly. 'You're a Hart, by Neptune, trained from your first steps to walk in a world of fire and water, blood and steel. Your father brought you up to be fast and strong. He trained you in the martial arts of east and west alike. What? Loose that on a brawling drunkard? You'd have killed him, lass. And then you'd've been hanged for it.'

Fleur gulped hard. He was right; she knew it.

''Tis as well your father took you to task from such an early age,' said William, his voice softening a little.

'Why, Uncle?' she asked.

'You'll be able to jump higher, swim faster, run further and swifter than any pirate you meet, girl.' He smiled. 'And you'll pack a punch that'll take 'em by surprise. Not a bad cache of secret weapons for the smallest pirate on the seven seas.'

He laughed heartily at that and Fleur leaned over to wallop him on the thigh.

'Ow,' laughed William, rubbing his leg. 'See? I told you that you packed a pretty punch. Tell me, girl,' he went on as their laughter subsided, 'did Henry teach you to wield a staff at all?'

'Aye,' said Fleur. 'We fought with quarterstaffs and sometimes fallen branches. Father said I was good – a natural.'

William's eyes suddenly sparkled like polished black marble. He was eyeing his niece as if appraising a ship in harbour. 'You may yet prove to be the family's greatest asset . . .' He nodded thoughtfully.

'Not if you insist on dumping me in some plantation when all I want is to be at sea,' muttered Fleur grumpily. 'With you, Uncle,' she added, hoping to appeal to his sentimental side.

William harrumphed and pretended not to hear. 'I reckon we'll spar a little with staffs tomorrow,' he announced. 'No point letting your skills get rusty. What would your father say?'

Fleur thought of her father, fighting bravely with the Hart staff against Blood and his men. Why had he kept the staff from her? she wondered. They might have trained with it all along. And now it was too late, for the staff lay in the hands of their hated enemy.

'Uncle,' she asked, 'do the Bloods share our skill with the staff, or the secrets of the east my father taught me?'

William shook his head. 'No,' he grunted. 'They say the Bloods draw their strength from a pact they made with the devil himself.'

'Hmph!' said Fleur dismissively.

'Take heed, child,' her uncle barked fiercely, sending a shiver through her despite the warm humid air. 'Meet 'em once with a cutlass in your hand and you'll soon see it be true. They'll fight like demons and cut your throat out with a smile.'

'Have our two families always hated each other?' asked Fleur fearfully.

'For as long as men have sailed in ships or fought with sword or staff, aye,' said William sombrely. 'But mark me, I shall live to see the end of it. The last great battle. I, William Hart, shall live to see my family take their rightful place and rule the oceans.'

The candle flickered and shadows danced on the wall behind him.

'Are you talking about the prophecy?' asked Fleur boldly, hoping to catch her uncle off guard.

'I've said enough,' he said firmly. 'And you' – he waved a finger at Fleur accusingly – 'you're sneaky.'

'But—' began Fleur.

'No. Not tonight. I have my reasons for not telling you everything, girl.'

Fleur fell silent. Her uncle, a little sorry to see her so deflated, looked down at his hands and impulsively twisted off one of a pair of identical rings that he wore on his little fingers. They were made from old, dark yellow gold and each was set with a large ruby. The jewels were the colour of congealed blood but they glinted scarlet whenever they caught a flicker of candlelight. He held up the ring he had removed and studied it thoughtfully.

'Rubies are one of the most precious jewels in the world,' he said, fixing Fleur with a piercing stare. 'They symbolize fire and blood. They're the king of gemstones, child, and these ones here have a star at their heart.' He ran a finger around the gold band of the ring. 'A circle has no beginning and no end. It is eternal. All the Harts wear one of these.' He leaned over and pressed the ring into her hand. 'This one was your father's – he gave it to me when he retired. Now it is yours.'

Fleur gasped as she slipped her father's ring onto the middle finger of her right hand. It fitted perfectly and the reflections of the dull light crackled over it like fire. 'Thank you,' she whispered.

William puffed on his pipe and watched her thoughtfully as she twisted and turned her hand in the light to admire the ring. 'I will tell you more, Fleur – that

I promise,' he said finally. 'I will tell you everything you want to know – all in good time.'

They all woke early the next morning to make a start on the repairs to the ship. William was soon barking orders at his niece again, much to Tom's delight. There was an unspoken rivalry for the captain's affections between his cabin boy and his niece. But Fleur felt more comfortable in her uncle's presence now. She was even bold enough to answer back now and then. She was still desperate to hear about the Hart prophecy, but she understood that William had his reasons for not telling her yet.

For his part, he seemed more human, less impatient and demanding. He was even willing to make conversation. But Fleur and Tom both knew not to push him too far: there would always be a fiery heart to a man like their fearsome captain.

The air grew hot and dead; with no cooling wind, sweat beaded on Fleur's face and neck and tickled her back. They toiled without a break until their stomachs growled with hunger and their legs began to buckle. Only then did they collapse in the shade to rest. The captain picked a spot next to the waterfall, where cold water fizzed over them as they nibbled on ship's biscuits, mangoes and juicy barbecued fish. Fleur had been scraping barnacles from the ship's stern; now she pointed towards the carving of a naked woman that adorned the prow.

'I thought it was unlucky to have women aboard?' she said.

William eyed the *Black Dragon*'s mascot and nodded. 'Aye, lassie. They ain't physically or emotionally capable and they distract the rest of the crew.'

Fleur tutted loudly as both he and Tom howled with laughter.

'Present company excepted, of course,' he added, 'and a handful of other notorious vixens.'

Fleur grinned and picked a fish bone out of her teeth. She nodded over at the carved figurehead again. 'What about Buxom Betty then?'

Tom snorted water through his nose as he burst out laughing.

'Buxom Betty! Now that's a good one.' William nodded approvingly. 'Well, firstly, she's hardly aboard, is she? She's shaped to the prow. And secondly, 'tis thought that a naked woman can calm the sea by shaming the storms.'

'What superstitious nonsense,' Fleur snorted.

Tom threw a biscuit at her. ''Tis the way of the sea,

Claw-cat. And if you're going to set foot on a pirate ship again, you'd better know our superstitions.'

'Like what?' she asked, dipping the biscuit in her water to soften it.

William's words came out in a tumble. 'Like . . . cats carry lightning in their tails and can summon the wind by sneezing – so anger the ship's cat and you'll call up a gale. Let's see . . . Ah, a silver coin placed under the masthead makes for a good voyage. Oh, and don't ever step on a ship with your left foot first.' He touched the heavy gold hoops hanging from his ears. 'We pierce our ears to improve our eyesight, but a gold earring is also a charm against drowning, and the price paid to Davy Jones to enter the next world should that fail!'

Fleur chuckled. Her uncle rubbed his bristly chin as he thought. 'Throwing stones in the water will cause storms, so best not do that. But pouring wine on the deck brings good weather on a voyage. Flowers are unlucky, so are priests – women you know about—'

Fleur waved her hands about to stop him. 'No more, sir!' she begged. 'I reckon you could carry on for ever.'

William nodded and stretched his limbs, then lay on his side while he loaded up his pipe with tobacco. 'Aye, there's probably some nonsense to cover everything.'

Fleur thought back to the night her father had been

murdered, and to what one of Blood's men had said about William: *You'll be thinkin' we believe in the legend, won't you? That if we say his name out loud, he'll come and have our hearts' blood.*

'And what of your legend, sir,' she asked more timidly. 'While we're talking about superstitions and the like,' she added. 'I've heard that if your name is spoken aloud, you'll be able to hear. Is that true?'

Her uncle threw his head back and laughed with gusto. 'Sometimes myths can be useful, child,' he replied.

Fleur pondered this for a few moments. 'So it's not true?'

'If it were true, I would be dashing all over the seven seas, as I'm sure my name is often muttered in vain.'

Fleur looked disappointed.

William lit his pipe and smoke curled into the endless blue sky. 'Although,' he began, closing his eyes, 'it does depend on how passionately a name is spoken. After all, how can the waves carry a whisper?'

Fleur shivered with delight, her mind brimming with wonder at her uncle's enigmatic response.

A sudden thump made them all turn. A small furry animal sat on its haunches barely out of their reach, watching them suspiciously. Without warning, it leaped forward, snatching up a piece of mango before retreating to peer at them from a nearby palm tree. Fleur stared up at it in amazement. She'd never seen anything quite like it. It was a cross between a monkey and a cat, with reddish-brown fur and a black and white face. Its long tail flicked and curled about it like a furry snake and its bulbous fingers and toes clung easily to the tree trunk. It stared at them with inquisitive red eyes as it nibbled on its prize.

'It's a lemur,' William said, smiling at his slack-jawed niece. 'There are plenty around these parts.'

'Tasty too,' Tom added, smacking his lips together approvingly.

Fleur glanced at him with disgust before turning to stare up at the strange little animal. It sat amongst the leaves, chewing vigorously on the mango flesh and tossing bits of the skin to the floor with a flick of its wrist.

'You couldn't eat him,' she exclaimed. 'He's as sweet as a kitten.' She crumbled up the remains of the biscuit in her hand. 'I wonder if he likes these?'

Fleur scattered the crumbs on the ground near the foot of the tree and waited. William rolled his eyes at her but watched with interest. The lemur watched too, its head cocked to one side as if considering its options, then sprang down and landed deftly by the biscuit crumbs. For a brief moment it glared at Tom, perhaps angry at being considered 'tasty', and then raced forward, snatched up the food and disappeared behind a rock, poking its head out shyly.

'See?' Fleur said, turning to frown at the others. 'He's clever. Like a little person covered in fur.'

William rolled his eyes again. 'You'll be talking to the fishies soon, I suppose, girl,' he teased.

'And there we were thinking you were made of *tougher stuff*,' Tom added.

Fleur looked back at the lemur; it was nibbling at the biscuit and scratching behind one of its ears. 'I ain't soft,' she muttered. 'That thing is almost like a little man and I don't fancy eating anything with a face that can smile at me from the pot.'

Her uncle laughed and spat out a fish bone. 'That's because you ain't been at sea long enough, girl.' He raised an eyebrow at Tom. 'A week of no food and you'd eat your best hunting hound . . . Two weeks and you'd gut your kin for sausages.'

At sunset William summoned Fleur to the beach to begin her first training session. Tom watched from a distance, hoping to pick up a few tricks, but he was soon asleep on the soft warm sand. The twilit sky burned like fire and golden light gathered in hollows and glowed on the surface of the lagoon like diamonds. Fleur and her uncle sat cross-legged, facing each other, their shadows slowly lengthening as the sun sank behind the horizon.

'Breathe deeply, girl,' rumbled William. 'Close your eyes and calm your spirit.'

'Why are we doing this?' asked Fleur impatiently, peeking at her uncle through her eyelashes. 'Can't we get on with the stick-fighting and the kicking and punching?'

He couldn't suppress a smile. 'We'll get to that. But first you have to learn to relax; centre yourself. If you go into a fight angry, you won't accomplish anything.'

Fleur folded her arms grumpily. 'Isn't kicking and punching someone an accomplishment fight-wise?' she asked. 'Anyway,' she added, 'I've never seen you having a sit-down before a battle.'

They both opened their eyes and glared at each other.

William puffed out his breath in frustration. 'Listen,' he muttered. 'A real fighter needs to be aware of everything. He—'

'Or she!'

'Fair enough. He *or* she has to sense every movement

of the battle around them, almost before it happens. That's the skill that keeps you off the tip of another man's steel, lass: learn it well.'

'I still don't see how sitting with my eyes closed is supposed to help,' said Fleur, mulling over her uncle's words.

'Awareness is reached gradually,' said William. 'Stage one is awareness of the self. Now do as you're told.'

She clamped her eyes shut again. 'All right,' she sighed, 'let's breathe.'

They sat in silence, breathing slowly while the gulls dipped and called overhead and Tom dozed on. Fleur's calm was shattered by a painful rap on the back of her neck.

'Ouch!' she exclaimed, toppling forward in the sand. Her uncle towered over her, holding out a hand to help her up. 'Why did you do that?'

'Stage two is awareness of other people,' he said, grinning then hauling her up roughly. 'You should have heard me coming, girl. I hardly made a secret of it.' He paced around in a small circle and his weapons rattled as he moved. 'See?' he said. 'I'm a regular Morris dancer.'

Fleur thrust her hands on her hips. 'Of course I heard you,' she barked. 'I just didn't expect you to whack me one, so I was waiting to see what you were up to.'

William looked pleased. 'Well, that's a start. But don't wait so long next time. The instinct is there, so listen to it. Never underestimate the element of surprise. You must be ready at all times, Fleur. At *all* times. This must become a way of life for you. Anything less and you'll wind up food for the fishies.'

She frowned. 'And what makes you think I can do this, sir?' she asked, suddenly unsure of herself. 'What makes you think I can be that good?'

'Because I believe in you,' he replied simply. 'You're a Hart and you've been schooled for this since you were a babe. Henry's lessons gave you many of the skills you'll need, and by the time I've finished with you, you'll be able to defend yourself against any attacker with your bare hands – and maybe your teeth from time to time.'

Fleur grimaced. 'That's sounds . . . um . . . interesting.'

William paced around restlessly and she could tell he was itching for a good fight. 'You must always assume that your opponent will be larger and stronger, which is something you'll be coming across plenty. There ain't no children in Alexander's crew.'

He looked at Fleur with eyes that were suddenly cruel and she shuddered. The reality for which Henry had trained her was almost too terrifying to contemplate.

'Defend yourself in any way you can,' he continued.

'But you don't just defend yourself,' Fleur argued, remembering how savagely he'd fought on the beach in Cornwall.

William sighed. 'That's because I'm bigger. Now then, try to attack from peculiar angles.' He twisted round in the sand, trying to show her what he meant. 'You're agile enough to contort your body to strike when the opponent believes himself safe. Use the backs of your forearms, your elbows, knees, heels, feet . . . You'll learn to tease your opponents into rash action, then take advantage of their hot blood and let it out!'

He lunged forward, drawing his cutlass; Fleur leaped back, startled. 'Well, what do you think of all that for starters?' he asked.

Fleur shrugged. 'Now you're talking.' She grinned. 'It's like I said. Punching and kicking.'

CHAPTER 14

Fleur quickly adapted to island life. Her bare feet were becoming as tanned and hardy as Tom's and she enjoyed the simple daily routine: fishing and hunting in the morning, foraging for fruit and fetching water in the afternoon, and working on the *Black Dragon* with William as much as possible. They tidied out the cabins and soon made them feel quite homely.

The captain seemed more relaxed than he'd ever been. It was as if someone had cut through the invisible shackles he wore. His mood brightened even further with his first batch of toke – a strong and sickly liquor which he had fermented from honey. But it was obvious that he was still desperate to get back out on the waves. And while all thoughts of Alexander Blood, or of revenge, or of reclaiming the Hart staff, were put aside while they fixed the ship and waited for a favourable wind, they still bubbled under the surface, fuelling the castaways' dreams at night.

In the early evenings William taught Fleur as much as he could of the pirating life. He also schooled her in combat, unlocking a talent for fighting that he happily acknowledged was worthy of a Hart. Henry had laid the foundations; William was honing those skills and giving his niece the confidence she lacked. He wanted to know how high she could jump, how hard she could hit, and how fast she was with the staffs he fashioned from sturdy branches, devising all manner of tests in an effort to find out. Tom joined them for some of the training sessions, although he hated it when Fleur bettered his efforts. He could punch harder than her, but she could hit the right spot every time. They were both skilled acrobats – Tom from his life on the rigging and Fleur from a childhood spent climbing trees. But Fleur had more stamina and stealth than Tom could ever hope for. She was faster too, and so deft with a staff that it made everyone around her dizzy.

Training the pair of them was good sport for William.

He tied them up with rope bonds and left them to make their own escape. He forced them to shin up the masts of the *Black Dragon* with sand bags tied around their ankles and wrists to weigh them down. He made them play catch with cannonballs until their shoulders ached too much to carry on. And of course he made them fight. At first Tom held back, not wanting to hurt Fleur. He learned his lesson soon enough: Fleur was so savage that it took everything he had to hold her at bay.

Fleur, in turn, showed the others how to shoot straight from her father's bow. But neither of them could match her unerring accuracy. She never let them shoot lemurs, despite her uncle's teasing as he rubbed his belly and smacked his lips. In fact Fleur's lemur had grown bolder as the days passed, even snatching food from her outstretched fingers. Parsley hated the creature though, and spat and hissed at it whenever it came near.

When the light failed each evening, the ill-assorted trio would light a bonfire on the beach and talk into the night. They'd lie flat on their backs, wriggling their bare toes in the warm sand and swatting away at the mosquitoes with palm leafs. William smoked his pipe and sipped his foul home-made toke. Tom would whittle driftwood while Fleur bombarded her uncle with questions. She begged to hear tales of the Hart brothers' adventures, which William recounted with relish.

It was a simple life, and there were moments when Fleur, Tom and William all began to forget that they had anywhere else to be. It was just the three of them.

And then, suddenly, they were no longer alone.

'Did *you* finish that turtle meat, Tom?' Fleur called from the beach. She'd acquired a taste for the juicy, salty turtle flesh lately, thanks to her uncle's cooking skills.

Tom was fixing a hole in the side of the ship and had worked up a sweat in the midday sun. He stepped into the shade as he watched Fleur wade across the lagoon to hand him a flagon of water. He gulped it down greedily before responding to her question.

'No. 'Twas probably your furry friend.' He sighed as his thirst was quenched and wiped his mouth with the back of his hand. 'My God, I'm burning up out here. I don't feel so good.'

Fleur frowned and shook her head. 'I don't think it was the lemur.' She stared thoughtfully at the dark fringe of jungle around the lagoon. 'Are you sure it wasn't you?'

'As sure as you were yesterday when you wouldn't admit to finishing the mangoes.'

Fleur's jaw dropped in protest. 'But I *didn't* finish them,' she protested.

Tom stretched his broad back with a wince. His bones were clearly aching, and he was pale beneath his tan. 'Who did then?' he retorted.

'Well, it wasn't me,' boomed the captain as he appeared from the other side of the ship and waded over to them.

The three of them looked at one another with puzzled expressions.

'There's other things that don't make no sense either,' Fleur said, lowering her voice.

'Like what?' her uncle asked.

'I wasn't certain before, but now I am. Clothes have gone, and water. And there's more . . .'

'Go on,' the captain prompted impatiently.

She looked about her nervously. 'I've seen footprints in the sand that aren't any of ours.'

Tom scanned the island slowly, shielding his eyes from the glare of the sun. 'Are you sure, Claw-cat?'

'Aye' – she nodded – 'at first I thought they were animal tracks, but I saw them again today, near the big red rock. And they're no beast's either. The tide stole 'em before I could show you.'

William stared hard into the jungle gloom, as if daring

whatever hid there to show itself. 'We're almost done here,' he said sternly, pointing towards the *Black Dragon*. 'We'll be off as soon as we're able.' He gathered up his tools and nodded briskly at them. 'Don't wander too far. We'd've have known by now if there were natives; if someone else is here, like as not they'll be up to no good. Now get some rest, the pair of ye. I'll keep an eye open.'

The cabins they had taken were furnished with proper beds so Fleur usually slept more soundly there than she had since leaving Cornwall, despite the lumps in her mattress. She threw herself on the bed, which emitted a huge puff of dust, ran a finger over her father's carved initials, then rolled onto her side and closed her eyes, wondering about the island's mysterious new visitor. But her dreams that night were dark and violent: the pale, malevolent face of Alexander Blood filled her vision. He had the Hart staff and used it to put a swift end to her. Her fingertips brushed the weapon as she reached out hopelessly, falling backwards into a bottomless grave full of hungry crackling flames. And as she lay there, consumed by fire, she could hear someone groaning her name, again and again . . .

In the morning she went into Tom's cabin, which was

next door to hers, eager to tell him about her horrible dreams. But her friend's face was ashen white and he was drenched in sweat. He was muttering her name like a mantra and she realized then that his voice must have bled into her dreams.

'Tom!' she gasped, dashing across to him. 'What's wrong with you?'

Tom's head lolled listlessly to the side and he stared at her with glassy eyes. He squinted, trying to focus on her face. 'Claw-cat? Is it really you this time?'

She nodded frantically and held his clammy hand in hers. 'Yes, Tom. It's me.'

He started shivering violently. 'I don't feel right.' He looked about the room fearfully. 'Is the storm still raging? The ship's tipping so hard we're bound to go under.'

Fleur stared down at her friend in shock. The boy was clearly caught in the grip of a powerful fever that was raging through his body. And there wasn't a doctor in sight.

A pale Fleur brought Tom some fresh water but his throat burned and he could barely swallow. She called her uncle, but try as they might, they could not calm his fever. As his flesh grew hotter, Tom began to see visions of his long-dead parents. He muttered to them in his delirium. By the time the sun began to sink below the horizon all William and Fleur could do was take it in turns to sit by him and wonder whether they were about to lose him. The thought terrified Fleur more than she dared to admit.

CHAPTER 15

Fleur ended up watching over her frail companion all night, but by the next morning she had no more hope for his survival. However, as she and William dozed next to Tom's bed, the mystery of their light-fingered visitor was abruptly solved with a knock at the cabin door.

'Hello. Um . . . can I come in please, sir?'

Fleur nearly jumped out of her skin at the sound. She sprang up, her eyes bloodshot and her face pale. Her uncle sprang to his feet too and took hold of the cutlass that hung from his belt.

'Who's there?' he shouted.

The door creaked open slowly and William and Fleur

readied themselves for the attack. Then their mouths fell open. A boy stood in the doorway, fidgeting nervously. He looked about fourteen, with thick, straight chestnut hair, freckles and intelligent, fine-boned features. His clothes were ragged and his wire-framed spectacles were cracked. A large weathered leather bag hung from his shoulder. He was covered in cuts and bruises and his pale skin was burned raw.

William brandished his cutlass and the boy shrank back from the doorway. 'Who the hell are you?' the captain demanded.

The boy stepped forward once more and cleared his throat to speak. His voice showed the benefits of schooling. 'Please, sir, I was the unhappy victim of a shipwreck in these waters. My name is Arthur Samuels.' He swallowed nervously. 'I was stranded on another island nearby.' His face twitched and he cleared his throat again. 'Everyone else, my father included, perished in the waves. I built a raft and set sail, I hoped, for the mainland, but I found only this island. I stayed for the food and fresh water. I am ashamed to admit to pilfering from your supplies, sir, but I decided against a direct approach. You . . . you seemed so fierce, sir, with all due respect.'

'Too right,' William roared, bending down to peer

into the boy's face. 'You should have followed your instincts.'

Arthur gulped and glanced over at Tom's shivering, sweating form, then held out his hand to reveal a pile of crumbled flower heads. They were pale pink with deep purple eyes at the centre. Fleur moved forward to have a look at them.

'Please, sir,' he began, glancing briefly at Fleur, 'this herb is called periwinkle – it's used to treat a wide array of ailments . . .' He swallowed again nervously as his voice quivered away to nothing.

William narrowed his eyes. 'Like what, boy? Come on, speak up.'

'Um . . .' he started. 'Um . . .'

The captain rolled his eyes in exasperation. 'Speak now or get out of my sight.'

Arthur looked as if he would love to run away, but he stood his ground, his knees knocking. 'Like insect stings, sir,' he replied hastily, 'and to stop bleeding and for lung congestion and inflammation and sore throats – and – and – and fevers!' He glanced at Tom.

'How do you know all this? Is it witchcraft?' William demanded, with a stare of such intensity that it made the boy squirm uncomfortably.

Arthur shook his head so frantically that his glasses

flew off his nose. 'Please, sir, it's not witchcraft.' He scrabbled on the floor for his spectacles. Fleur pushed them towards him with her toe and he picked them up eagerly.

'My father taught me. He was a doctor,' the boy continued, his voice just above a whisper. A tear strayed down his sunburned face; he wiped it away, embarrassed. 'He was many other things too. He travelled the world, learning from different lands and drawing wisdom from them all. He learned how to use herbs and flowers as medicine after the doctors at home failed to cure our mother from smallpox.'

William hmm'd thoughtfully as he plucked one of the crumpled flower heads from Arthur's palm. He held the delicate thing between his coarse fingers and studied it with a look of scorn. 'Are you sure it'll help, boy? A good cabin boy is hard to find, and if more harm is brought to him by your ministrations, I swear on my sword I'll strip your guts for fiddle strings.'

Arthur looked to Fleur for support but she stared at him as sternly as possible. 'And that'll be after I pluck each eye from its socket.'

The boy gulped hard and nodded furiously under their withering gaze.

William loomed over him like an angry bear and growled out his orders: 'Get it done.'

Arthur set to work immediately; the captain dozed by Tom's bed, keeping an eye open to watch the young visitor as he toiled. Under Arthur's careful instruction, Fleur assisted him. First they crushed the periwinkle petals and sweetened them with honey; then Arthur added some dried herbs from the pouch that he wore around about his neck. William's gaze narrowed at this last addition, but for want of any better ideas both he and Fleur had decided to trust the boy. Arthur propped Tom up in a sitting position and Fleur held his limp hand as the gloopy, strange-smelling potion was poured down their patient's throat.

'What now?' asked William impatiently.

'We should bathe him,' said Arthur, more confidently. 'In cool water.'

'The shock'll kill him,' the captain protested, rising to his feet.

Arthur faced him boldly and shook his head. 'No, sir,' he replied, his voice trembling only a little. 'It will cool his fever. It will save him.'

Somewhat bruised from having been faced down by a child, the fearsome pirate William the Heartless spent the rest of the day and the following night pacing nervously while Arthur and Fleur tended to Tom. The decks groaned under his big sea boots, and the wind seemed to mould to his mood, gathering force and bringing hard rain to the island. The *Black Dragon* rocked violently in her moorings and the fish in the shallows were tossed up and stranded along the shoreline. At dawn, the storm and Tom's fever broke together. William, Arthur and Fleur gathered about his bed as he opened his eyes and took in the new arrival for the first time.

'Have we been rescued, Captain?' he croaked, his throat dry. 'Only, isn't he a bit short for a pirate?'

Arthur was officially received aboard the *Black Dragon*. William promised to let him stay with them until he could be dropped at a suitable port, with money in his pocket. Fleur had been impressed by the newcomer's healing skills and was warming to him. Her uncle, however, wasn't quite so ready to welcome him into the fold. He led Arthur into the stuffy sleeping quarters below decks and pointed to the tatty hammocks strung about like gap-toothed smiles. He didn't even think of offering the boy a cabin.

'Pick a hammock and that'll be your berth while we stay here,' he said gruffly, chewing on his dirty nails.

Arthur edged into the room and stared about the dingy space with wide, searching eyes. Fragile sunbeams reached in where they could like probing fingers. Here and there they revealed unexamined piles of clutter and unidentified scuttling things that darted for the shadows when they realized they were being observed. The smell of rotten wood, swollen with stagnant salt water and animal excrement, was overpowering.

'Am I really expected to sleep in here?' Arthur asked, backing against the wall nearest the exit and staring into the gloom in disgust.

William glared at him and nodded briskly. 'Yes, you damn well are, you ungrateful whelp.' He spat a crescent moon of filthy nail onto the floor. 'Though you're welcome to sack down on the deck if you prefer. Ordinarily, with strangers, I slit their throats and throw 'em overboard. I suppose I could offer you the same courtesy.'

Fleur appeared behind her uncle and shook her head at Arthur warningly.

'This will be lovely,' said Arthur with an unconvincing grin. 'Ahoy there, Cap'n, and all that. Ahem.'

William suppressed the urge to laugh. He was enjoying having somebody to tease since Fleur had stopped fearing him. Not that he regretted her newfound confidence around him. She was a fine addition to the family. Arthur was more fun to goad anyway: he was cut from different stuff to them. Despite his knowledge and experiences, he was still as fresh as a kitten.

Fleur nudged William gently in the ribs and stood on tiptoe to whisper in his ear. 'Please show him some compassion, Uncle. Remember, he saved our Tom.'

William sighed and lit his pipe. 'Look here, sparrow,' he said in a kinder voice. 'There's cabins to be had on this ship before my crew get here, but those that are empty still need a good clean – most are piled with cannonballs and old weapons. I'll help carry what's too heavy for you. I can't say fairer than that. There ain't no beds in there neither, so unhook yourself a hammock and strap it up yourself. Find me when you need me.' And with that he turned and strode off, puffing on his pipe.

Fleur leaned against the door frame and nodded over at Arthur.

'I've always wanted to sleep in one of these, like a real sailor,' he told her, then swung himself enthusiastically into the nearest hammock. It tipped, twisted and dropped him to the floor as deftly as a Greek wrestler. He lay in a crumpled heap, gasping for breath. Both he and Fleur could hear William's mutters long after his footsteps had receded.

★

In the days that followed, Fleur nursed Tom back to full health while Arthur gave a hand with the repairs. Though shy at first, Arthur soon proved to be a useful shipmate. He seemed to have a remedy for every ailment and his knowledge of herbs and potions was exceptional. When Tom complained that his head was throbbing, the boy had quickly produced a willow bark and feverfew paste with ingredients from his precious pouch, which he smeared across Tom's forehead. The pain vanished before Tom had time to wonder whether it was working. When William smashed his leg against a rock, caught by an unexpected wave, Arthur had smeared citrus-scented marjoram shrub onto his bruised shin. The swelling was soon eased. At night he made everyone rub lemon oil onto their skin to keep off the mosquitoes – a routine nobody minded after the first bite-free night. There was a quiet assuredness about the clever scatter-brained boy that comforted Fleur. And with Tom still poorly it was good to have someone of her age around to talk to. Arthur was refreshingly different to the pirates she had grown used to.

One blistering, cloudless afternoon Fleur came back from hunting to find Arthur staring up at the Chinese characters drawn on the side of the *Black Dragon*.

'Pretty drawings, ain't they,' she said brightly, throwing down a wild piglet.

Arthur looked round, noticed her prize and smiled, pushing his spectacles up the bridge of his sweaty nose. 'Yes, I suppose they are.'

Fleur started wading across the water to him. 'William says it's Chinese writing,' she explained.

'That's right,' Arthur agreed, nodding eagerly. '*Haaklùhng*: *lùhng* is the word for dragon. They're a symbol of good luck in China.' He pointed up at the torn silk flags hanging limply from the masts. 'They have those flags on their ships to protect them. There's a legend which says that a dragon lives in the clouds and watches over respectful sailors. When the dragon grows angry, he makes typhoons and terrible storms. Bright flags please the dragon. Red's the best colour, apparently.'

Fleur stared at him in surprise. 'How do you know Chinese writing?' she asked, open-mouthed.

'My mother was half Chinese.' He looked away shyly. 'Father met her when he travelled to the east with some silk traders. Anyway, I'm good at other languages as well. Father said I had an unnatural ability to remember things.' He dropped his head sadly at the thought of his deceased parents. 'I remember everything . . .'

'*Parlez-vous français?*' Fleur asked brightly, desperate to change the subject.

'*Oui, bien sûr,*' he replied. '*Y español, und Deutsch, italiano*—'

'All right, all right, *ça suffit!*' said Fleur, laughing. 'That's enough.'

'What about you?' asked Arthur, smiling too. 'Where did you learn?'

'My father taught me,' she explained.

They strolled back around the lagoon, chatting happily, then sat down together on the warm sandy beach. The dipping sun slanted through the masts of the *Black Dragon*, sending splinters of sunlight across the water.

'Where's your father now?' Arthur asked.

Fleur had been trying not to think too much about her father, worried that grief might consume her. She didn't even talk to Tom much about Henry. But there was something in Arthur's kind, gentle eyes, as well as their shared recent loss, that made her want to tell him everything.

'He died in a fight. He was trying to protect me and my uncle,' she replied quietly.

Arthur nodded. 'Mine too. He made sure that I had a raft to cling to when our ship went down and he fought off the men who tried to steal it from me.' Tears swam in his eyes. 'The current dragged him under – he was exhausted. There wasn't enough room for both of us out of the water. I tried to grab him . . . but . . .' His words trailed into nothing.

Fleur reached out and squeezed his hand briefly. He smiled at her gratefully, tears rolling down his cheeks.

'You must think me terribly unmanly after the company you've been keeping, Fleur,' he said, laughing a little through his tears.

She shook her head. 'It's a relief to have you here, to be honest, Arthur. We could use a brain like yours – and a little less thuggery.'

They smiled at each again, dipping their hot feet into the cool water of the lagoon as they watched the sun go down.

CHAPTER 16

Fleur and Arthur's friendship blossomed, much to Tom's obvious annoyance.

'The pair of you are as thick as thieves,' he moaned as Fleur laid food and water by his bedside. Parsley was curled up at the foot of his bed, purring loudly. 'He's like your bloomin' shadow or something.'

Fleur flopped heavily into a chair by the bed and pinched a piece of stewed pork from his bowl. 'What am I supposed to do?' she asked. 'Ignore him?' She popped the meat in her mouth and rolled it around her tongue. 'Mmm, that tastes nice. Arthur added these herbs and—'

'Arghh!' exclaimed Tom, thumping his fist down on the bed and startling the sleeping cat. 'That's what I'm talking about. Arthur, Arthur, Arthur! That's all I ever hear! I'm having Arthur dreams at night! Arthur, Arthur, bloomin' Arthur. Give me strength!'

'Well, get better and come and join us then,' snapped Fleur, irritated. 'Honestly, Tom, what's your problem?'

He turned away from her sulkily, folding his arms across his chest.

'Tom!' Fleur said sharply. 'Arthur saved your life. You should at least be grateful for that. I know I am.'

He looked back at her and his harsh expression crumbled. There was a vulnerability about him now that Fleur had never seen before.

Tom shrugged and tried to smile. 'I suppose I feel a bit left out stuck down here,' he admitted quietly. 'And, well, Arthur is so clever and learned. Of course I'm grateful that he saved me . . .' He paused and stared down into his lap. 'Fleur, why would you want to know someone rough and wild like me when there are boys like Arthur around?'

Fleur looked at her friend in astonishment. 'Are you jesting with me, Tom?'

Tom turned to face her with a look of confused innocence that made Fleur want to wrap him in her arms and squeeze with all her might. Instead she reached for his hand and took it in both of hers.

'Arthur is interesting and clever,' she began.

Tom tutted and tried to pull his hand away, but Fleur held it tightly.

'But we're as different as sand and water,' she added quickly. 'You and me, Tom, we're made from the same stuff. When you had the fever, and we thought we might lose you, well . . . I . . .' Her words trailed away at the painful memory. She paused and took a deep breath. 'I feel like I've known you for ever. Do you know what I mean?'

Tom nodded eagerly and blushed. 'Aye, I do,' he said enthusiastically. 'That girly boy could never climb the mainmast in a gale.'

'I'm sure he couldn't,' Fleur agreed.

'Or shoot straight from the prow of a rolling ship,' he said, warming to his theme. 'And I bet he couldn't—'

At that moment Arthur's head appeared in the doorway. He had a battered old book of science tucked under one arm. 'Hello, chaps,' he said breezily. 'Feeling better, Tom?'

Tom grunted unintelligibly and forced a smile.

Arthur turned to Fleur. 'Good, good,' he said. '*Mens sana in corpore sano*, and all that, eh? Fancy a game of mah jong, Fleur? I found some old tiles in one of the cabins. I'll teach you if you like?'

'That would be very nice, Arthur. You don't mind, Tom?'

'No, no, of course not,' said Tom through gritted teeth, wondering as usual what Arthur was talking about. 'You go on. I promised Parsley a game of chess anyway.'

Arthur, noting Tom's bad mood, stepped forward and held out his hand. 'We haven't been formally introduced yet, what with you being poorly and all that. Arthur Samuels. Pleased to make your acquaintance.'

Tom looked at Arthur's outstretched hand as if it were a three-week-old fish and scoffed. 'What the hell are you doing?'

Arthur's face fell and he withdrew his limp hand. 'Um. Just saying hello. Um, formally.'

Tom rolled his eyes. 'We don't stand on ceremony out here, *Arthur*. We ain't like your lot. We ain't dandies or gentlemen. We're pirates.'

'But . . . I . . . I only wanted to be polite,' Arthur stammered. 'I'm part of your crew now.'

Fleur cringed and closed her eyes. Arthur shouldn't have said that. Tom had devoted his life to his captain: he had weathered all the bullying from the other pirates; he had never known kindness, love or privilege, and it had taken years of hard work and regular thrashings to prove himself a valued member of the crew. He wasn't about to let the newcomer have it quite so easy.

'You wish to be part of this merry band of ours, do you? But I know your type. Fed on pap and suckets like a baby,' he spat scornfully. 'You probably think you're better than us, don't you? With all your fancy words and books.' He pointed at the volume Arthur was still clutching. 'Well, books are naught but fuel for the fire in our world, worm. You ain't welcome and you *ain't* part of my crew.'

Arthur reddened as Tom glared at him with his fists clenched and his jaw set.

'Don't talk to Arthur like that, Tom,' said Fleur, stepping between them. 'You don't know anything about him.'

He glared at her with some surprise. 'I know all I shall ever need to,' he snapped, pulling himself up in his bed.

She held up her hands. 'Tom, William has promised to take Arthur to a suitable port and leave him there. He'll only be travelling with us for a short time.'

Tom stared back at Arthur and nodded. 'Why didn't you say so?' he said with a sly smile. 'Welcome aboard, Arthur.'

★

The great pirate captain William the Heartless was brought almost to the point of madness by his crew of orphans. It would be a blessing for all of them, Fleur decided, and her uncle in particular, when they were finally reunited with some real pirates. William's well of patience had run dry: he desperately needed capable sailors to help him finish the *Black Dragon*. Fleur could only do so much and Arthur was just getting in the way. The boy was constantly eager and knowledgeable, yes, but clumsy with it, and Fleur had grown used to the captain's howls of rage echoing incessantly around the cove. One of Arthur's most annoying habits was to ignore William's instructions, thinking he could complete the given task better and more quickly: he was always wrong.

'Arthur, where's the rowing boat?' William barked as the small group sat about on the main deck, drinking a warm brew of island herbs and spices that Arthur had concocted. The delicious aroma of cloves, vanilla beans and cinnamon steamed from their hot tin cups. Fleur was exhausted from her training with William and kept drifting off to sleep and jolting awake again. A rather frail Tom had joined them, still wrapped in a blanket, with Parsley's warm body stretched across his cold feet. The friendly lemur was perched on a cannon nearby, nibbling on a bunch of plump red grapes.

At William's question, Arthur leaped to his feet at once and dashed from one side of the ship to the other, leaning over the rail to stare down into the water. As he dashed about, his eyes grew wilder and more frantic.

William downed his drink and thumped the cup on the deck. Tom rolled his eyes at Fleur as they readied themselves for yet another Arthur-fuelled explosion.

'What's wrong, lad? Tell me plain,' the captain said evenly.

Arthur turned to face him, his face as pale as moonlight. 'I tethered it to that rock as you asked, sir.'

William frowned; one of his eyes twitched nervously. 'But it's not there now.'

The boy bit his lip and shifted his weight from one foot to the other. 'Please, Captain, I swear I tethered the boat up properly, just as you showed me.'

William stood and stared out to sea. Bobbing in the distance, almost too far to see, was the tiny boat. Fleur could hear her uncle grinding his teeth – never a good sign. He narrowed his eyes as he rounded on Arthur. 'Boy?'

'Yes, sir?' Arthur replied with military precision.

William spoke in a low, measured tone. 'You did tie a clove hitch, didn't you?'

Arthur gulped and looked sheepish. 'Um . . . I . . . a clove hitch is . . .'

The captain circled the boy menacingly and Fleur sent up a silent prayer. The worst of her uncle's rages, she knew, began quietly.

'Arthur? Answer me, lad, and don't be afeared. A clove hitch, boy — you take a turn around the rock with the rope, then feed the working end of the rope diagonally up and then across the standing part.' He was miming the tying of the knot with expert movements. 'Then another turn, tuck and beneath the diagonal? Like I showed you? Aye? Tell me you tied a clove hitch and all will be well.'

Arthur couldn't look him in the eye. He hung his head in fear and shame. 'I . . . I think . . . that is to say . . . I think I tied another knot. The camel hitch, sir.'

William's eyes bulged in their sockets and an angry flush shot up his neck and across his face. Fleur opened her mouth to intervene but Tom held a finger to his lips to silence her. It was never wise to interrupt the captain's rages.

'You — did — *what*?!' His staccato outburst rose in volume with each word. There was a small scuffle, a splash, then a surprised and slightly indignant squeal as the nearby lemur sprang off the edge of the ship in shock, straight into the lagoon below.

'A child!' William raged. 'Defy *me*! I suppose you're the better sailor, lad? Is that it? Tell me, are you a better, more experienced sailor than I? Well, you know best, with all your years of seafaring experience.'

Arthur shook his head slowly but couldn't quite bring himself to speak.

'You can't use a camel hitch to moor a rowing boat, you land-loving oaf,' William spat. 'If the rope gets wet the knot'll slip easily. And that boat was full to the brim with wood for the fire too.'

Arthur nodded miserably.

'So you've lost us our rowing boat and, as a special treat, we've no fire to cook our fish tonight neither.'

'I'll fetch more, sir,' the boy pleaded. 'Please, if I go now I'll have an armful by sundown.'

The captain backed away, scowling. 'An armful?' he scoffed. 'Aye, well, it might warm a toddy for me. But what about my rowing boat? Will you bring back one of those too?'

Fleur and Tom exchanged frustrated looks but knew better that to join in. Instead they clasped their mugs with both hands and remained silent, although Tom could barely suppress a smirk.

Arthur shook his head again and his bottom lip wobbled. 'I'm so sorry, Captain Hart,' he mumbled fearfully. 'I thought I was doing the right thing.'

William slammed his fist hard against the ship's rail. 'Sorry isn't good enough, you sprat. You're not worth ship-room! Isn't it always the way with you young 'uns? You think you know right but you seldom do. This is my world you are living in, boy, and you'll do as I say.' His heavy breathing slowed as he fought to control his anger.

'Yes, sir,' Arthur said quietly. 'I'll try harder, I promise.'

'*No!*' The captain was instantly back to boiling point. 'Don't try any harder or you'll kill us all.'

And with that, he stomped off down the gangplank and along the sands, cursing loudly and waving his fists at the sky. 'And what's with all these damned children?' Fleur heard him yell, just above the sound of the surf, as he receded into the middle distance. 'Punishment for my sins, is it?'

Arthur looked over at Fleur and Tom, shame-faced and silent. Nobody knew what to say.

'I thought it was the right knot to tie,' Arthur said eventually. 'Damnit' – he reddened – 'sorry to curse.'

Fleur stifled a giggle: she was used to far coarser

language than that among her pirate brethren. Tom just looked at him as if he was stupid.

Fleur picked up his tin cup and offered it to him. 'Come on,' she said. 'Drink this. And don't worry about it, Arthur. He'll calm down. Just try to listen properly and do as he says. The captain ain't a man to trifle with.'

Arthur took the cup gratefully and took a gulp of the hot, sweet liquid, burning the roof of his mouth. 'Ouch!' he yelped, dropping the cup. He sighed heavily. 'It's not my day.'

Tom could barely conceal his amusement, but Fleur smiled at him kindly. 'The best thing to do is keep quiet and work hard,' she reiterated. 'Do whatever he asks and don't challenge him.'

'But you do,' Arthur said quietly; he always seemed to notice everything. '*You* challenge him.'

Fleur shook her head. 'Not always. I watch his moods carefully, like the changing tides. The captain hated me to begin with, see? I'm not so sure how he feels about me now though. I tried to ask him once, but he never actually told me.'

Arthur looked surprised. 'But it's obvious. He cares about you deeply. You must know that, Fleur?'

She burst into laughter and sprayed her drink down

the front of her clothes. 'Captain Hart doesn't care that much about nothing and nobody,' she said, shaking her head. 'Except this ship and the treasure he might plunder with it.' She turned to Tom. 'Ain't that right.'

But Tom just looked at her and shrugged. He was suddenly very quiet and seemed troubled. Arthur, however, was adamant.

'No, Fleur. You're wrong,' he insisted. 'But you'll see . . .' He looked up at the darkening sky thoughtfully and his face hardened. 'May I excuse myself? I have something to do.'

She nodded at him, lost in thought. Tom snorted at the boy's politeness and snuggled down under his blanket. They didn't even notice Arthur leaving.

After a while Fleur turned to Tom. 'I suppose Arthur was talking nonsense,' she began. 'The captain doesn't really care about me, does he?'

Tom looked at her with a strange, blank expression. 'I don't know,' he replied evenly.

Fleur picked at a piece of peeling varnish from the deck. It curled away like a fingernail. 'I mean, he doesn't really like *anyone*, does he?' she began again, desperate for Tom to contradict her.

The boy looked at her wearily and sighed. 'He's your uncle, Fleur, flesh and blood and all that,' he said quietly. 'You've so much in common. So much shared history.'

'But that doesn't mean he cares about me. Arthur's just an idiot.'

Tom leaned towards her slightly. 'No, you're the one being an idiot.' Fleur scowled at him, but he ignored her. 'Don't you see?' he said with exasperation. 'You belong to one another, Claw-cat. The captain needs you just as much as you need him.'

Fleur's heart skipped. She desperately wanted that to be true. 'Do you really think so?' she asked eagerly, embarrassed to show how much she needed her uncle's affection.

But Tom didn't seem to hear her. 'Where did Arthur go?' he asked instead, changing the subject.

'The axe is here, so it's not firewood he's gone for,' Fleur replied. 'I wonder where he is?'

Tom tried to stand, but his weak legs gave way beneath him.

'It's all right,' Fleur said, pushing him gently back onto the deck. 'Wait there. I'll find him. He's probably just hiding away somewhere.'

She ran about the ship and down to the beach, calling out Arthur's name, but the boy was nowhere to be found. The captain reappeared as she made her way back to the ship. He was still simmering.

'Have you seen Arthur?' Fleur asked as they walked up the gangplank together.

Her uncle sighed as they made their way across the deck to where Tom lay. 'Why? What's the brainless bilge rat done now?'

'He's disappeared.'

'Good!' William snarled, much to Tom's amusement.

Fleur scowled at them both. 'He doesn't mean to be any trouble. You could both see how upset he was about losing the boat,' she admonished, turning to glare directly at her uncle. 'And you shouting at him like that only made things worse.'

He opened his mouth to protest but she refused to let him speak.

'Shouting ain't going to bring that boat back, and you know what Arthur's like,' she said. 'If he can't make things right, he gets himself in a terrible state.'

She stared out furiously to sea, and as she did so, a terrible thought struck her. 'Can Arthur swim?'

She dashed to the side and peered across the ocean, searching desperately for signs of a swimmer. Panic began to claw at her throat. They all knew that Arthur was foolish enough to make for the lost boat. William brought out his spyglass and squinted into it against the glare of the setting sun.

'He really would chance it, wouldn't he?' he murmured. 'Brave little fool. The pull of the tide's strong today.'

A strange little squeal escaped Fleur.

'Don't worry, Fleur,' said Tom. 'He's probably gone to get wood and just forgot to take the axe.' He laughed unconvincingly.

Fleur shook her head and fixed her gaze on the choppy waves beyond their sheltered moorings. 'You don't even like him, so don't pretend that you care,' she snapped. 'It would just be too cruel if he died. All he ever wants to do is help and you two are always so horrible to him.'

Troubled looks were exchanged between William and Tom.

They paced the deck nervously, William scanning the horizon with his spyglass while Fleur muttered prayers for Arthur's safe return, her face white and her hands trembling. All the sorrow and grief she had repressed since losing her father was bubbling to the surface at the thought of losing someone else she cared about. Even Tom was anxious. Arthur had already survived much adversity and helped them in so many ways. Despite his annoying ways, the brave fool had earned the right to a place in their little world. The waves curled and slapped against each other. As the light began to fail, Arthur's safe return seemed ever more unlikely. And then they saw him.

'There he is!' shouted Fleur, pointing at a tiny speck on the waves that could have been a large clump of seaweed if it hadn't been waving.

William peered through his spyglass and grinned. 'Aye, it's him. Unless there's some other naked idiot standing in my boat.' He passed Fleur his telescope. 'The boy's a numbskull,' he said warmly, 'but he's determined, I'll give him that. Who would've thought it, eh?'

Fleur sighed happily as Tom slung an arm protectively around her shoulders. 'I just don't want to lose anybody else,' she murmured.

William nodded down at her, and his expression was almost kindly.

It took Arthur a long time to row back to the shore, where Fleur, Tom and William were waiting. Two empty barrels had been sacrificed for firewood, which gave Arthur something to aim for as he rowed through the dark, and the day's catch was crackling on the flames. When the little boat finally reached the shallows, William strode out and dragged it safely back to land.

'Arthur!' Fleur cried, running into the sea. Water

soaked her clothes as she stumbled out to greet him. Tom watched moodily from the beach.

Arthur smiled and raised a weak but triumphant fist in the air. 'I got it,' he croaked. 'Hooray for me.' Then he fell back into the boat with a groan.

'Swimming out wasn't actually that hard,' said Arthur between mouthfuls of delicious blackened fish. His appreciative audience was gathered around the fire; even Tom had refrained from his usual insults and asides. He couldn't help admitting to a grudging respect for Arthur now.

'I only had to swim with the tide to catch up, though I swear I felt a shark brush against my legs once or twice.' The boy shivered and wiped a flake of fish from his lips. 'Rough as a cat's tongue, it was . . . No, it was rowing back that nearly killed me. Fighting the sea all the way. I thought my arms would drop off – or that I would be pulled out to sea. But' – Arthur directed his question at William – 'I did it, sir. Didn't I?'

William nodded gravely in return. 'Aye, laddie, I reckon you did. And proved yourself as brave as you are reckless. Two excellent qualities in a pirate. Well done. You're a diamond matey now.'

He threw a juicy mango at the beaming boy. Arthur

caught it with unusual grace and turned the fruit in his hands proudly. Coming from William, it was as good as a medal.

As the tiny crew got back to their chores, readying the ship for departure, Fleur knew that her time with her uncle was running out. Whatever the change in him, he still had no intention of letting her join him on his adventures. Nor was he about to let her face Alexander Blood with him in their final battle. All he cared about was delivering her to St Kitts in one piece as he had vowed to do. But she still dreamed of vanquishing Blood and avenging the death of her father. Her skin prickled and her heart raced as she gave her mind free rein: if only Henry had known how much the sea would come to mean to her, she thought, he would never have asked his brother to make that promise.

William grew impatient again. He and his ship were ready to leave now, but without extra manpower they needed a strong blast behind them to cut through the powerful undercurrents that surrounded the island. But the wind had died away. So, to stop himself from going mad, William spent his time training Fleur and Tom, with Arthur joining in as much as possible. While he barked orders, they practised wielding knives, firing pistols, fighting with staffs and hand-to-hand combat: they learned how to knock the air out of a man's lungs and deaden arms and legs with a sharp punch in the right place. Of course, they saved these moves for a sand-stuffed dummy mounted on an oar. The less dangerous moves they practised on each other.

It was an endless source of irritation to the boys that Fleur often bested them. Arthur took his beatings with good grace, but Tom could not bear to lose to a girl and frequently resorted to shows of brute strength – the only way he could assert himself.

'Come on,' he dared Fleur at the end of a particularly long day's training. 'I bet you can't take on the captain with a staff.'

'Of course she can't,' said Arthur, coming to Fleur's defence. 'No one could.'

'Thanks, Arthur,' the captain called out to them, grinning.

'I'm not talking to you, bookworm,' Tom sneered at Arthur. 'I'm talking to Good Queen She-warrior over here. What do you reckon, Fleur? Let's see you channel that energy. Go on.'

'Don't listen to him,' said Arthur. 'He's just being stupid. You don't have to do anything.'

Fleur stood there, thinking. 'It's all right,' she said

eventually, glancing over at her uncle. 'I'm not doing this to prove anything to Tom, I just reckon I might be able to beat him.'

William rose to his feet. 'Is that right, child?' he asked challengingly.

Tom sniggered and stood aside as Fleur squared up to her captain. They'd fought with staffs many times, but both had been holding back.

'This is going to be brilliant,' Tom chirped mischievously.

'Fleur, don't,' cried Arthur.

'Shh!' she said.

William pointed at the sturdy branches they had been using to practise with earlier. 'Tom, bring those over to us, will you, boy?'

Tom suddenly looked a little concerned. 'Are you actually going to fight her, Cap'n?'

William raised an eyebrow at Fleur. 'Do you want me to play-fight, Fleur, or come at you like I would Alexander Blood?'

She swallowed nervously. 'Give it all you've got,' she replied, more bravely than she felt.

He turned to Tom and nodded seriously. 'Aye, lad, I'm going to fight her to the death.'

Tom backed away with the staffs, but William laughed

and beckoned him forward. 'Don't worry, boy, I'll just maim her a little.'

Tom looked from Fleur to William and reluctantly handed over the staffs. He sat back down on the sand next to Arthur; both boys were pale with worry.

Fleur closed her eyes and dropped her shoulders, breathing slowly and evenly as her uncle had taught her. Then she planted her feet squarely on the sand and began to breathe more deeply, feeling the power in her muscles and the weight of her body, anchored to the beach by her iron stance. She opened her eyes and lifted the staff.

'Let's do it.'

The captain nodded, then hit her staff with his, throwing her backwards. Fleur quickly righted herself and charged at him with controlled fury. In a whirl, they danced around each other, clashing staffs and jumping aside to avoid blows. At first William held back, but Fleur attacked him like a savage. The thunk of the staffs and their loud grunts echoed across the bay. Arthur put his hands over his eyes, peering through his fingers. Tom just sat bolt upright, chewing on his bottom lip nervously.

'Ouch!' Fleur cried out in pain as her uncle's staff clipped her on the back and forced her to the ground.

Tom jumped up. 'Stop! I'm sorry, Fleur. Stop now or he'll kill you.'

William flashed Tom a bemused look and held out his hand to Fleur. Their eyes locked and sparked. Fleur ignored his proffered hand and jumped to her feet, shaking sand from her clothes. Pain rocketed through her spine from the blow, but she pushed it to the back of her mind – she knew this was the only way to truly earn respect from a man such as William. This was a fight she was determined to win. Or die trying.

Adrenaline coursed through her and she started twirling the staff, tossing it from hand to hand like a baton. Soon it became a blur against the sky. William's smile faded as he watched his niece focus on him, her expression grim. Then, with a bloodcurdling yell, she launched into action, her staff an extension of her, like an extra limb. She was a tornado, whirling and spinning away from each blow the captain tried to land. They both jumped and crouched, spinning their staffs above their heads and under each other's feet, until they were dizzy and bruised.

Then Fleur lunged forward, knocking William backwards with her staff. He staggered away so that there was space between them. She sprang forward again before he had steadied himself, thrusting with the tip of her staff and vaulting over him in a somersault. She soared up, kicking him hard in the chest. He stumbled back again, clumsily sweeping his staff through the air, but Fleur knocked it aside and forced him down onto the sand. Then she placed a foot over his chest and stared down at him, grinning.

'And now I kill you,' she said breathlessly.

William shook his head, then beamed at her in delight. 'Well, well, lassie. It seems I've met my match.' He winced with pain as he rubbed his chest. 'I'll look forward to seeing what you can do with the family staff.'

'Blimey,' said Tom, slack-jawed. 'She actually did it.'

'If I hadn't seen it with my own eyes . . .' said Arthur.

Fleur dropped her staff and collapsed next to her uncle, glowing with pride. She really *had* done it: she had beaten William the Heartless in a fight.

'Haven't you realized it yet?' asked Tom, grinning over at her. 'This is the Dread Pirate Fleur. And she can do anything.'

CHAPTER 17

Even though they all knew that their days on their beautiful island hideaway were numbered, it was still a surprise to hear William announce that the wind had turned and it was at last time to set sail. Suddenly none of them felt eager to leave the place.

'It's always like this after too long on land,' said Tom, trying to comfort the others as they clambered aboard. 'We'll soon find the rhythm of the waves in our hearts.'

'Has anybody seen my lemur?' asked Fleur, scanning the beach sadly. 'I wanted to take him with us.'

'I reckon Parsley's had him,' Tom teased, 'or else the captain.'

'Stop it, Tom,' said Arthur. 'Fleur's become very fond of him.'

'It's the way it is, Arthur.' Tom shrugged. 'If you spend your days on a pirate ship, you've got to get used to saying your goodbyes.'

There was no sign of the lemur on board either. Fleur tossed a bowl of fresh fruit over the side for him in case he came back to find them gone. 'A ruddy waste,' said Tom grumpily.

Then, with a southerly breeze filling the salt-stained sails, they joined their captain at the giant rudder. The *Black Dragon* was ready to fly.

The ship finally sailed out into the ocean with her head held high. It had been years since she'd been dashed against the rocks and left to perish; now she was ready to speed gracefully through the water.

'Come, hearties, let's get her under way,' William shouted. 'Crowd on sail and let her run before the wind.'

He stood on the poop deck, carefully steering a path through the shallow lagoon to the ocean. It was strewn with rocks rising from the sandy depths, and the tides charged and crashed around as if enraged. Their secret island was uncharted and only the most skilful of sailors could have navigated his way out. Tom manned the sails and Fleur stood by William, astrolabe in her hand, carefully leading them towards the open sea. The ship bumped and ground her way over water so shallow that they were barely floating at all – and then the sea bed suddenly dropped away and they were bobbing comfortably on the wide roof of the ocean.

William ordered them not to look back at the island that had saved them all – it was supposedly bad luck; but none of them – even the captain himself – could resist taking a sneaky glance. As they surged forward, Fleur stood at the bow and let the wind and sea spray blast her from all directions. She clung to the rigging and laughed out loud as the *Black Dragon* rose and plunged through the water. It made her feel more alive than anything else. All she needed was the wind at her back, the sea beneath her and the sky above to be happy. She was going to miss her little lemur friend, along with the peace and solitude and the soft moan of the sea on the sands, but it felt so wonderful to be riding the waves again.

It had taken them an entire day to navigate through the dangerous currents and vicious-looking rocks that surrounded the island. Fleur had wondered why no one had found the *Black Dragon* in all that time, and now she knew. When they first entered the troubled waters back on the *Libertine*, she hadn't appreciated what a treacherous journey it was, made ever harder by the fact that William's crew were all so young. But night followed day, and sure enough, they had made their way through.

The trade winds blew steadily and they were soon approaching a string of islands, including that of Ile aux Forbans. Myriad little islets and coral archipelagos flowered like rose gardens as the *Black Dragon* approached its destination. The waters below them teemed with life: moray eels, turtles, lion fish, sharks and barracudas cast long shadows on the sea bed. They approached the south side of the island and sailed into a sandy bay shaded by coconut palms and mango trees. A handful of Madagascan children ran along the beach waving up at them. They wore nothing more than rags and were giggling happily, obviously not intimidated by their pirate visitors.

William checked his ship. 'Fleur, the main sail looks like washing hung out to dry – pull her fast,' he commanded, then took the helm and tasted the wind. The breeze whipped his tangled hair away from his face to reveal that he was smiling.

Thanks to Henry's tutoring of other languages,

Fleur already knew that Ile aux Forbans was French for Pirate Island. Her uncle told her that it was a popular base for men like him, sitting as it did on two important trade routes, the Red Sea and the Indian Ocean: passing ships were overflowing with wealth ripe for the taking. It was a perfect hidey-hole for pirates as the island's ample bays and creeks protected them from tropical storms. Underground tunnels ran beneath the earth like worm-holes for a speedy escape, and it was well provided with fruit and fresh water. The Madagascan natives and their pirate neighbours shared the island without any trouble and treated each other with respect.

'Heave to!' the captain called out. 'Bring her up in the shade of this rock.'

The *Black Dragon* slowed and the anchor was tossed into the clear blue water with a loud splash.

'We're here, me hearties, we're here,' William announced at last. 'Gather what you need and follow me.'

They all dispersed and returned moments later armed with some of their meagre belongings. Fleur had strung her bow and arrows across her back and tucked the astrolabe into the leather pouch on her belt.

'My legs are wobbling,' Arthur groaned as he made

his way down the gangplank. 'I feel as if the sea is still moving beneath me. I can't steady myself.'

As soon as his feet hit the sand, he staggered to the ground, much to the amusement of everybody else.

William roared with laughter. ''Tis the way it is, lad. The sea is in your blood now.'

Arthur scowled when the captain hauled him up, but smiled to himself when no one was looking. It was true: the sea had stolen them all.

As William led them along the curving strip of beach, their feet sank into the fine, soft sand. Fleur kept stumbling in her haste to keep up, but he marched ahead, leaving a churned-up trail in his wake. He was heading for a grassy plateau where palm trees bowed low and clustered together like gossiping hags. Seagulls circled and swooped above their heads, kaw-kawing loudly.

'Is it far, sir?' asked Arthur, shifting the weight of his leather bag from one shoulder to the other.

'We're all but there,' the captain replied. 'I don't like to be too far from the sea when I'm here.' He paused and stared at the sand with a frown, then bent over to pick up a large, shiny gold coin.

'What's that, Cap'n?' Tom asked.

William flipped the worn coin over in his fingers

thoughtfully and looked out across the island with a faint smile. 'A Spanish doubloon.'

Fleur ran to catch up, bending forward to ease the stitch that stabbed at her side. 'Why are you smiling, Captain?'

Her uncle handed her the coin, his smile broadening. 'Because there's pirates all around us. I'm back amongst my own.'

His digs were no more than a small wooden hut hidden within a ring of palm trees. A couple of hammocks hung outside it like cobwebs. It sat a little way from the waves that gently lapped at the sand.

'Is that it?' asked Fleur as they approached the ramshackle building.

'Aye, it is, and it belonged to my father and his father before him and has been good enough for us all,' replied William abruptly. He stopped walking and turned to face her. 'What were you expecting, girl? A palace?'

Fleur quickly shook her head. 'Oh, I wasn't being rude, sir . . . I was just asking.'

He scowled and quickened his pace.

'But you could probably buy a palace if you wanted to, couldn't you, Captain?' Arthur enquired cheekily.

William stopped dead in his tracks and whipped

round again. 'I could, but why would I want to, boy?'

Arthur swallowed. 'Um . . .' he offered.

The captain tutted and indicated all around them. 'Why spend my gold on a gilt cage when this is all I need?' He eyed Arthur sternly. 'Now, any more questions and I'll skin you for dinner.'

The door came away from its hinges when he wrenched it back, revealing a very basic room that smelled musty. There were empty rum bottles, candle stubs and unwashed tin plates everywhere. Maps were strewn over the floor, shredded to ribbons by tiny animal claws. The bed was a rumpled mess of scratchy blankets, and a bloodied sword had been tossed into a corner, where huge ants swarmed over it. William had the grace to look ashamed. He kicked aside a pile of clothes and removed a tin dinner plate from the bed.

'I seldom have company,' he muttered by way of explanation and threw the plate into the corner with the sword.

Fleur looked about the room with disgust; her uncle saw her expression and shrugged. 'I suppose you'll be telling me it's not good enough to sleep in now, girl,' he said with a warning glare.

She glared back. 'Actually, you're right,' she replied, hands on hips.

They all looked at her with gaping mouths and she blushed. 'It's in a terrible mess and it needs a clean,' she blustered.

William frowned. 'You're not expecting *me* to clean it, are you?'

Fleur stood her ground. 'Not all by yourself – we'll help you.'

The captain looked startled and then chuckled suddenly. 'All right, girl. I suppose it won't take us long if we all chip in.'

Tom opened his mouth to protest, but Fleur shot him a warning look and he clamped it shut again immediately.

William was right: it didn't take them long once they got started. Every now and then someone would disturb some nasty creature, but once the rubbish was hurled outside there wasn't really that much left to scrub. Soon the hut was as clean as it ever could be and they went down to the beach to watch the sunset. Tom sat in one hammock, silently whittling; in the other Arthur lay snoring, a book written by the scientist Robert Boyle open on his stomach, its pages fluttering in the wind. William smoked and fidgeted in the shade and Fleur studied him surreptitiously. It wouldn't be long before his new pirate crew joined them – it was evident that he was desperate to spend time in the company of his peers. Fleur curled into herself as she sat on the cool sand. She felt sad: everything was about to change again.

CHAPTER 18

'Ahoy there, Captain. Ahoy.'

Fleur and the others were sitting outside the spotless hut when the wind carried the shout over to them. William searched the distance with his telescope and then waved. He turned to Fleur, his eyes gleaming.

'It's Jack and my crew.'

Fleur snatched the telescope from him eagerly and pointed it in their direction.

'Hey there, mackie,' William called out to Jack. ''Tis good to see thee, brothers.'

Jack strode over and embraced his captain, who patted him hard on the back. The lieutenant nodded over at

Fleur. ''Tis good to see thee in one piece, child.' He raised a wrist bearing his precious pearls and chuckled. 'I've managed to hang onto 'em without you this time.'

Fleur smiled at his warmth and nodded back at him.

Then he looked over at Arthur suspiciously. 'Who's this?' he asked. 'He's too pale for a native.'

'A castaway. Found him on the island,' William explained abruptly. 'We'll drop him off at the next port.'

Jack nodded, ignoring Arthur's polite smile, and grasped Tom in a clumsy hug. He clapped the cabin boy roughly on the back, then promptly started introducing some of the new crew. They were a grizzled, hard-looking band of sailors; they lounged around cracking filthy jokes, and Arthur cowered away from them fearfully. Fleur gazed at him in surprise: she had forgotten that people were terrified of men such as these.

After the captain had spent some time talking to his new crew, he took off to a local drinking den with Jack. Dressed in their finest clothes, the two men marched down the beach, laughing raucously and taking swigs from a bottle of neat rum. Fleur, Tom and Arthur sat outside the hut, drinking coconut milk and roasting chunks of lobster and goat meat on a driftwood fire. The whole world glowed with gold as the sun went down.

The distant waves sounded like the rushing of wind in a forest; closer at hand, the foaming white water rushed towards the beach, sparkling and crackling with bubbles.

Parsley sat on Fleur's lap, eagerly nibbling on scraps of food. Beside her, Arthur and Tom vied constantly for her attention. Fleur enjoyed the fact that they were so different: while Arthur was educated from books and his father's teaching, Tom's practical experience was such that the newcomer could only have dreamed of. The cabin boy and the scholar argued into the night until both boys' faces grew hot.

When Tom finally sprang to his feet and declared he was going for a walk, Fleur could tell he was itching to give Arthur a good thrashing. Arthur had got under his skin from that first day and stayed there. With a scowl Tom threw Parsley up on his shoulder and strode away into the night, muttering under his breath. And as she watched him go, Fleur realized to her astonishment that he was just like William.

The captain arrived home drunk in the early hours, singing filthy sea shanties. He passed out in one of the hammocks and snored loudly until dawn. When sunrise streaked the sky, he woke grumpy and dishevelled and cloaked in melancholy. Fleur joined him on the shore and they both stared at the frothing surf in silence. When he finally turned to her, his eyes were glistening and his voice was hoarse: she knew what he was going to say before he uttered a word.

''Tis time to bury him.'

A winding path of shingle and sharp rock wound its way up the Ile aux Forbans. Trees bowed low and their leaves whispered as the cool evening breeze played in the branches. The rest of the island seemed to tumble away from the lofty peak; at the foot of the cliffs below the graveyard lay a deep cove where the bones of sunken ships reached up out of the water like phantom hands. There was a chill to the place, almost as if someone had left a door open connecting it to the icy underworld beyond. Graves and tombs were everywhere, some roughly chiselled with skull and crossbones, others with wordy epitaphs. The locals respected their dead and everything appeared well looked after, but it was clear that they still feared those who were buried there. Broken acorn shells had been scattered liberally in an attempt to keep the spirits away, but ghosts were everywhere.

Arthur seemed very excited: he knelt down beside a huge headstone bearing a picture of a skeleton running away from the hangman's noose. Fleur found his naivety and misplaced enthusiasm irritating and charming in equal measure.

'I had no idea that pirates buried their own,' Arthur whispered to Fleur when he crept back. 'If the army gets them, they're hanged in chains of iron or buried head down when the tide's out so that their soul may never find rest.'

Fleur looked over at William and prayed that the army never took him alive.

To her surprise, a large number of pirates turned up to pay their respects to Henry Hart. They all gathered in the glow of the lanterns, dressed in their most flamboyant clothing: golden trinkets adorned their sumptuous velvet waistcoats; shocks of coloured feathers sprang from their hats. In spite of the warmth of the evening, they wore exquisite long coats, and their buckled shoes sparkled. The mourners stood in groups, smoking and muttering amongst themselves, but a hush descended as Jack and three others slowly carried Henry's barrel over to a clearing and set it down carefully.

'As you all know, Henry was a heroic captain and a decent man,' William stated simply; he looked over at Fleur and his voice wavered with emotion. 'He was also my brother and a father who made a choice to save his family. I always resented him for that but now I have only respect.'

He paused, and Fleur smiled over at him sadly.

'But his spirit will always belong to the sea, and to that he will return,' William finished, glancing down at the waves crashing far below them.

As they lowered the barrel into the earth, the shantyman began to sing a mournful song. His voice was low and solemn and some of the men joined in, but most were silent and thoughtful. There were many there who had known Henry; they had greeted Fleur warmly, speaking of their admiration for the magnificent pirate captain. Fleur stood beside her uncle and let salty tears roll down her face; she no longer cared that everyone could see her. She still missed her father so much; it felt as if someone had scooped out her insides and left her hollow. This was the first time she had finally understood that he was never coming back. No one would ever love her as much as her father had.

As the service continued, Arthur and Tom shot her kind, sympathetic smiles, but William was as unreadable as an Egyptian tomb. He didn't even blink as he stared upon the barrel, but Fleur knew in her heart that this was the only way he could stay strong. When the tips of his fingers found hers, she took his hand and clung to it.

★

'There are so many graves here,' Fleur commented, as she stared out across the graveyard after the funeral was over. Most of the mourners had gone on ahead to drink their sorrows away. On his captain's orders, Tom had reluctantly taken Arthur off to explore the island, leaving Fleur and her uncle alone. The longer they stayed in the garden of the dead, the more alive the place seemed to become. As the sun sank low and the shadows lengthened, Fleur began to feel that the empty graveyard was actually becoming very crowded indeed.

William sensed her discomfort and gestured towards a row of plots next to Henry's freshly dug grave. 'These ones here belong to the Harts.'

'Really?' Fleur scrambled to her feet. 'Is my grandfather here?'

He nodded. 'He and many others. Come, child, I'll introduce you.'

He led her down the lines of graves, pointing out cousins, uncles and more distant ancestors. Most of the headstones had the family crest carved into them – a noble-looking hart stag. On some of the older ones, the crest had worn away almost completely.

As Fleur inspected the family plot, she suddenly realized something. 'I'd like to be buried here, Uncle,' she said. 'Beside my father. But they're all men.'

William nodded. 'Aye, you'd be the only lassie here, no doubt.'

'Not the only – the first,' she replied firmly.

He smiled at her and reached for his pipe. As he stuffed it with tobacco, Fleur gazed around again, and as she did so, an overwhelming sense of belonging crept over her, helping to fill the lonely void that her father's death had left. She could almost hear her ancestors whispering to her from their sandy beds: *You're a Hart, a Hart. You belong to us.*

She turned to see that William was studying her thoughtfully. 'What's the matter, Uncle?' she asked.

He blew a smoke ring into the air. ''Tis time I told you everything.'

They came to a halt and he leaned against a tomb, pulling a bottle of grog from the pocket of his long coat. The evening was growing colder and Fleur shivered.

'Here, lassie,' he said, offering her a drink. 'You'll be needing a tipple.'

Fleur reached for the bottle. 'What is this?' she asked.

'Toddy,' said William. 'My own grog drawn from palm trees.'

She sipped gingerly at the cloudy liquor, then coughed and spluttered as if her lungs were about to explode.

'Yeucchh,' she exclaimed. 'It's sickly sweet and really strong.'

William snatched the bottle from her. 'Just as it should be. Let me have it, child – quick, quick. It has to be drunk on the day it's made or it turns sour.'

Fleur watched him swallow most of the bottle. He wiped his mouth with the back of his hand and his eyes narrowed as he addressed her, suddenly serious.

'This is going to sound like nonsense to you, girl, but it is what it is and I'll tell you what needs to be told.' He took another gulp and cleared his throat.

Fleur's eyes widened and she felt a rush of anticipation. 'Is it about the staff?' she asked excitedly.

'It is.' Her uncle nodded. 'But don't run ahead of me – just listen. I'm telling you first 'cause you're a Hart and you need to hear it in it purest form, not handed down as gossip from others. And second, because you're a damn fine mariner, if I'm any judge of these things – which I am; anyhow, I reckon you're ready.'

Fleur flushed with pride. 'Why now?' she asked. 'What were you waiting for?'

William stared off into the distance. 'I was trying to protect you,' he explained gently. 'You're Henry's daughter through and through, which means there's much of me running through your veins as well. And if truth be known, I didn't want you to fall prey to the legend of the staff the way that I have – or at least did. You should know the truth, child, but you need not follow my obsession.'

Fleur opened her mouth to speak, but her uncle waved a hand to silence her.

'What I tell you now comes with a warning, Fleur. Don't let the staff's secrets unhinge you: they've pushed me to the brink of madness and that ain't a happy place to be. There's magic and myth in this world and I'm not so sure where the staff sits any more. Somewhere in between, perhaps. There're those who say it's nothing but false rumour, but I happen to think there's a nugget of truth in every tale that's stood the test of time.'

William sipped his drink and sighed. 'What do you know of how the world began, girl?' he asked, meeting his niece's eye with a solemn stare.

'Eh?' said Fleur, wondering how on earth to answer such a question. 'You mean the Garden of Eden? Adam and Eve and the apple tree? All that business?'

'Aye, well, that's one part of the tale, or one way of telling it at least. I've travelled enough of the world to realize that different folk have different ways of explaining the same thing. But what of the ocean, girl? Can't say as

I remember the Good Book having much to say on't myself. Not till Noah's flood at least.'

'I suppose not,' said Fleur. 'I don't think Eden was on the coast, at any rate.'

Her uncle snorted and continued. 'Now the Bible tells us how God made the world in six days,' he said, his voice dropping to a reverential whisper, 'but a day for God and a day for man are different things, girl, and the Book of Genesis doesn't like to bother its readers with details. The building of the world took longer than all the time that's come since, Fleur. The first day alone would stretch back from now to the time of dragons and giants. Aye, there was ages and ages for the world to grow before God gave Adam shape; before bird and beast and field and forest. But even then, at the beginning of things, the world was not empty. The first things that God put in the world were the Elementals, each one an aspect of His own great spirit. Fire and Water, Earth and Air – guardians of the realms that would be and keepers of the creatures that would come to live there.

'As the Lord's creation grew, the Elementals gained in power and influence. And as life arrived in each realm, the guardians gave a little of their own borrowed spirit to their new subjects. Earth to the creatures of land, Air to the birds and the buzzing bees. Fire to the worms and serpents and those that burrow underground – and Water to all the fishes of the rivers and seas, and to the giants of the deep. For another great age there was balance and beauty in the world that God had made.

'But He grew lonely – you know that part, it's in the book. The Elementals were not company enough for their Lord, busy as they were guarding his creation. So He made a man out of the Earth, the first of the Elementals, and breathed Fire into his heart and Air into his lungs. But God knew that without a soul man would be just one more animal in his menagerie, and not the companion He desired. And for this greatest gift he looked to Water.'

Fleur waited impatiently through what she considered a somewhat overly dramatic pause. William drained the rest of his toddy, tossed the bottle among some tombstones and picked up his tale at last.

'When Water gave up its spirit – that small part of God himself – to be the cloth of man's soul, He first had to take back the part of it that He had given to the fish and to the dark creatures at the bottom of the ocean. That is why of all God's creatures, the fish are the dumbest, and why the giants stay in their depths also, for they no longer have the wit to rise and do so only by accident. So man got his soul and Water lost his, and for ever after the oceans would be a place of wild storms and rolling waves.'

'So this is the Harts' big secret?' Fleur scoffed, entertained but sceptical, to say the least. 'That we're a family of heretics?'

William laughed loudly at that. 'By God, you're as sharp as a shark's tooth when you want to be, girl,' he said, slapping Fleur on the back so hard that she nearly swallowed her tongue. 'Hold your horses,' he went on. 'It's only half told yet. Now, the soul of the ocean is a mighty thing, so that after a spark of it was taken for every man, woman and child that would ever be until the end of days, the Lord God found He still had a little left over. A little of the pure spirit of all the waters of the world. And this He forged into a jewel, a ruby of incomparable worth, for it is said to harbour a great power that will be given only to its true master . . . or mistress,' he concluded. 'That ruby heart, said to have been fired in heaven and cooled in an iceberg in the frozen North, is the very same jewel that is set in the Hart staff – your birthright, Fleur – stolen from you by Alexander Blood on the night of your father's death.'

Fleur's eyes widened as she remembered again the pull of the ruby.

'Now tell me,' William said. 'Do you know what magi are?'

Fleur shook her head.

'They be shamans, girl, sorcerers from the east. A gnarly old magus gave the ruby to our ancestor, Jacob Hart, in Persia, see? And he told him the secret.'

'Aye, sir?' Fleur was engrossed.

'He told him that the legend speaks of a Hart of our bloodline – one who has heard the song of the ocean – who will gain possession of the staff's enchanted ruby and end the terrible feud that has consumed our family for so long. 'Tis said, moreover, that they will have a talent that suits the ruby's magic.'

'What does that mean?' asked Fleur, confused.

Her uncle smiled. 'The finest blade has no more bite than a butter knife in the hands of a novice swordsman,' he explained. 'Likewise, that staff and the ruby it carries hold great power, but they will not reveal it easily.'

'I still don't understand, Uncle,' Fleur admitted.

William lowered his voice almost to a whisper and leaned in close as he spoke. 'P'rhaps not, lass, but 'tis said that should the right soul find the ruby – the right combination of talent and true spirit – they'll not just beat their foes in battle. They'll be able to harness the power of the ocean itself. Imagine that, girl. Magical dominion over the waves. Handy in a storm or set-to, I reckon.'

'But that's silly,' said Fleur. 'You've possessed the stone, and my father did too. You didn't exactly rule the oceans, did you?'

'Did we not, girl?' said her uncle, suddenly cross. 'I'll thank you to remember the name of the pirates who've held sway from Penzance to the Indies since ever the first ship set sail.'

'Aye,' grumbled Fleur. 'But that's not the same as real power of the magic kind, is it?'

'I'll give you that, lass,' said William, relaxing a little. 'A prophecy can play out in many ways. Any Hart that takes hold of the stone can be said to rule the seas, in a fashion. The ruby, if you believe such things, has made pirate kings out of generations of our men. But 'tis still said that a Hart who is pure in bloodline will one day truly fulfil the prophecy.'

'But how will this pure Hart harness the power of the ocean?' asked Fleur.

'That I don't know,' William admitted with a shrug. 'I'll tell you this though: whatever the truth of the legend, the Bloods fear it, some of 'em. That staff's a mighty standard to carry into battle, if nothing else.'

'So is it magic or not?' asked Fleur, frustrated by her uncle's riddling speak.

'Perhaps. It could be the ruby's still waiting for the right man's touch.'

'Or woman's,' added Fleur.

'Aye,' said William, narrowing his eyes thoughtfully. 'And God willing we'll live long and sail far enough to find out.' He leaned back. 'Anyway, whether you believe it or not, that's the prophecy, that is. Eight hundred years old, and long overdue, if you ask me.'

They sat in silence, looking up into the black night. Bats dipped and spun overhead in their sky ballet.

'I believe you, Uncle,' Fleur said firmly, shivering now more with excitement than the chill of the graveyard. 'As I told you before, I knew there was something special about that staff from the first moment I clapped eyes on it. I could feel its power as real as you and me sitting here now.'

William stared at her hard and narrowed his eyes. 'And like I said, girl, don't become obsessed with the staff's secrets. It could be your undoing.'

'But how?' Fleur asked.

'That's enough,' he warned. 'Now you know the long and the short of it. You can make of it what you will. But don't bother me with any more questions.'

Fleur nodded silently and their eyes met. Neither said any more but they were both thinking the very same thing: Fleur was the only living Hart who hadn't yet laid hands on the staff.

William decided to stay on the island for a few days before they set sail again for the Caribbean. His crew weren't in a hurry to leave either. They all knew how hard life aboard a pirate ship could be, and Ile aux Forbans was paradise on earth. They were also keenly aware that Alexander Blood would soon discover that William had survived: a huge battle was inevitable. So they made the most of their time. The pirates spent most of their shore-leave drinking in the local taverns with beautiful, exotic native girls. But over the lazy, drunken days they still managed to load the ship with as much as they could take to trade and eat: fresh vanilla, fish, coconuts, tobacco, snuff, grain, coffee, wild goats and much more. The *Black Dragon* sank deep into the sea, groaning with the weight of it.

As soon as William's cronies found out that Arthur was a competent healer, a queue of pirates with ailments started to snake from the door of William's hut. Jack hadn't managed to recruit a ship's doctor yet, so Arthur was in heavy demand. He dealt with every person with the same gentle, intelligent kindness and was treated much better than he would have been otherwise. Even

Jack came to him complaining of a gangrenous toe, although he made quite sure that no one else knew about it.

When they were alone together, Fleur and Tom spent most of their time lazing on the beach, chatting about nothing in particular and wondering about the Hart prophecy. Having told his niece their family secret, William clearly didn't wish to speak of it again. Instead he reminded her that chasing myths could drive a person mad; he had better things to do. With his crew in place, his thoughts were turning once again to Alexander Blood.

But it was all Fleur could think about. The staff might have driven William to the brink of insanity, but perhaps that was because he wasn't the one who was supposed to claim its secrets . . .

One day she and Tom were lying on the shore, letting the warm sea water lap their feet. Parsley was padding about nearby, chasing the waves out to sea.

'It might be me,' Fleur speculated. 'I might be the one to claim the prophecy.'

Tom burst out laughing. 'And Arthur might not be a fool.'

As Fleur sat up, a tiny crab scuttled away from them. A huge barnacle had glued itself to its orange shell, making the crab teeter like a drunk. 'And what do you mean by that?' she asked.

Tom shrugged, leaving the impression of an angel in the sand beneath him. He grinned to himself. 'I mean that Arthur's a fool and you ain't a sea god.' He glanced at her scornfully. 'Come on, Claw-cat. You must know it's all nonsense. If a pirate as worthy and great as Captain Hart couldn't claim it, I doubt anyone can. And even if it wasn't just a big fat myth, you're only a girl, remember.'

Fleur punched him on the arm. 'Ouch!' he cried and sat up abruptly. 'What was that for?'

'Stop saying that I'm only a girl,' she said indignantly. 'You know it makes my blood boil. And Arthur's not a fool – he's really clever and you know it.'

Tom looked daggers at her and they both stared out to sea. Rolling pebbles were dragged down as the backwash raked the shingle. 'I suppose he makes good company for you when I'm not around,' Tom muttered grumpily after a while.

Fleur considered him out of the corner of her eye, but he was staring steadfastly into the distance. He was still acting like he was jealous!

'Aye,' she began carefully. ''Twas good to come across him. He's pleasant company for a lubber.'

'There's more fire in a small dead fish,' Tom snapped back quickly. 'You're welcome to him.'

He suddenly grabbed a large stone and stood up, hurling it out to sea as far as he could. Not to be outdone, Fleur got to her feet, picked up a flat disc-shaped stone and sent it skimming over the tops of the waves. *One, two, three, four, five* graceful arcs, and then it fell into the sea with a satisfying plop. Tom pretended not to be impressed.

'My father taught me,' Fleur explained.

Tom continued to stare towards the horizon, although his jaw twitched spasmodically. 'I didn't ask,' he pointed out.

She eyed him with a smile. 'Right.'

'And Arthur *is* a fool,' he added adamantly.

CHAPTER 19

When the day of departure finally arrived, Fleur found herself a little sad to be leaving Ile aux Forbans. She couldn't sleep during their last night on the island, and while she tossed and turned, Tom slept soundly on the floor next to her; it drove her mad. At dawn she was watching the sunrise dribble through cracks in the hut with the first birdcall. Fleur gave up on sleep entirely. She pulled on her uncle's coat as quietly as possible, and crept out of the hut past the snoring Arthur and William.

In the pirate graveyard, the morning air was thin and chill. A mist hovered over everything. Fleur met nobody along the winding shingle path, and all was quiet except for the chattering birds. Fresh acorns had been scattered liberally around the Hart family plot in an attempt to keep the ghosts at bay.

Someone had laid a bunch of black orchids on the fresh earth of Henry's grave: most of the flowers still had their roots intact, as if they had been torn straight from the earth and tossed there. Clouds rolled across the pale morning sky. A fingernail of moon was still visible against the gloom and the North Star glimmered weakly. Fleur shrugged off her uncle's heavy coat and laid it on the dewy ground. Then she sat down, leaned back against Henry's grave and, brushing a tear aside with one hand, began to tell her father all about her adventures so far.

By the time Fleur was ready to leave, the morning sky was blue with promise. She shifted and stretched, enjoying the warm rays of the sun, then sat up and stared down towards the rolling surf.

'I thought I'd say goodbye too, lassie,' said a gruff voice behind her.

Fleur spun round, surprised to see Jack standing behind her with a sad smile on his weatherbeaten face. He wore his baggy ship's breeches and a loose shirt, but none of the weapons that usually hung about him.

He looked different unarmed: more vulnerable and human.

'May I?' he asked, indicating a spot next to Fleur.

She nodded and swivelled round to face him properly. She'd never been completely alone with Jack before and the situation felt awkward. They sat in silence for a while, listening to the crashing of the waves and the call of the birds.

Finally Jack pointed at the orchids on Henry's grave. 'That looks like the captain's work to me, wouldn't you say?'

Fleur nodded and smiled; Jack grinned back at her.

'I miss your father too, Fleur,' he said quietly, then swallowed hard. 'And I'd say I was crueller to you because of it. It was easier to snub you than to think of you as Henry and Rose's little one.'

'I thought it was because you had me down as bad luck,' Fleur told him.

'Well, there was a bit of that too,' he admitted. 'Though I reckon you've proved us all wrong there, young miss.'

Fleur nodded at him, her green eyes sparkling, and a startled expression came over Jack's face.

'Why, you're the very image of your ma,' he said.

They were silent for a while; when he spoke again,

his voice was warm and kind. 'Henry was a good friend to me and I always respected him. I was more'n a little jealous of the Hart brothers, I'll admit. In the old days they were inseparable. A force to be reckoned with. No one could break their bond.' His expression darkened. 'Till things went wrong.'

Fleur shuffled forwards and hugged her knees, curious to hear what the lieutenant had to say. 'What do you mean?' she whispered.

Jack took a swig from his flask and offered it to Fleur, but she shook her head. He shrugged and drank again. 'Maybe I'm speaking out of turn here, Fleur,' he said, corking his precious liquor, 'but I think Henry would have wanted you to know all there is to know. William is a law unto himself. He's as wild as the sea itself, capable of great deeds and terrible cruelties. Has he told you of his wife and son?'

'He has,' said Fleur, remembering the pain on her uncle's face as he had recalled their fate at the hands of Blood's men.

Jack's face twitched and he closed his eyes for a moment, lost in his own painful memories. 'It sent him to a dark place, Fleur. William always thought that he should have been the one to fulfil the Hart prophecy. He carried that staff around like it was part of him. And for a while he acted as if it gave him the right to do whatever he wanted.'

'What about my father? Did he think the prophecy might be about *him*?' Fleur asked.

Jack smiled and deep wrinkles appeared around his red eyes. 'Your father shared William's passion for the sea, but he never felt the need to rule over it. After he lost Anna and his boy, William planned a path of vengeance, hoping to spill enough blood to awaken the staff's power.' He paused and steeled himself. 'It sent him quite mad,' he continued quietly. 'William was hell-bent on fulfilling that prophecy and eliminating as many of Blood's kin and crew as he could. Kill all the Bloods, end the feud, fulfil the prophecy. See?'

'What did he do?' Fleur whispered, shivering despite the warmth from the morning sun.

'Do ye really want to know, lassie?' asked Jack darkly. 'It might alter your opinion of him.'

Fleur nodded miserably. She had to know the truth, even if it meant knocking her uncle off his pedestal.

'He gathered together a group of cut-throats and villains, more vicious than any I have ever sailed with. Those men weren't pirates, they were devils. I barely slept for fear they'd kill me in my sleep for sport.' Jack stroked his neck uncomfortably as he remembered his former shipmates. 'Now then,' he continued, 'William didn't tell Henry or me what he was up to, but he stormed the *Libertine*, murdering the crew while they slept in their hammocks. Alexander managed to escape, of course, and William took his ship from under him.'

'So the *Libertine* was Blood's in the first place?' Fleur cried in astonishment.

Jack nodded and took another fortifying sip of rum. 'That's only half of it. Henry discovered that William was planning to murder all the womenfolk of the Blood line. A great and bloody vengeance for what Alexander had done to him.'

Fleur gasped with horror, her head spinning. 'Did he . . . ?' she spluttered.

Jack turned away from her searching eyes.

'Did he?' she repeated more boldly. 'Please, Jack, I have to know.'

Jack met her gaze. 'I won't lie to you, girl,' he said eventually. 'But I beg you to remember that he was crazed, Fleur. He was not himself. There was no slaughter in the end, mind, but no peace neither – not for the Bloods, not for William, not yet for your poor family.'

They sat in silence for a few moments, Fleur reeling from the possibilities.

'Tell me,' she croaked finally.

Jack plucked a wild flower from the grass and rolled it between his fingers, crushing the fragrant petals as he spoke. 'Henry found out what his brother was planning and took me into his confidence. Piracy can be cruel and bloody, as you know, but the Harts had always protected womenfolk. And we couldn't let William toss his soul to the devil so readily. Henry took the Hart staff, making it look as if it had been carried off by thieves, and hid it well,' he explained. 'William, though he had no idea where to start, was determined to find it again. He was still determined to rule the oceans using its power. I for one thank God he never fulfilled that prophecy. A man in his state of mind with power over the waves might've drowned the whole world.

'Now, Henry told William that he'd have no part in such horrible revenge. He went as far as to swear that he'd warn the Bloods if ever William made his move. It was that betrayal, as William saw it, that opened the rift between 'em that they never closed in life. All Henry wanted was to protect his brother, see. And you and your ma too.' Jack stared out to sea, his eyes awash with tears. 'So that was the end of it. Henry gave up the sea and his birthright as a Hart, which is the bravest thing he could ever have done.'

'What of William?' Fleur asked quietly. 'What did he do next?'

'Well, he never did take his revenge against the Bloods' womenfolk. Perhaps he listened to his brother after all. Or perhaps he was only waiting till the staff was in his possession once more. We spent years looking for that wretched stick, travelling the world over. William was never the same man again – I don't think any man ever truly returns from a brush with madness. And without his brother there was something missing that couldn't be replaced. Still, as the years passed, his anger lessened some and he convinced himself that the Hart prophecy was a mere fairytale. Then you turned up and it got him pondering again.'

Fleur sank her head into her hands in despair. 'I didn't mean to cause any trouble. I don't want him to turn evil again. I don't want to end up like that myself. Maybe it's a good thing I'm leaving him after all.'

Jack stared at her in surprise. 'No, no, Fleur. You've missed my whole point,' he said warmly. 'Don't you see? You've calmed William; given back some of what he lost when his brother left. Family, girl. A sense of purpose and belonging. Why, you've made a better man of him. And no doubt a much worse pirate.'

They smiled at each other at that.

'Jack,' asked Fleur, 'why do you think my father kept the staff a secret from me?'

He tilted his head to one side thoughtfully. 'I have my own theory about that, girl,' he replied. 'I think he believed in the prophecy more than he liked to admit, even to himself. He trained you well — and not just to protect you from the odd enemy who might've come calling.' He shook his head and studied Fleur closely. 'No, I think Henry always knew you'd hear the call of the ocean — you can't escape from your own destiny. Maybe he hoped that one day you'd take to the waves together.'

'Do you honestly think that?' Fleur gasped.

Jack shrugged and smiled. 'He'll have noticed your affinity with the sea, and your skill in combat. He'd've been blind not to.'

Fleur's heart swelled with pride at the compliment.

'Knowing your pa, I reckon he was terrified that *you* were the one who'd fulfil that damned prophecy. A father wants the best for his little 'uns, but he wants it to be simple too. Find someone to love, have children of their own, happy lives — that sort of thing. No father wants his daughter to become the all-powerful embod-iment of an ancient myth. Am I making sense?'

'I think so,' said Fleur. 'Maybe the staff is bad. Maybe

it can only bring pain and sadness and I should just throw it into the sea – if we ever get it back, that is.'

Jack shook his head and winked slyly. 'I don't think so. There's them who say the legend speaks of one who is *pure of heart*, you see – not simply of the Hart bloodline: something William always chose to overlook.' He smiled to himself. 'Words get muddled up down the ages, Fleur. Anyhow, there ain't many that's pure of heart in the pirating game. Keeping your soul shiny is nigh on impossible in our line of work. But you're different, girl: you ain't murdered anyone for starters, which is good going for a pirate.'

'Not yet, at any rate,' Fleur admitted.

Jack laughed and fell into a fit of coughing. 'I just wonder,' he said, clearing his throat noisily, 'what would happen if you got your hands on that ruby heart. William once hoped to unlock its power with the force of his hatred and anger. But I reckon you've something a might fiercer in your arsenal. Something the staff might have been waiting for all along. The older I get, the more I think that the greatest power doesn't come from rage, but from something else entirely.'

'And what's that?' asked Fleur, her eyes wide.

Jack looked down at Henry's grave, then clambered to his feet, batting the dust from his breeches as he did so. 'Don't tell anyone I said it or I'll split your skull, girl,' he warned, 'but I think they call it love.'

As the *Black Dragon* set sail for the Caribbean, there was a burst of activity onboard. All hands were on deck, with William in his element, barking orders and stomping around happily. Elsewhere, Carlton Bart, the sailing master, was below decks, poring over his maps and charts, while Toby Butler, the new cook from the west coast of Ireland, was tucked into a quiet corner with a favourite book – the poems of John Donne. Toby was a fine cook, but he'd rather have been a librarian, and was easily distracted from his kitchen duties. A pile of unpeeled yams and a basket of freshly caught fish still lay beside him: the crew would be eating very late that day.

In the crow's nest Fleur and Tom stared out across the water, mesmerized by the waves undulating below. As the ship cleared the shallows and slid out into the wide basin of clear blue water, Fleur noticed huge dark shapes gliding around beneath them. She was about to ask Tom what they were when a low rumbling moan shook her to her very bones.

'What's happening?' she asked, grabbing Tom's arm in fright.

He grinned and pointed at the water off their

starboard side. Fleur saw the surface of the water break and ripple as something huge rose up. Arthur was hopping about the poop deck excitedly, holding the captain's brass telescope to his eye. The rest of the crew barely registered the commotion, but Fleur's heart was in her mouth. Suddenly a head the size of a hill appeared, and a plume of white spray shot upwards, almost high enough to soak her perch.

'Sea monsters,' she gasped. 'What are we to do?' She pointed shakily at the vast creature below.

Tom clutched his sides and burst out laughing.

'Stop it!' she snapped. 'What's happening?'

'They're only humpback whales, Claw-cat,' he teased.

Fleur was as embarrassed as she was relieved. 'I've seen whales in Cornwall, but they were the size of sharks,' she replied, staring down at the gigantic mammal as another plume of water shot up.

'That there is how they breathe,' Tom explained. 'They ain't fish, see, they breathe air, like us, and hold it under the water. They gather here every year with their babies. Look, there's a young 'un now.'

A calf had surfaced alongside their giant visitor, and was eyeing the sides of the ship with curiosity. Its mother lifted her vast leathery tail and slapped it down hard as a warning for others to keep their distance.

'They're huge,' Fleur gasped in awe, 'and there are so many of them.'

'Some folk think they're sacred, others think they bring nothing but bad luck,' said Tom, suddenly quite serious. 'If you ask me, there's more to 'em than we know.' He shrugged. 'Then again, what would a cabin boy know?'

Fleur watched in wonder as the whales were joined by other members of their pod. Their haunting song filled the air around them and made the water vibrate against the *Black Dragon*'s hull. She became lost in the rise and fall of their plaintive cries that seemed to bounce across the surface of the entire ocean. At times they seemed to be calling her name, warning her that something was coming. Finally she shook herself free of the hypnotic song.

'Tom,' she said softly, 'I think cabin boys can know an awful lot.'

As she stared out over the ocean from their lofty vantage point, rank on rank of breaking waves foamed towards them like an approaching army. With her sails full, the *Black Dragon* cut through the water like a knife though butter. Soon Ile aux Forbans was a dot on the horizon. Ahead was an endless azure-blue sea.

'Come on,' sighed Tom reluctantly, beckoning Fleur down from the crow's nest. 'No doubt the captain will have work for us to be getting on with.'

Fleur nodded and was about to start her descent when Tom grabbed her by the arm.

'What is it?' she asked. 'Have you seen more whales?'

Tom shook his head grimly and pointed off the port side. 'Ship.'

Fleur followed his gaze to see a large vessel charging towards them at full speed. The bowsprit cut through the water like a spear. They were bearing down fast.

'It's a brigantine, isn't it?' she said.

'Aye,' murmured Tom distractedly.

The sails of the approaching ship were straining hard, as if an angry god was urging them onwards.

'It's coming at us hard,' Fleur said. 'Do you think they see us?'

The colour had drained from Tom's face. He was rummaging in his pocket for his spyglass. 'If we see them, they see us,' he told her, putting it to his eye. He paled even further as he peered at the oncoming ship, and the hand that held the spyglass began to tremble.

'What is it?' Fleur asked urgently.

But Tom was already over the side of the crow's nest and bellowing down to all the crew as he half climbed, half tumbled to join them on deck.

'Ship ahoy!' he yelled, as loud as his lungs would allow, ''Tis the Bloods in our own *Libertine*. We're under attack!'

'Stand by, my bullies!' the captain bellowed from the poop deck. 'Man the guns.' As a breathless Fleur joined Tom by the mainmast, her uncle spotted them and barked his orders. 'Tom, hoist the colours. And Fleur' – he pointed over to Arthur – 'take the lily-liver down below and keep him out of sight. This is about to turn ugly.'

Tom set off to raise the flag with an 'Aye, aye, Cap'n'.

Fleur turned towards Arthur but her uncle stepped down from the poop deck to head her off. 'Stop there, lassie.' In three long strides, he was beside her. He grabbed hold of her arm and pulled her to him roughly. 'I don't want you taking no risks in this fight,' he said firmly.

Fleur shook him off. 'But I'm crew, Captain. So no special treatment.'

Below his tricorn hat, William's eyes shone proudly but he shook his head. All around, the crew raced to their stations carrying cannonballs and deadly blades.

'No!' he said. 'This ain't something you'd survive, Fleur. And they'd treat you worse once they saw you were a girl too. Keep that bandana on and stay hidden with Arthur here if you hope to see out the voyage under my command.'

'But, Captain,' Fleur protested, 'I know this ship as well as you do. I can help. I *want* to fight.'

Her uncle yanked her to him but she wrenched herself away, rubbing her arm. They glared at each other with the same stubborn gaze.

'You have no idea what these animals are capable of, girl,' William warned. 'You're no match for 'em. And I can't be sure that I am, neither.'

He gestured towards Arthur, whose face was pale with fear. 'Take 'im down now, girl,' he ordered. 'There's no time left.'

Fleur froze. Those were the exact words her father had said to her on the night of his murder. Her eyes began to fill with hot tears. Would her beloved Uncle William fare better than her lost father against Blood and his cut-throats? The sound of cannon fire brought her back to the present. As they heard Blood's first volley splash harmlessly into the water off their port bow, William bent to kiss Fleur's cheek. When he spoke, his voice was thick with emotion.

'Go.' He turned away from her. 'Man the larboard guns and double 'em up!' he shouted as the *Black Dragon* readied to return fire. 'Tell them to aim high, lads. Let's swab their poop deck with buckets of their own blood. Ezra Dunne, look lively now. Pound 'em, lads. *Pound 'em.'*

Fleur stood rooted to the spot as she stared up at her uncle, magnificent in battle. Arthur tugged at her sleeve, but she pulled her arm away and blinked as tears blurred her vision. William looked just like her father, when he'd faced the same enemy on that terrible night. He drew his sword and stood god-like amidst the chaos.

'Fight with all you have!' he roared, and his troops cheered. 'To the death, men, and beyond.'

'Fleur, come on,' said Arthur, pulling her away.

'I don't want to hide. I want to fight,' she protested as they snaked their way through the running pirates, down towards the bowels of the ship. 'I'm *not* a coward. It makes no sense to bury me away down here when I know in my heart that I'm supposed to be part of this somehow.'

As they ran along the gun deck, they heard Jack shouting orders to the crew. With the *Libertine* almost upon them, the cannon and musket balls were no longer falling short of the *Black Dragon*'s sides. The sound of splintering wood and the screams of injured men added to the chaos.

'Load 'em with hot coals, boys!' Jack yelled as he

distributed the blazing lumps from an iron scuttle. 'We'll give 'em the hot galley broadside when they come amidships.'

Glancing towards the doorway, Jack spotted Fleur and Arthur hovering. 'Get below, you two, and stay safe,' he cried out as a cannonball crashed through the ship's side a few yards to his right. 'A peg leg don't look right on a young 'un.'

They scuttled deeper into the ship until the sounds of battle were muffled and they could talk again at normal volume.

'Go on without me,' said Fleur, utterly decided now. 'But don't hide in the bilges because it's sure to flood.'

'Not without you!' Arthur protested weakly.

But Fleur pushed him towards the door that led to the hold. 'I'll join you in a while,' she assured him with a nod.

'But—' Arthur began.

Fleur silenced him with a stamp of her foot. 'But nothing! We all have the right to make our own choices. And this is mine. I have waited for revenge for so long. You can do what you like, but I'm going to fight. And I'm going to win.'

Arthur nodded at Fleur with respect. 'I wish I was as brave as you, but I'm not, I'm ashamed to say. Tom was right when he said I was a chicken-heart.' He leaned in to kiss Fleur's cheek in the same spot where William had prickled her earlier. 'But I know you can do it.'

Fear and excitement in equal measure coursed through Fleur's body as she made her way back above deck. She made a brief detour to grab her father's bow from her miraculously intact portside cabin, then burst out into the smoke and light and noise of battle.

'Aloft to repel!' roared the captain as he raced through the smoke past Fleur. 'Keep hammering that waterline, Jon Martins! Fear not, I have a plan, men, and 'tis almost time.'

He looked so fearsome with his cutlass held high that Fleur prayed she would not be spotted disobeying his direct order to stay below. When he was out of sight again, she ventured further onto the deck. She ducked and dodged as musket balls thudded into the wood around her, shielding her eyes from the flying shards.

Peter Fenn, a gunner who had always been kind to her aboard the old *Libertine*, was loading shot and scrap metal into the smaller cannons. When he caught sight of Fleur, he scuttled over to her and pulled her down into a crouch. 'Are you mad, missy?' he asked her, his eyes bright and wide. 'The cap'n wants you below decks.'

'I'm going there now,' Fleur lied. 'But tell me what's happening first!'

'Blood's men are about to board, lass,' spat Peter. 'We weren't ready for 'em. So hide yourself if you've any wish to live another day. And if all else fails, be ready to swim for it.'

Fear took hold of Fleur like iron bands. She stared hard at Peter, looking for some sign of hope or humour. But there was none. All around, her uncle's men were falling, their limbs shattered, their bodies torn by the onslaught of Alexander Blood's broadside barrage. What had she, a mere girl, been thinking? That she could help? How? By adding her blood to the puddles on deck, perhaps, to slip up the boarders when they came?

An unexpected noise, barely audible above the clamour, brought Fleur back to herself. She shivered, shaking off the paralysis of fear, and strained to hear it. Parsley! The ship's cat was peeping out from behind the wreckage of a shot-blasted barrel, wailing like a banshee. He was obviously terrified.

'Parsley!' called Fleur, beckoning to him. 'Parsley! Come on, boy. Come on. I'll look after you.'

The cat's ears twitched at the sound of his name. His eyes darted about until he saw Fleur. With a bound, he leaped out from his hiding place and scampered towards her, mewing excitedly. Fleur opened her arms to gather him up. Suddenly there was a deafening crunch and a puff of red, and then Parsley was gone.

It took Fleur a moment to figure out what had happened. There was a huge hole in the side of the ship where a cannonball had torn through. There was another hole in the opposite side. And in the middle was a dark crimson patch where Parsley had been. A direct hit. She choked back a sob and surveyed the scene again. The cannons had stopped and Alexander Blood's men were casting ropes between the ships. In a moment they would be aboard, and the slaughter would begin.

A tear rolled down Fleur's cheek. She wiped it away and was appalled to see smears of Parsley's blood on her fingertips. She was beaten: there was nothing she could do up here but die. She got to her feet unsteadily, and turned for the door that led back to the hold, where her friends would need her soon. But the door was blocked. A tall, lean figure barred her way. His cross belt was stuffed with pistols – so many that they looked like a hand of bananas – along with some vicious-looking daggers. His mouth was fixed in a cruel grin, displaying a row of crooked, blackened teeth. Black ribbons flapped from the braids in his flame-coloured hair and beard. And above his head he held the Hart staff.

Rage flashed through Fleur as she recognized Captain Alexander Blood. Her fists clenched and her muscles twitched. That staff belonged to her family, by God and she would have it! Blood pumped through her like hot oil, awakening her senses. With one smooth action, she took her father's bow from her shoulder, pulled an arrow from her quiver, brought the bow up fast and fired. Blood swerved and the arrow nicked the side of his head, slicing off the lobe of one ear and sending a large gold hoop clattering to the deck. The pirate roared in pain and shock, and charged at Fleur, brandishing the Hart staff like a spear.

She reached for another arrow, but he was too fast. As she dived left to avoid the sharp tip of the staff's narwhal horn, Blood shouldered her to the deck. The wind was knocked out of her as they skidded across the bloody boards, scratching and kicking and clutching for each other's weapons. The precious staff was knocked overboard and for a moment Fleur stared after it in shock. The one-eyed pirate picked her up, literally hurling her across the deck. She crashed and skidded across it; then the ground disappeared beneath her as she slid through the open gash in the ship's side and tumbled, thrashing and shouting, into the waters below.

The world beneath the waves was calm. Fleur's hair

fanned out around her head and she watched as tiny bubbles rose up from her mouth and nose. Then, without thinking, she took a deep breath and foul sea water filled her lungs. She choked and took in even more salt water. She tried to kick for the surface, but her chest burned and her head began to spin. She could feel the strength leaving her body and her mind began to wander. She had stopped struggling and let the sea carry her to her destiny. It was all so clear now: she was about to die.

As her strength failed, Fleur saw something falling through the water nearby. Straight and true, it cut through the sea towards her until she realized what it was. The Hart staff! With the last of her energy she pushed out towards it, her hands outstretched. At least, thought Fleur, she would take this prize and let it sink them both to the bottom of the sea. It would never be claimed by a Blood again. As the staff slid within reach, her fingers wrapped around its polished wood, finding the ruby that adorned it. And then something amazing happened.

Many times, afterwards, Fleur would try to remember the precise feeling of that first touch, or piece together the events that saw her own life saved and the fortunes of her uncle and his crew miraculously turned. But she could never quite recapture the exact sense of fulfilment, power and promise that the ruby brought, or give a good account of her own incredible actions that day. She couldn't even say for sure whether she or the staff was the instrument of the Harts' revenge. What she could do, however, was remember the fight itself in great detail. And if these details seemed impossible or fantastic, well, there were a great many battle-hardened pirates who'd swear to their last drop of rum that that's just how it played out; some would add that the devil had had a hand in it for sure.

This much, Fleur knew. As she grasped the staff, her mind cleared and her lungs found some impossible reserve of air. She felt the same strange energy and power course through her that she had experienced when she had beaten William in the fight. Musket balls pierced the water but Fleur darted out of their path. She didn't even have to think about it – she simply moved instinctively. Her reflexes were sharp and her body had never felt stronger. The same awesome song that had filled her head before began rising from the depths, as if every creature in the sea was calling to her at once. Then Jack's words came to her in a whisper that cut through everything: *The legend talks of one who is pure of heart, you see; not simply of the Hart bloodline.*

And then suddenly everything made sense. 'I will live!' Fleur screamed inwardly. Her blood was fizzing with excitement and her hand felt like it was burning where she clutched the staff. She looked down and saw light pouring from the ruby, enveloping her hand in a brilliant red aura. Could it be . . . ?

But there was no time to doubt it, she had to act fast. She kicked her legs hard and swam to the surface, ignoring the bursting pressure in her ears. It was as if something powerful had jumped into her skin and was hurling her forward. With a gasp, she burst through the surface and paddled there a while, gaining strength.

'Fleur, Fleur . . . *Fleur*!'

Amidst the gunfire and explosions, someone was shouting her name. Fleur looked up and saw Arthur peering through a huge hole ripped in the side of the ship. Even from a distance she could see that his face was red and wet with tears.

'I thought you were dead!' he shouted down, before bursting into a fit of hysterical laughter. 'Hang on, I'll be back soon.'

Fleur kicked her legs, shivering in the cold water while above her cannon fire blazed across the gap between the two ships. She looked down at the ruby and saw that its light had faded; she began to wonder if she had imagined its smouldering glow. She felt more like herself again too, and her teeth chattered and her limbs felt numb as she trod water with the heavy staff. But sure enough, Arthur was quick to return.

'Here, catch hold of this,' he shouted, throwing down a tumble of knotted rigging.

Fleur reached out and clutched the rope eagerly. There was a brief scuffle above and she saw that Tom's flushed face had replaced Arthur's pale one.

'Claw-cat!' he bellowed above the roar of the battle. 'Arthur told me what happened. Can you make it up here?'

Fleur nodded and pulled herself out of the water, careful not to drop the staff.

'Is that what I think it is?' Tom shouted.

'It is,' she replied. 'Now shut up and let me climb.'

But her arms were exhausted, her wet clothes felt like lead weights and the long staff was tucked awkwardly under one arm, making the climb even harder. Arthur and Tom encouraged her from above, and soon they were heaving her though the hole and into Jack's cabin. Fleur collapsed on the floor in a soggy heap, panting for breath. Tom wrapped a blanket around her, crouching beside her protectively. He couldn't drag his eyes away from the staff.

'I watched you fall,' Arthur said, his voice thick with emotion. 'I feared the worst . . .' His words trailed away and he cleared his throat, embarrassed. 'I found Tom . . . he wanted to come and make sure you climbed up safely.'

Tom nodded towards Fleur's bow and quiver of arrows, lying nearby. 'I got those for you too, just in case.'

'Thank you, both of you,' Fleur said, trying to control her shivers.

Arthur rubbed at his teary eyes with dirty, trembling hands and spoke in panting staccato bursts. 'Sorry. I told you I wasn't brave – crying like a baby and hiding away in here. Alexander's men are winning. It won't be long now.'

Fleur and Tom said nothing for a few moments, both exchanging the same worried look. They were all terrified, but Arthur was falling apart. Fleur pushed an arm from under the coarse blanket and squeezed his hand.

'Thank you, Arthur,' she said warmly. 'That's me *and* Tom you've saved now. I'd say that was pretty heroic *and* brave.'

He blushed and looked down at his feet. 'It was nothing,' he mumbled.

'It was everything,' she told him, tilting his face upwards with a gentle finger under his chin.

Arthur glanced over at Tom, suddenly embarrassed by his tears. 'What must you think of me?' he said sadly.

Tom grinned at him warmly. 'Actually, quite a lot,' he replied. 'That rigging was piled up on the main deck, right in the middle of the fighting. You risked your life going up there to get it, Arthur. I didn't know you had it in you.'

Arthur shrugged, his panic melting away as he basked in their praise. 'I ran so fast that no one saw me,' he boasted.

Fleur and Tom chuckled and he grinned back at them. A loud explosion rattled the cabin walls, but none of them flinched.

'Bravery comes in all shapes and sizes, Arthur,' said Fleur, shaking off the blanket and reaching again for the narwhal staff.

'Is that . . . is that really the Hart staff?' Arthur asked.

Fleur nodded and rose to her feet. 'Aye,' she said, studying it. She listened to the sound of gunfire closing in around them.

Tom scrambled to his feet next to her. 'It's magnificent,' he gasped, running his hands over the narwhal horn.

Fleur stood as tall and proud as her slight frame allowed. 'This staff is my birthright, and with it I will turn the battle.'

She picked up her bow and quiver of arrows and slung them over her shoulder. As she turned to leave, Tom pulled her back.

'But you'll be killed.'

Fleur unclamped his hand from her arm. 'No I won't,' she replied calmly. 'The prophecy says—'

'We *know* what the prophecy says – you told us,' Arthur interrupted. 'But even the captain doesn't know if it's true. I'm a scientist – well, I've read lots of books anyway – and I'm beginning to realize that everything in this world has an explanation behind it, Fleur. There's no such thing as magic, it's just stories. One of your ancestors probably made up the legend to scare his enemies. Can't you see that?'

Fleur's hands tightened around the staff defiantly, her resolve firm. 'It's real,' she insisted, 'if I make it real. Those men killed my father and I'm going up there now and I *will* turn this battle.'

Tom backed away from her: he knew nothing could dissuade his stubborn friend when her mind was made up. 'I'm coming with you then,' he said firmly.

Arthur swallowed his fear and stood next to Tom. 'Me too,' he said, with as much bravery as he could muster.

Fleur tilted her head to the side and frowned. 'But you might die.'

'Oh well.' Tom shrugged. 'It's going to happen sooner or later.'

They all smiled at each other. Then, with a deep breath, they burst out through the cabin door and into the thunderous fray in the corridors beyond.

CHAPTER 20

The battle for the *Black Dragon* had reached a crescendo. Blood's men swarmed about the decks, swinging from the rigging of the *Libertine* to clamber through the ragged holes left by the barrage of cannon fire. The roof of the hold was burning fiercely, sending a plume of acrid black smoke spiralling into the clear blue sky. Amidst the smoke, swords and daggers glinted as they cut through the air.

Peter Fenn spied them immediately and dashed over. He was splattered with other men's blood. 'We need you, Tom,' he said. 'Come quickly.'

Tom nodded at Arthur briskly and turned to Fleur.

'Stay alive,' he said huskily.

'You too,' she replied.

Taking a deep breath, Tom turned and ran straight into the heart of the battle. Fleur stood in shock for a few seconds, then grabbed Arthur's hand, leading him through the smoke and fire, darting between battling men.

'Can you see the captain?' she shouted as she struggled to overcome a mounting sense of despair.

'No,' yelled Arthur, ducking to avoid a short-handled dagger that missed his head by a whisker. 'Wait!' He grabbed Fleur by the shoulder and pointed over towards the stern. She followed the line of her friend's outstretched arm, straining to see what it was that had caught his eye.

Then her heart plummeted into her stomach. William and Alexander Blood were locked together in a desperate struggle, knives drawn, fists clenched, jaws set, eyes wild with murderous rage. Both men were bloodied and bruised, but they showed no signs of slowing. The fight would surely be to the death.

Fleur started to run over to them, but Arthur held her back. 'What are you planning to do?' he asked urgently.

'I don't know yet,' she replied honestly.

Arthur smiled at her, his mouth twitching with barely

concealed fear. 'Don't suppose I can do anything to stop you?'

'Don't suppose you can,' said Fleur, shaking her head firmly. And she darted through the smoke to join her beleaguered captain.

She ran with the staff held out before her like a spear. William and Blood were wrestling now, rolling on the deck in a blur of teeth and fists and flashing blades. As Fleur approached, her uncle seemed to be getting the better of his foe. He had freed himself from Blood's grip long enough to get his fingers around his enemy's throat. The pirate captain spluttered and gasped under William's crushing hands. Then something changed. His grip suddenly relaxed, while Blood's bulging eyes and swollen face were returning to normal. He was laughing; on William's face Fleur saw only shock and pain.

She struggled to understand what she was seeing. Was William hurt? She screamed as she ran full tilt towards the fearsome Captain Blood. Her banshee wail caught him off-guard and he rolled out from under William, who landed heavily on his back. Blood crouched beside his foe and roughly pulled a small serrated silver blade from between the fallen pirate's ribs. Fleur recoiled at the sight, sliding to a halt an arm's length from her snarling enemy.

Blood pulled himself up to his full height, threw back his head and laughed. Then, ignoring Fleur completely, he planted one heavy boot on William's throat, drew his long rapier and stared down at his foe. Fleur's heart raced. She wanted to help, but what use could she be? She watched hopelessly as her fallen but still defiant uncle gritted his teeth and glared into the eyes of his assassin. In a moment he would feel the cold steel of Blood's blade as it pierced his heart. And he was helpless. *But you're not, girl*, said a familiar gruff voice in Fleur's head, shaking her to her senses.

'No,' she said aloud, holding the Hart staff out before her and stepping boldly towards Captain Blood. 'Stop it!' she shouted, loud enough to be heard over the ongoing racket of the battle. 'I said, stop what you're doing. *Now.*'

The one-eyed pirate looked her up and down – an impudent child with a fighting stick – and laughed again, long and loud. All the while, he was pushing the tip of his sword hard against William's chest so that he struggled not to cry out in pain.

'I thought I'd already killed you,' the pirate captain jeered. 'Plucky little thing, ain't you. I reckon there's room for a boy like you on my ship if you don't fancy dying today.'

Fleur stepped closer to him and raised her chin. 'I

wouldn't join your crew if you were Noah and your ship the ark,' she said proudly. 'I'd sooner drown.'

'That can be arranged,' he said, and with flick of his long arm, he disarmed her, sending the precious staff sliding across the deck, out of reach. Without the staff Fleur could feel her courage ebbing away; she wanted to sink to her knees and surrender. At that moment Peg-leg appeared through the smoke, holding a small jagged knife that was red with fresh blood. He spotted Fleur and a cruel, hungry smile crept over his face. She gasped as a hundred thoughts whirled in her head. Was this the end of everything? The ship, the crew, the prophecy, her uncle, her life . . . ? But as she stared into the faces of her enemies, a strange calm came over and she let her hands drop to her sides.

'What's this? A lamb to the slaughter, eh?' Blood taunted. 'Here, William, looks like the fight's gone out of your half-pint champion. Ha ha!'

Fleur stood firm, like a tree rooted to the spot as she spoke. There was noise and smoke from fresh explosions all around her but she didn't flinch. She stared directly at her enemy. 'You caused my father's death,' she stated matter-of-factly before glancing over at Peg-leg. 'And you're the pig that pulled the trigger that brought him down.'

She removed the bandana that had been hiding her growing black curls. Blood frowned, then stumbled backwards as realization flooded his face. 'Henry . . . You mean Henry Hart, don't you?'

Peg-leg shuffled forward, jabbing his bloody knife towards Fleur. 'I told you she was a girl, Cap'n.'

Blood shot his henchman a glare. 'You didn't tell me she was Henry Hart's girl though, did you, you hop-a-long fool.' He studied Fleur intensely, regaining his composure. 'And now I see it as clear as day. What a blind bat I've been. I could have slit your throat back on that island. I dare say you were at the inn that night we ended your miserable father too, eh?'

'Yes.' Fleur nodded, her voice loud and clear. 'I'm Fleur Hart and I was there. And by God, I'm here to avenge my family,' she declared, breathing deeply and evenly.

Blood laughed as Fleur swung Henry's bow from her shoulder and pulled an arrow from her quiver. 'You going to shoot me, missy?' he guffawed.

She pointed the arrow at his chest, not quite able to control the trembling in her hands. The crew moved to overcome her, but he waved them away.

'Don't worry, lads, she ain't got what it takes to let that arrow fly. This girl is no killer – I can see it in her eyes.'

Fleur stood firm, with the arrow aimed squarely at her enemy, her whole body quaking with fear. She squeezed one eye shut and aimed for his heart. But he was right: she didn't have it in her to kill him. Even though she despised him with everything she was, she still couldn't do it. The bow wobbled in her hands as his men goaded her.

William writhed on the floor and Blood thrust his boot down harder on his neck. The fallen captain gurgled alarmingly and started to turn blue.

'Shoo, little goose, while I take care of your uncle,' Blood sneered. 'And never you mind – I'll get to you soon enough. The world will be a better place when I've rid it of you wretched Harts.'

'No!' Fleur shouted, her heart pounding as she glanced down at William.

Quick as a flash, she tilted her bow upwards and fired the arrow, straight and true. It soared through the rigging, where it cut clean through the rope that held the ship's huge boom. It swung free, crashing into the pirate captain and his men, bowling them over like skittles and sweeping them through a large gash in the side of the ship into the waters below. The boom swung back and forth dangerously. Stunned pirates from either side scattered across the deck, ducking and rolling out of its way.

Fleur ran to her uncle's side and helped him up. 'Are you OK?' she asked as he dusted himself down, wincing in pain.

He drew himself up to his full height and grinned broadly. 'Never better, child, thanks to you.' He glanced over at the gaping hole through which Blood and his men had disappeared. 'Shall we see what's left then?'

Fleur nodded eagerly and they raced over to the side of the ship. Blood's tricorn hat hung where it had been snagged on the splintered wood. The battle had ceased now, but there were still scuffles here and there where the invading crew fought on. In the churning waters below, the pirate captain and four of his men were thrashing about, shouting for help. Sharks circled around them – great black-eyed scavengers grown bold with the scent of blood. Fleur noticed that Peg-leg was among the swimmers. He held his wooden leg in one hand and was knocking the other men aside with it.

Blood gazed up at the Harts imploringly. 'Help us,' he cried urgently.

William spat into the water. 'Never!' he yelled back.

Fleur tugged at his shirt and shook her head solemnly. Her uncle rolled his eyes to the heavens. 'You're not serious, girl?' he asked.

She looked down at the struggling pirates. 'It shouldn't end this way, sir. I didn't mean to kill them – to let them die would be murder.'

William slapped the ship's rail in exasperation.

'Please, Uncle,' Fleur said quietly. 'Hold him prisoner, cast him adrift, but please don't let it end this way. I won't have his blood on my hands.'

He stared intensely at his niece and saw only grave sincerity on her face. Something glinted in his dark eyes; then it was gone. He knew all about the torture of guilt and wasn't about to let Fleur carry that burden. With a heavy sigh he nodded his assent, scanning the deck for a rope, then looping one end around the barrel of a heavy gun and tossing the other over the side.

'Happy now?' he asked her; she smiled gratefully back at him. Then he turned to Jack and his crew, who had gathered nearby. 'Make sure you don't let the oily bilge rats get away when they reach the top. It's straight to the brig for them, boys.'

The beleaguered crew managed a feeble cheer of approval.

William needn't have worried. In the churning waters below, a terrible scene was unfolding. Instead of taking their turn to climb the lifeline to safety, Blood and his men were clambering over each other, punching and kicking and tugging at one another's sodden clothes as they tried desperately to get hold of the rope.

'Hold back, you villains!' Blood bellowed. 'Show some respect for your captain!'

'You never showed any for us,' spat Peg-leg.

Blood shoved the man's head under the water. He came up cursing and choking, and dragged his captain away from the rope again.

'I'll string you all up when I get the chance,' shouted the pirate captain. 'You'll kill us all, you fools.' He drew a knife and began hacking at anyone within reach. Fresh blood filled the water and the sharks thrashed around in excitement. The first man to be taken was the furthest from the rope. He screamed once, threw up his arms and vanished into the water, which soon turned red with blood. The rest redoubled their efforts to reach the lifeline, but they had not learned their lesson. Instead of cooperating, they fought to be first out of the water, while the frenzied sharks picked off one man at a time, snapping them up in their terrible jaws. Fleur and her shipmates watched in helpless horror. Soon, only Blood and Peg-leg were left, gore-soaked, terrified, but still scrabbling for the end of the rope that William had thrown.

'Let me up, damn you,' spluttered Blood as he dragged

himself out of the water again. 'Let me climb first so that we both may live, fool!'

Peg-leg, scared though he was, at last relented, letting go of his captain's leg. Suddenly a shark came up from beneath, taking off his good leg in one bite; another shark reared out of the water, trapping the screaming pirate in its cavernous mouth. Blood cried out at the sight and spun wildly on the end of his rope. Peg-leg, thrashing in terror, caught his captain on the head with his wooden leg and sent him back into the crimson water, where the gathered sharks circled, tearing at him until there was nothing left. As for Peg-leg, only his wooden leg remained. An eerie silence fell across the *Black Dragon* as the survivors looked down at the empty waters in horror.

William cupped his hands around his mouth: 'Men of the *Libertine*,' he shouted, 'your captain is dead!'

The crew had thinned as the battle claimed its casualties, but the dozen or so hardened pirates that remained of the boarding party had been stunned into inaction. All eyes turned to William as he continued.

'Throw down your weapons!'

'Never!' shouted someone from the stern. The others joined in, rattling their cutlasses and baring their teeth at Captain Hart and his men.

'Very well,' he said firmly. 'I take back what I said. Carry on.' He reached for the Hart staff and tossed it to Fleur with a wink. 'You're better at this than me – go get 'em, girl.'

Fleur caught the staff and went into action. The men around her were stunned by the young girl's talent. She moved like a tiger from prey to prey, whirling the staff like an extension of her arm, cracking heads and scooping legs out from under the enemy. She had never known that she could fight like this. Fleur had seen enough killing and was not going to add that to her sins, but she left a trail of groaning and unconscious victims in her wake.

Elsewhere William had rallied his troops and they were driving Blood's men back towards the *Libertine*, or simply shoving them overboard when the opportunity rose. He managed to find Fleur amongst the confusion. The wound in his ribs was oozing dark-red blood and he had to steady himself against her. At that moment Tom and Arthur came tearing up, both looking tired and a little the worse for wear. Fleur grinned at her friends before turning her attention back to her uncle.

'We need your bow, girl,' he shouted above the din.

'Of course,' she said, unhitching it from her shoulder and offering it to him.

'*I* don't want it – *you*'ll need it,' said William. 'Fleur, do you reckon you could hit the *Libertine*'s binnacle from here?'

'Aye,' said Fleur with confidence as she squinted over at the raised section of the deck where the *Libertine*'s wheel was mounted. 'But why?'

'Because,' said her uncle, grinning again, 'when I heard Alexander had plans to take my ship, I packed every corner on that old brigantine with nice dry powder. If I can't have her, no one can.'

'Gunpowder?' asked Arthur, his eyes widening.

'No, wig powder,' said William, sighing. 'Aye, lad, gunpowder. So, Fleur, if you can land a burning arrow on that binnacle, victory is ours, I reckon.'

While Fleur stretched her bowstring and lined up her shot, Arthur and Tom ran off in search of fire. Arthur returned with a tar-dipped rag, which he wrapped around the head of one of Fleur's arrows. Tom brought an unbroken lantern up from below. Fleur dipped the arrow into the lantern's flame and the ragged head poured forth an oily black smoke. She drew back her bowstring and took aim through the smoke again. Then she let the arrow fly.

They all held their breath as they watched its arc between the two ships. Up and up and up it flew, then down and down, to land with a solid thunk in the oak of the *Libertine*'s binnacle. A cheer went up among the small group on the *Black Dragon*. On the *Libertine*, everything went up! The powder beneath the binnacle ignited with a fiery roar, sending great chunks of wood in all directions and triggering a chain reaction that set off every ounce of explosives concealed in the length of William's old ship. Within seconds she had been blown to smithereens; the ragged remains floated on the surface of the sea.

If Captain Blood's death had turned the battle in favour of William, then the loss of their ship finished off the crew of the *Libertine* completely. The last of the boarding party downed their cutlasses and surrendered. Jack appeared, limping badly. He had lost part of an ear, and dark blood had congealed all over his face and neck. But his smile was as bright as the sun burning above them. William ordered Arthur to tend to the wounded and issued a generous jug of rum to each man. Then they assembled by a lifeboat holding Blood's snarling crewmen, which hung over the side of the ship. His eagle circled overhead, screeching loudly.

'Why don't you just kill them?' Tom asked his captain earnestly. His loathing for them was as fierce as William's.

'Believe me, lad,' said William, glancing over at Fleur,

'there's nothing I'd like better than to run the beggars through, but not like this – it's not how things are done, boy. These men are dregs and nothing for us to worry about.' He looked down at the swirling waters and raised his voice so all could hear him clearly. 'Let it be enough that all will know that their great leader, Alexander the Bloody, was struck down by a young girl.'

Tom looked disappointed and muttered: 'Well, I'd still like to run 'em through with my sword.'

'Ha!' muttered Mario, the Italian rigger, who had lost an eye in the battle. 'I'd like to see you try.'

'Don't push your luck,' said William, and with a swish of his blade he cut the ropes that held the lifeboat, and sent it plummeting into the water below with an enormous splash.

Fleur leaned against the ship's rail and watched as the vanquished pirates struggled to retrieve the oars that were hurled down after them. They started to row south, and their defiant shanties lingered in their wake.

'That was horrible,' said Fleur, turning away from the departing boat. 'I can't believe Blood died so horribly.'

'Aye,' said William grimly. 'And mark this, he died not by a Hart's hand, but by his own greed. There be other Bloods on the ocean, but I reckon they'll see no more need now to keep on with this feuding.'

'You mean no more pointless killing and plotting?' asked Fleur, amazed. 'Really?'

'Aye,' said William. 'I reckon it's time to get back to some good honest old-fashioned piracy.'

From the *Black Dragon*'s lower deck a cheer went up. Fleur looked round to see the crew saluting their victory.

Tom turned to her, his eyes sparkling. 'We did it, Claw-cat.'

Fleur blushed and smiled. She blushed — and smiled — even more when Tom threw his arms around her and hugged her warmly. Arthur stood a little to one side, watching his friends shyly. He knew that the bond between Fleur and Tom was stronger than any he could hope for with her. He could read Fleur's heart better than Fleur herself. They made a nice couple, Arthur thought to himself, resolving never to stand in their way again.

'Ahem!' William coughed theatrically. 'If you don't mind . . .'

Fleur and Tom sprang apart in sudden embarrassment. Then, overcome with exhaustion, Fleur sank slowly to her knees.

She woke up surrounded by William and his grateful crew. Some of them hadn't known that she was actually a girl and had been as shocked as Blood's crew when she had revealed her true self. Fleur was trembling so violently that Jack gave her a nip of rum. The crew all took turns to thank her for saving their beloved captain, giving her gold coins or lucky trinkets. She had shown her mettle and proved herself to them once and for all; a new-found respect glowed in their eyes. From now on, it seemed, a girl would bring them only good luck.

William, though, grew quiet and thoughtful. He had a promise to keep – and that meant St Kitts. Fleur was to live with her cousin, as he had solemnly promised.

CHAPTER 21

The next couple of days were long and difficult. Men were still dying from their wounds, in spite of Arthur's skill, and by the end of the week the crew of the *Black Dragon* had halved in number. The survivors, however, were a hardy bunch, who took up the work of their fallen shipmates with gusto. They repaired the damaged ship in record time, so that once the last funeral had been held, and the fever had passed from the wounded who remained below, a stranger would never have guessed at the fierce struggle that had taken place just a few days before.

The mood of the men also began to return to normal

– though there was much talk about the need to swell their numbers quickly.

After the battle Tom had made a point of shaking Arthur's hand, and although they would probably never really see eye to eye on a great many things, a friendship of sorts had begun to form between them.

As for Fleur, her uncle kept her busy, testing her abilities to the limit and drilling her with the narwhal staff. Since the battle, she had not experienced the same surge of power as when she'd first touched the ruby in her hour of need, but it still hummed when she held it. Hummed, or purred perhaps, like a contented cat.

'Remind me why we're doing this,' said Fleur as she back-flipped off the side of the ship to land deftly at her uncle's side. Her anger at William's determination to ditch her on St Kitts had returned. 'You're only going to dump me with some woman I don't even know. What's the point of being a good fighter if I'm stuck on some island doing needlework?'

'Excellent,' said William, nodding at her graceful move and ignoring her words completely.

'And what about the prophecy?' she snapped.

He raised an eyebrow quizzically.

Fleur scowled at him and stood with one hand on her hip, the other twirling the staff like the sails of a windmill.

'Let's be honest,' she said boldly. 'I'm getting results with this thing. Don't you want to know where the story ends? If I end up ruler of the oceans, you could be my cabin boy.'

'No, Fleur,' he replied, chuckling to himself. 'You know that our ways have to part for a while. A pirate captain cannot rewrite his vow to suit his circumstances.'

Fleur dodged his sudden lunge, knocked away his cutlass with ease and held the tip of her staff at his throat.

'And anyhow, powers or not,' he continued, 'a little skill of your own won't hurt so I'll continue training you while we're together. And' – he knocked the pointed tusk away from his bristled chin – 'I'm glad to say, you're improving all the time.'

'Aye,' Fleur said bitterly. 'For all the good it'll do me. I'll wager the moment you raise anchor you'll have forgotten your troublesome niece altogether.'

William smiled down at her with such warmth that his weathered face looked quite kindly. 'Maybe once,' he said quietly, 'but you've been a tonic to me – you know that, Fleur, don't you?'

She shrugged miserably and her uncle's smile faded. 'Before you came along I might as well have been dead,' he went on. 'I didn't care about nobody, specially myself.' He sniffed. 'But you reminded me how to live.' He pointed up at the flag being hoisted high up on the mainmast. Instead of the Jolly Roger, he was flying the Hart stag. 'Look, lassie, I had it made for us on Ile aux Forbans – 'tis in honour of you. We'll meet again, I swear it.'

Fleur was just about to ask for something in writing when Jack appeared, carrying William's tricorn hat on a large silver plate.

The captain frowned at his lieutenant suspiciously. 'What's all this about, man? I've been looking for that.'

Jack winked at Fleur and pointed at the new curls reaching down her back. She'd stopped wearing her bandana now that all William's crew knew she was a girl.

'The secret's officially out then?' he said. 'The crew are all still talking about your combat skills.'

Fleur raised a hand to her hair, and was surprised by how much it had grown. 'Aye' – she nodded – 'Finn's retired for sure. And don't start treating me like a girl now because of it.'

Jack laughed and nodded at William curtly. 'So, Captain, are we to understand that a girl is officially a member of our crew now?'

William narrowed his eyes and looked from Fleur to Jack. 'Aye,' he said guardedly. 'Until we reach the Caribbean, that is.'

Jack held the plate out to him and bowed slightly. 'Would you like some seasoning on your dinner then, sir?'

William rubbed at his bristly chin in bewilderment. 'What are you talking about, you damned idiot?'

Jack shrugged, the corners of his mouth twitching. 'It's just – and correct me if I'm wrong here, Fleur – but I recall you saying, Captain, that you'd rather eat your own hat than let a woman join your crew.'

Fleur burst out laughing, along with her shipmates, and William snatched his hat from the proffered plate with good grace.

'But I never said a *girl* couldn't join my crew, now, did I?' he said, chuckling.

Jack nodded at them both with a grin and walked away.

Fleur turned to her uncle and opened her mouth to speak, but then Arthur appeared, barging in between them unceremoniously.

'Please, sir,' he asked nervously, 'can I come with you?'

William looked confused and Fleur sighed with exasperation.

'But you are already coming with us, ain't you? We're taking you to the first port and leaving you there – with money in your pocket was my pledge, if I remember rightly.'

'Yes,' blurted Arthur in reply, 'and I'm thankful for that. But . . .' He paused uncomfortably and tugged at the hem of his shirt. 'But I don't want to leave *you*. I mean, I want to be part of your crew.'

The captain burst out laughing and slapped his thigh in disbelief. Arthur looked on with hurt and hope in equal measure. After a while, William had recovered himself enough to continue.

'But you don't even like sailing, boy,' he said to Arthur, stifling a chuckle. 'You're made for bigger things than life in the rigging. If you join my crew, life will be harder than anything you've ever known. You should take your leave while you can. Grow up in comfort, lad, and when you're a gentleman you can tell your friends the tale of when you shared a desert island with William the Heartless.' He turned to leave.

'I can help you,' Arthur said quickly. 'I've got lots of useful skills. And after all, you still haven't found a ship's doctor, have you?'

William shook his head and rubbed his bristly chin as he eyed the boy. 'Not yet,' he admitted.

'Well, I can help with that,' Arthur continued eagerly. 'And I . . . well, I can help with other things too. I pick things up quickly – Jack-of-all-trades, me. Oh, surely I could be of use to you?'

'Hmmm,' rumbled William, frowning.

Arthur laced his hands together imploringly. 'Please, sir, I've nowhere else to go.' His voice wobbled with emotion and his eyes reddened. 'I'll work hard and do whatever you tell me without complaint. I'll even sack down on the deck if it helps.'

William couldn't help but laugh at that and Arthur reddened.

Above them, in the ship's rigging, Tom had been watching the scene unfold. He sprang down to the deck, as agile as a monkey, landing between his captain and Arthur.

'I thought we were leaving him at the nearest port, sir,' he hissed urgently.

Fleur glowered at him while William narrowed his eyes and looked from Tom to Arthur and back again.

'Sorry, Arthur,' Tom went on apologetically, looking over at the other boy. 'I know we've made our peace an' all, but it took me ages before I'd earned my place on Captain Hart's crew.' He glanced quickly over in Fleur's direction. 'It's not fair that you should have it so easy.'

William quizzed his cabin boy sternly. 'So you would let the orphan fend for himself, Tom? I wonder how you would have felt had I done the same to you?'

His stare was so penetrating that Tom turned away, his ears and cheeks burning. Arthur spluttered indignantly but wisely decided to stay quiet. Tom started to say something else but William butted in.

'We *don't* have a ship's doctor yet and you did save Tom from his fever,' he mused.

Tom looked horrified. 'But, Captain!'

'Exactly, Tom, *Captain*,' barked William. 'Now silence, boy, I'm thinking.'

He stepped up to Arthur with his hands behind his back. He rocked backwards on his brass-buckled shoes and hmmm'd before he spoke again. 'And you'll do precisely what I command?'

Arthur beamed at him, his eyes shining. 'Of course,' he assured him. 'Anything.'

The captain paced around him slowly. 'And they'll be no making allowances. Do you understand?'

Arthur nodded vigorously.

'And you won't get no share of any treasure neither.

Not until you've proved your worth. Call it an apprenticeship.'

The boy nodded again, only slightly less enthusiastically.

William pointed at him and narrowed his eyes. 'And the moment you mess things up, you're off the ship. At a good port and with something to spend, mind you. I'll keep my word on that. Long as you remember. One step out of place and you're gone.'

Tom groaned loudly and stormed away.

'So be it.' William nodded, his mind made up. He peered at Arthur with such a hard, penetrating gaze that the boy cringed under his scrutiny. 'You're crew now,' he growled. 'That means you belong to me.'

Halfway through the long slog to St Kitts, Fleur was sitting up on the quarterdeck with Tom one evening, turning the narwhal staff over in her hands. She was going to miss the weapon – it had begun to feel like an extra limb – but she had to leave it with William once he dropped her off. After all, her skill in fighting and defending herself was hers to keep, with or without the staff, and it would be safer in William's care if the Bloods ever came calling again.

The *Black Dragon* rose and fell in the heavy swell and

Fleur steadied herself against the bulkhead. With a weary sigh, she ran her fingers over the jagged sharks' teeth embedded at the base of the staff.

'I just don't understand it at all, Tom. Not at all.'

Tom rolled his eyes and peeled a banana. 'Are we seriously going to go over this again?' he groaned.

Fleur had been rattling on about the injustice of her imminent departure at every opportunity lately. 'Yes!' she snapped. 'We are, actually.'

Tom sighed and nodded. He knew she was desperate to talk about what had happened to her in the battle and whether the prophecy was real or not. He knew that the very idea thrilled as much as scared her. But he was worried that their friendship would vanish as Fleur's strength and confidence in herself grew; he thought he could already feel a distance between them. After all, he reasoned, why would someone as potentially powerful and important as her want to spend her time with a lowly cabin boy? There was already talk on the ship that she would one day take over her uncle's role. He wished he could tell her this, and more besides, but he didn't have Arthur's way with words. He'd been appalled to learn that his rival was going to be sticking around: what hope did he have to shine now? And in the battle, all he'd done was carry the shot for the gunners and shoot anyone climbing up to the crow's nest. Compared to his shipmates, and especially Fleur, he felt useless.

Fleur lifted the staff so that she could admire it properly. Inca gold glinted in the moonlight. 'I don't think he's thinking things through properly, that's all,' she continued. 'I mean, look how useful I am on this ship these days.'

Tom winced at this and tossed his banana skin over the side. Preoccupied with her thoughts, Fleur completely failed to spot her friend's grumpiness. She was finally realizing who she was and what she could be, and thoughts and emotions were furiously bubbling to the surface.

'I don't know whether there's any truth in this prophecy thing or not, to be honest, but how does William expect us to work it out if we're not together? It makes no sense, him leaving me in the Caribbean.'

Tom shrugged and Fleur trailed a fingertip around the staff's precious ruby.

'I mean, it has to be real – you saw me fight, Tom. It's like something takes hold of me, and I seem to know where each attack will come from before it lands . . . And like I told you before, I can hear the mutterings of the sea when I listen hard enough. But I can't explain any of it. Not properly. And sometimes I think I'm just making it up.'

Tom shrugged. 'Maybe the captain's worried you'll scare the crew with your powers?'

He registered Fleur's furious look and tried again. 'Well, maybe it's a point of honour then?' he suggested. 'The captain did make a promise to his brother, didn't he?'

Fleur nodded and blew air from her cheeks in exasperation. 'Arrrgh!' she growled. 'Why can't you say something that makes me feel better?'

Tom turned to leave with a 'Harumph'.

Fleur frowned and caught him by the elbow. 'What's wrong?' she asked outright, hand on hip. 'What have I done to make you angry, Tom?'

Tom turned round again and fiddled with a knot in the wood beside him. 'Nothing,' he mumbled. 'I mean . . . well . . . nothing.'

Fleur threw her arm in the air in frustration. 'Tom, I'm not stupid, you know. Something's wrong. Why won't you tell me?'

Tom stared down at his bare feet and wiggled his toes uncomfortably.

'Please, Tom?' she persisted.

He couldn't meet her eyes. 'I'm just a simple boy,

Fleur,' he murmured eventually, his mouth dry. 'All I want is to serve under Captain Hart and learn all I can till I'm good enough to captain my own ship. I've never known much about anything but sailing and the sea – and this whole prophecy thing, to be honest, turns my head inside out. It don't make no sense, Fleur, if it's true, and nor does the world no more.'

'I'm sorry,' she blurted out, her face red.

Tom looked up at her and his blue eyes burned like a summer sky. 'It's not you,' he said soothingly, but Fleur shook her head.

'I've been talking about myself all this time. I've been stupid. And I never stopped to think.'

Tom interrupted her quickly. 'No,' he insisted. 'I'd be the same if it had happened to me. Don't you see, Fleur?' He swallowed. 'I'm jealous of you.' He dropped his head into his hands with shame. 'I wish the captain was *my* uncle. I wish he lo— respected me the way he does you. I wish I'd been trained and loved since I was a young 'un. I wish I was you. You have a destiny, Fleur, and I wish it was mine too. If the prophecy is real and there is magic in that staff, who knows what you will be capable of? But if your power came from within, and you yourself harnessed those skills from self-belief and hard work, then you are a true warrior and have earned the right to this ship. What do I have?' He peered up at her; now he was red too. 'Sorry.'

Fleur was astounded. 'You fool, Tom,' she began, laughing a little despite herself. 'I've lost count how many times I've been jealous of you since we met in Cornwall. I'll always be a little bit of a disappointment to him, see, Tom, 'cause I'm just a slip of a girl.'

They both grinned at each other then, and the tension between them drifted away, and as it did Fleur's heart began to burn with an unfamiliar feeling. As Tom's blue eyes sparkled at her, she felt like she missed him, even though he was right there beside her, and his steady gaze made her tremble. As much as she enjoyed Arthur's company, he could never mean as much to her as Tom. The cabin boy was as brave and strong as Fleur, with the same hunger for adventure and love of the ocean. It was like they were cut from the same rock.

'Look,' she said, 'you're the only person I can really talk to and *know* you'll understand. You're my closest friend, Tom. So I'm sorry if I've made you feel that I don't need you, because I do. I know we'll be apart soon, but if you vow to be on my side in spirit, I promise you'll have my loyalty for ever.'

Their eyes met and Tom nodded slowly. He would keep that promise. And somewhere, deep inside, he made another promise, to himself and to Fleur. He'd keep that one too, or the devil take him. And at that very moment the boy became a man.

CHAPTER 22

With the wind behind them and the waters kind, the *Black Dragon* reached St Kitts sooner than Fleur had hoped.

As she stared out from the prow, she hated the lush tropical paradise awaiting them. She hated the smooth, soft, sugar-white sands punctuated by coconut trees, and the calm, warm waters below. This heaven was her hell.

'Two points to starboard and keep her steady, man,' William shouted as the ship slowed to a halt and the anchor was tossed into the water.

Fleur stared up at the spectacular cloud-fringed peaks

that were all but covered by a vast emerald-green forest – and groaned. They had arrived.

Most of the crew remained by the ship, but William had gathered together a few of them, including Tom, to accompany him and Fleur to their destination. A disconsolate Arthur loaded them up with water, fruit and biscuits; with much throat-clearing, clumsy hugs and emotional goodbyes, the small group set off.

They followed the path as it climbed the sides of a huge dormant volcano; the rim of the crater was vast. After stopping briefly to drink from a lake and sit in the shade of beautiful trees beside orchids and wild raspberries, they entered a forest filled with chattering green vervet monkeys and brilliant tropical flowers. They looked down on grey beaches formed from the island's dark igneous rock. When the mountains led away from the placid coast and among swaying fields of sugar cane, Fleur knew that they had arrived at her cousin's plantation.

William marched them up the hillside, across acres of immaculate, rolling landscaped gardens dotted with hibiscus and passion flowers, towards a white wooden mansion. He climbed the few steps to the porch, then paused for a moment at the solid wooden door before thumping on it loudly.

A beautiful native woman opened it and peered through, her eyes filled with terror at the sight of the pirates. She tried to close it, but William rolled his eyes impatiently and jammed a foot in the gap.

'Woman, we ain't here for trouble. Go and get your mistress.'

The maidservant raced off into the house, glad to escape the company on the threshold.

Finally a well-dressed woman appeared in the doorway; Fleur could tell immediately that she was by no means pleased to see them. Her mouth was turned down, her lips pale and bloodless from the effort of maintaining her stern expression. The top half of her face, meanwhile, was busy shooting withering looks, first at the motley company, then down at Fleur, and finally at her uncle, who could barely conceal his own disdain.

'William,' she said curtly, with a nod of the head.

'Hoa, Myra.'

The mistress of the house pursed her lips. She bore a slight resemblance to Fleur, but age and ill-temper had twisted her once fine looks. Her skin was as rough as sackcloth and her goose-grey hair was thin.

'I can't say 'tis good to see thee.'

'Nor I,' he replied matter-of-factly.

They glared at one another, mutually repulsed but held together by the bonds of blood.

'So,' she began, 'this is the girl, I suppose. Which means they've finally done for him, eh?'

'Aye.' William nodded, his glare warning her not to speak ill of Henry. 'My brother is dead and I've brought his daughter to you for safekeeping, as was promised and paid for.'

Myra measured her cousin with cold eyes. Fleur shivered as if to shake off the look.

'We haven't the room for you really, child. But I suppose we'll make do.'

Fleur looked around and had to bite her tongue. There was obviously plenty of room for her and any number of people in that huge mansion. It seemed that her cousin Myra was as reluctant for Fleur to take up residence as she was herself.

'You'll have to earn your keep, mind,' Myra went on, 'but you look hardy enough.'

William held out a large leather bag, the surface cracked from years of salt water. It looked heavy.

'This is for you. You've been paid handsomely already, but this'll make sure the girl wants for nothing. Mind you spend it on her now,' he added, his eyes narrowing as Myra's eyes widened.

Fleur looked up at her uncle and tears welled up in her eyes. But she swallowed them back, determined not to cry.

Myra snatched the bag from William and tore it open, eyeing the glittering contents. 'Hmph,' she grunted. 'Only gold? I was hoping there'd be gems in there too.'

He made to take back the bag but Myra whipped it out of reach.

'You ungrateful witch,' he bellowed. 'Just make sure you look after the lassie like she was your own. You've Henry to thank for all this,' he reminded her, sweeping an arm across the broad expanse of her plantation. 'Do your duty as you promised or I'll be back – and in a less generous mood.'

Myra glared at him but knew the threat was real. She grabbed Fleur's arm with bony fingers and yanked her over the threshold. 'So be it, William the Heartless,' she muttered. 'So be it. Now leave my land before I set the hounds on you.'

William ignored her and took a step towards Fleur. He fished around in one of his deep pockets, pulling out his trusty telescope. Dropping to one knee so that they were the same height, he held it out to Fleur.

'Here, lassie, this is for you. Watch the waters for my return. I shall be back.'

'When you are, the law will be waiting for you,' said Myra spitefully.

'Then they'll hang me for murder, among other crimes,' growled William. 'Anyhow, we both have our reasons for not wanting them at our door, don't we, woman?' he warned cryptically, sending Myra scuttling into the house with a trail of muttered oaths. William gave his trembling niece a warm smile, but she could not return it.

'Please, Uncle, take me with you,' she begged him. 'I can't stay here. I'll go soft, I'll waste away. We need to stay together, that's obvious. You know as well as I do that there's something in that prophecy.'

He placed his strong hands on her shoulders. 'Fleur, whatever we've seen, the fact is that prophecy's still more likely to be folklore and gossip than anything else. Ruler of the oceans – I ask you!'

Fleur gulped as fresh misery descended. 'That's not fair and we both know it,' she moaned.

William shook his head gently. 'Let it go, lassie. Don't let the secrets of the ruby heart consume you as they once did me. I know you felt its power and potential' – he lowered his voice – 'same as me and your father and every Hart before us. And I believe you when you say you can hear the voice of the sea. Reckon I've some knowledge of that myself. But chasing a dream will unhinge you, child. If something is meant to be, it will find you. That I can promise.'

Fleur squeezed her eyes shut for a few moments as his words sank in. The hope that she might be the one to claim the ruby heart had been driving her forward. It had helped to fill the void left by the death of her father, and had given her the strength to face her enemy. But what was left of her new self without the prophecy that brought it into being?

'Who am I without that?' she said aloud. 'I thought I was special, Uncle. I thought I'd finally found where I fitted in the world. Who am I now?'

He chuckled, not unkindly. 'You're my niece and a true Hart, Fleur.' He cupped her chin with pride. 'And you're much more besides. It's you who have achieved so much, not some magical ruby set in a staff. The path you're carving is all your own. You'll find a place where you're happy. And it needn't be here,' he continued. 'The sea's call will grow too loud to ignore. Our paths *will* cross again and I'll be keeping an eye on my favourite niece, make no mistake.' He tapped the side of his nose and winked. 'I'll listen for my name on the waves, girl. Just remember not to whisper.'

'But—' Fleur began.

'But I have to leave you here,' William interrupted. 'This was Henry's wish and I promised to honour it. You will be safe here.'

'I don't want to be safe. I want to be with you . . . to be at sea. I can't breathe here. Please, Uncle. Don't leave me,' she pleaded, unable to stop the tears rolling down her face.

He was quiet for a time, as if considering the suggestion, but then shook his head adamantly. 'I'm sorry, Fleur. I swore an oath to your father.'

Fleur searched the eyes of her shipmates for support, but they had turned away awkwardly as her gaze met theirs. All except for Tom, who was staring at William beseechingly – though even he knew better than to challenge his captain. Instead, he stepped forward shyly and handed Fleur a cream pink-tinged conch shell.

'I picked it up on Ile aux Forbans.' He held it to her ear. 'Listen. The sea's voice is trapped inside, so you can listen to its chatter whenever you want to.'

Fleur closed her eyes and listened to the shushing sound. 'Thank you,' she said, taking the shell and clutching it to her chest.

Tom went beetroot red and stared at his feet. 'Goodbye, Claw-cat,' he said.

'Goodbye,' she echoed feebly.

Her uncle nodded his approval and straightened suddenly. 'Till we meet again. And remember, you're a Hart. The tides will bring us together again sooner or later.'

He turned to leave, then stopped suddenly and took her in his arms. She clung to him, feeling her ribs being crushed. The tears came hot and fast now: with her uncle's departure, her world was shrinking. Finally he broke the embrace and strode away from her, beckoning his men with a cry of 'To the *Black Dragon*! All aboard!'

As the group started off towards the beach, Tom hung back, glancing over his shoulder. Fleur sobbed as she watched them go, and was still sobbing, alone in the doorway of the great house, until there was nothing left of them but a path trodden through the sugar cane and a sail on the horizon.

In the days that followed, Myra and her equally unpleasant husband made it abundantly clear that Fleur was not a welcome guest in their home. Despite the wealth of accommodation on offer, she was given a cramped and shabby bedroom in the servants' quarters and a long list of cleaning duties to keep her busy.

'You're a thorn in my side, child,' Myra snapped one

morning as she handed Fleur another pile of dirty laundry. 'Remember, I've taken you in out of the kindness of my heart, so do as you're told and be grateful.'

Anger bubbled in Fleur's stomach. Cousin Myra had done very well indeed out of her arrival, whatever she might say.

'You Harts are nothing but trouble,' she went on as Fleur struggled with the grubby sheets. 'I'll be honest and tell you now that I wish I'd never set eyes on you. You're a wrong 'un – I could tell that the moment I first saw you. Like your uncle, and your father too.'

Fleur could hold her tongue no longer. If this woman had any idea what she was capable of, she was sure her treatment would be different. 'Aye, a Hart,' she replied, her voice calm and measured but brimming with fury, 'that I am. And proud of it too.'

Myra glared at her with disgust. 'Hold your tongue, child. The likes of you ain't fit to wipe my feet on. Devil's blood!'

'No, Hart blood,' blazed Fleur.

Myra cried out in horror. 'Impudent beast!'

Anger ripped through Fleur suddenly and she grabbed the woman by both arms without thinking what she was doing.

Myra pushed her away. 'Get off me, you stupid girl.

How dare you assault me like that. You'll get the back of my belt if you do that again.'

'But—'

'You'll shut your mouth and do as you're told while you live under this roof. Now get out of my sight.' And she kicked Fleur square in the behind as she turned to leave.

Fleur stamped off to a safe distance and found a wall to beat out her frustration on. This was to be her life, then – cleaning up after a hateful old witch who grew fat on her father's plunder.

She left the laundry lying in a little-used stairway and retreated to her lonely room to pore over the souvenirs of her adventures. She took out William's telescope and gazed through the window and far out to sea; even from a distance she could hear its call. Next she held Tom's shell to her ear and imagined the gentle sloshing of the sea against the *Black Dragon* as she lay anchored in some sandy bay or smuggler's cove. Then she turned the shell over in her hands, held it to her mouth and, thinking of her beloved uncle, spoke his name like a prayer: *William Hart, William Hart, William Hart . . .*

Fleur was woken by sound of raised voices and the clattering of heavy boots in the hallway. She was unable to make out what was being said, but she gathered from the shrieks coming from her cousin Myra that some pretty colourful oaths were being thrown around downstairs. Myra's shouts of protest continued after the other voices had died down, and the sound of footsteps reached the stairs. Fleur's breath quickened. Was she in danger? After all, her father had sent her here for safety's sake. Perhaps Alexander Blood's family had found out where she was holing up and had arrived with a bloodthirsty pirate army?

Flitting silently around the moonlit room, she gathered up her few possessions, slung her bow across her shoulder and moved towards the open window, ready to make a quick getaway. The footsteps grew louder and louder, until they halted suddenly at her bedroom door. Breathing hard and clutching her hastily packed bag, Fleur backed away from the door. She kept her gaze steadily on it, until she could feel the windowsill pressing against the backs of her thighs.

Then the door flew open and Fleur was blinded by the glare from a burning torch. Slowly her eyesight adjusted to the light, and a tall figure came into focus, torch held high in one hand, the narwhal staff in the other. His voice, when he spoke, was as loud as cannon fire and as deep and warm as a barrel of rum.

'I kept my oath to your father, wouldn't you say? I brought you here, didn't I? Don't remember nothing specific about leaving you.'

Fleur's eyes widened and her heart filled with love and hope as she heard the voice of her uncle, her *captain*.

'I have need of your skills and time is pressing,' he said. He tossed something at her and she caught it deftly: the Hart staff. 'I've reason to pay a visit to the witch trials in Penance Bay.'

'Witch trials . . . ?' stammered Fleur incredulously.

'Aye, lass, that's what I told you.' He reached out a hand and grinned broadly. 'Well, girl,' he asked, 'have you the stomach for a journey?'

THE END

Acknowledgements

Thanks to Toby Starbuck for sifting through this book with a ruthless eye and a brilliant mind. I simply couldn't have done it without him.

Thanks to my mum and dad for all the babysitting, M&S dinners, encouragement and relentless support when I went feral with deadlines.

Thanks to my agent, Sarah Such, for her belief, input and encouragement from the outset of this story.

Thanks to all at Random House, especially Charlie Sheppard and Harriet Wilson, who were both a joy and an inspiration to work with. Also Annie Eaton for giving me the chance, Sophie Nelson, who totally had my back with the copy-edit, and Adam Relf who drew the beautiful illustrations and who, along with Rhys Willson, created the excellent jacket.

Thanks to Bluebell Whyman for inspiring me to write this story about a feisty girl pirate in the first place, and to all the kids down the street where I live, who constantly remind me that adventure is everywhere. But a special thanks to Ally, Jess and Cleo for listening to the very first chapter of this book and telling me to write more.

Thanks to those at United Agents who were so

positive and supportive of me while writing this book, despite difficult times, especially Rosemary Canter and her team. Thanks to Terry Wong-Lane for the Cantonese, and my friends and family for putting up with me while I basically ignored them all for a year.

And finally, a huge nod of appreciation to *The Pirate Primer* by George Choundas for all the swashbuckling language tips and excellent pirate put-downs. I can now swear like a true sea dog.

If I've forgotten to name anyone here, I'm so sorry and deserve to be dunked from the yardarm.